Mike Resnick

THE OTHER
TEDDY ROOSEVELTS

THE OTHER
TEDDY ROOSEVELTS

Mike Resnick

Subterranean Press 2008

Original Publications:

"Bully"—*Asimov's,* 1991
"The Bull Moose at Bay"—*Asimov's,* 1991
"Over There"—*Asimov's,* 1992
"The Light That Blinds, the Claws That Catch"—*Asimov's,* 1992
"The Roosevelt Dispatches"—*F&SF,* 1996
"Redchapel"—*Asimov's,* 2001
"Two Hunters in Manhattan"—*The Secret History of Vampires,* 2007
"The Unsinkable Teddy Roosevelt"—*Oval Office Oddities,* 2008

First Edition

ISBN
978-159606-137-8

Subterranean Press
PO Box 190106
Burton, MI 48085

www.subterraneanpress.com

To Carol, as always.

And to Bill Schafer,
fine publisher,
fine editor,
fine friend

Contents

2007:

INTRODUCTION

So why would anyone spend so much time writing science fiction stories about Theodore Roosevelt?

Well, they have a lot in common, science fiction and Roosevelt. Both of them deal with ideas. Both of them are entertaining. And most of all, both of them are bigger than Reality.

You think not?

Let's take a look at Roosevelt's life.

Roosevelt was born in New York City in 1858. As a boy he suffered from a debilitating case of asthma. Rather than give in to it, he began swimming and exercising every day and like every pulp hero you ever read about, he built himself up to where he was able to make the Harvard boxing team.

But he'd been making a name for himself before he went to Harvard. Even the Gray Lensman and Doc Savage weren't exclusively brawn, and neither was Roosevelt. An avid naturalist to the day of his death, he was already considered one of America's leading ornithologists and taxidermists while still a teenager. Nor was his interest limited to nature. While at Harvard he wrote what was considered the definitive treatise on naval warfare, *The Naval War of 1812*.

He graduated Phi Beta Kappa and *summa cum laude*, married Alice Hathaway, went to law school, found it boring, and discovered politics. When Theodore Roosevelt developed a new interest, he never did so in a half-hearted way—so at 24 he became the youngest man ever elected to the New York General Assembly, and was made Minority Leader a year later.

He might have remained in the State Assembly, but on February 14, 1884, not long after his 25th birthday, his beloved Alice and his mother died in the same house, 12 hours apart. He felt the need to get away, and he went West to become a rancher (and being Theodore Roosevelt, one ranch couldn't possibly contain him, so he bought two).

Not content to simply be a rancher, a sportsman, and a politician, like hundreds of pulp and science fiction heroes he became a lawman as well, amd hunted down and captured three armed killers in the Dakota Badlands during the fearsome blizzard that was known as "The Winter of the Blue Snow". Could Hawk Carse or Lije Baley have done any better?

He began building Sagamore Hill, the estate he made famous in Oyster Bay, New York, married Edith Carew, and started a second family. (Alice had died giving birth to his daughter, also named Alice. Edith promptly began producing sons—Kermit, Theodore Jr., Archie and Quentin, as well as another daughter, Ethel.) In his spare time, he wrote a number of well-received books. Then, running short of money, he signed a contract to write a four-volume series, *The Winning of the West*; the first two volumes became immediate bestsellers. He was also an avid correspondent, and it's estimated that he wrote more than 150,000 letters during his lifetime—and what science fiction writer, I ask you, is not an avid correspondent?

He was now past 30 years of age, and he decided it was time to stop loafing and really get to work—so he took the job of Police Commissioner of the wildly corrupt City of New York...and to the amazement of even his staunchest supporters, he cleaned the place up, just like heroes from The Shadow to Lincoln Powell. He became famous for his "midnight rambles" to make sure his officers were at their posts, and he was the first Commissioner to insist that the entire police force take regular target practice.

He made things so uncomfortable for the rich and powerful (and corrupt) of New York that he was kicked upstairs and made Assistant Secretary of the Navy in Washington. When the Spanish-American War broke out, he resigned his office, enlisted in the army, was given the rank of Colonel, and assembled the most famous and romantic outfit ever to fight for the United States—the fabled Rough Riders, consisting of cowboys, Indians, professional athletes, and anyone else who impressed him—and what classic space operas don't have a crew of romantic misfits just like that? They went to Cuba, where Roosevelt himself led the charge up San Juan Hill in the face of machine-gun fire, and he came home the most famous man in the country.

Less than three months later he was elected Governor of New York, a week after his 40th birthday. His new duties didn't hinder his other interests, and he kept turning out books and studying wildlife.

Two years later they kicked him upstairs again, finding the one job where his reformer's zeal couldn't bother anyone: he was nominated for the Vice Presidency of the United States, and was elected soon afterward.

Ten months later President William McKinley was assassinated, and Roosevelt became the youngest-ever President of the United States, where he served for seven years.

What did he do as President?

Not much, by Rooseveltian standards. Enough for five presidents, by anyone else's standards. Consider:

- He created the National Park system
- He broke the back of the trusts that had run the economy (and the nation) for their own benefit
- He created the Panama Canal
- He sent the Navy on a trip around the world. When they left, America was a second-rate little country in the eyes of the world. By the time they returned we were a world power.
- He became the first President ever to win the Nobel Peace Prize, when he put an end to the Russian-Japanese war,
- He mediated a dispute between Germany and France over Morocco, preserving Morocco's independence.
- To make sure that the trusts didn't reclaim their power after he was out of office, he created the Departments of Commerce and Labor.

When he left office in 1909 with a list of accomplishments equal in magnitude to any Galactic President in science fiction, he immediately packed his bags (and his rifles) and went on the first major safari ever put together, spending eleven months gathering specimens for the American and Smithsonian Museums. He wrote up his experiences as *African Game Trails*, still considered one of the half-dozen most important books on the subject ever published. Clearly he had a lot in common with science fictional hunters from Gerry Carlyle to Nicobar Lane.

When he returned to America he concluded that his hand-chosen successor, President William Howard Taft, was doing a lousy job of running the country, so he decided to run for the Presidency again in 1912. Though far and away the most popular man in the Republican Party, he was denied the nomination through a number of procedural moves. Most men would have licked their wounds and waited for 1916. Not Roosevelt. He formed the Progressive Party, known informally as the "Bull Moose Party", and ran in 1912. It's thought that he was winning when a would-be assassin shot him in the chest while he was being driven to give a speech in Milwaukee. He refused all medical aid until he had delivered the speech (which ran 90 minutes!), then allowed himself to be taken to a hospital. The bullet would never be removed, and by the time Roosevelt was back on the campaign trail Woodrow Wilson had built an insurmountable lead. Roosevelt finished second, as President Taft ran a humiliating third, able to win only 8 electoral votes.

So *now* did he relax?

Fat chance. This is Theodore Roosevelt we're talking about. The Brazilian government asked him to explore a tributary of the Amazon known as the "River of Doubt". He hadn't slowed down since he was a baby, he was in his 50s, he was walking around with a bullet in his chest, all logic said he'd earned a quiet retirement—so of course he said Yes.

This trip didn't go as well as the safari. He came down with fever, he almost lost his leg, and indeed at one time he urged his party to leave him behind to die and to go ahead without him. They didn't, of course, and eventually he was well enough to continue the expedition and finish mapping the river, which was renamed the Rio Teodoro in his honor. (I don't really need to compare him to the hundreds of explorers who inhabit the worlds of science fiction, do I?)

He came home, wrote yet another bestseller—*Through the Brazilian Wilderness*—then wrote another book on African animals, as well as more books on politics...but his health never fully recovered. He campaigned vigorously for our entrance into World War I, and it was generally thought that the Presidency was his for the asking in 1920, but he died in his sleep on January 6, 1919 at the age of 60—having crammed about seventeen lifetimes into those six decades.

He was so fascinating, so talented in so many fields, so much bigger than Life that I decided (and I hope you agree) that he belonged in the one field that could accommodate a man with those virtues—science fiction, where he could finally find some challenges that were truly worthy of his talents, from civilizing the Congo to facing down a vampire on the streets of New York.

So here they are—the assembled alternate histories of that most gifted of Americans, Theodore Roosevelt.

—Mike Resnick

1888:

Red WHITECHAPEL

Back in the 1970s, when some experts had decided that Jack the Ripper was a member of the British royal family, I took a good look at their reasoning, decided they were wrong, and wrote an article on who *I* thought the Ripper had to be. I had hoped it might generate some discussion, or at least a bit of controversy, but it sank without a trace.

Move the clock ahead a quarter of a century. I decided to offer my conclusion to a much larger audience—the science fiction readership of *Asimov's*. My Teddy Roosevelt stories had become quite popular by then, so it was an easy decision to make him the hero. He had ample reason to be in London in the late 1880s—by then his reputation as a naturalist and ornithologist had crossed the ocean…and so had his reputation as a deputy sheriff out in the Dakota Bad Lands. Who better for a harassed and befuddled police force to turn to for help?

Besides, Roosevelt succeeded at almost every task he undertook, and since I was writing *alternate* histories, he didn't fare too well in some of them, so I figured it was time to let him win one.

The novelette was nominated for the Hugo Award in 2001, so clearly *someone* must have agreed with me about the Ripper's identity.

"*F*rom Hell, Mr. Lusk—
Sir, I send you half the Kidne I took from one woman,
prasarved it for you
tother piece I fried and ate it was very nise

> *I may send you the bloody knif that too it out if you only wate a whil longer*
>
> *signed*
> *Catch me when yu can*
>
> *Mishter Lusk"*
> —*Jack the Ripper*
> *October 16, 1888*

> *"I have not a particle of sympathy with the sentimentality— as I deem it, the mawkishness—which overflows with foolish pity for the criminal and cares not at all for the victim of the criminal."*
> —*Theodore Roosevelt*
> *Autobiography*

The date was September 8, 1888

A HAND REACHED OUT of the darkness and shook Roosevelt by the shoulder.

He was on his feet in an instant. His right hand shot out, crunching against an unseen jaw, and sending his assailant crashing against a wall. He crouched low, peering into the shadows, trying to identify the man who was clambering slowly to his feet.

"What the devil happened?" muttered the man.

"My question precisely," said Roosevelt, reaching for his pistol and training it on the intruder. "Who are you and what are you doing in my room?"

A beam of moonlight glanced off the barrel of the gun.

"Don't shoot, Mr. Roosevelt!" said the man, holding up his hands. "It's me—John Hughes!"

Roosevelt lit a lamp, keeping the gun pointed at the small, dapper man. "You haven't told me what you're doing here."

"Besides losing a tooth?" said Hughes bitterly as he spit a tooth into his hand amid a spray of blood. "I need your help."

"What is this all about?" demanded Roosevelt, looking toward the door of his hotel room as if he expected one of Hughes' confeder-ates to burst through it at any moment.

"Don't you remember?" said Hughes. "We spoke for more than an hour last night, after you addressed the Royal Ornithological Society."

"What has this got to do with birds?" said Roosevelt. "And you'd better come up with a good answer. I'm not a patient man when I'm rudely awakened in the middle of the night."

"You don't remember," said Hughes accusingly.

"Remember *what*?"

Hughes pulled out a badge and handed it to the American. "I am a captain of the London Metropolitan Police. After your speech we talked, and you told me how you had single-handedly captured three armed killers in your Wild West."

Roosevelt nodded. "I remember."

"I was most favorably impressed," said Hughes.

"I hope you didn't wake me just to tell me that."

"No—but it was the fact that you have personally dealt with a trio of brutal killers that made me think—hope, actually—that you might be able to help me." Hughes paused awkwardly as the American continued to stare at him. "You *did* say that if I ever needed your assistance..."

"Did I say to request it in the middle of the night?" growled Roosevelt, finally putting his pistol back on his bedtable.

"Try to calm yourself. Then I'll explain."

"This is as calm as I get under these circumstances." Roosevelt took off his nightshirt, tossed it on the fourposter bed, then walked to an ornate mahogany armoire, pulled out a pair of pants and a neat-ly-folded shirt, and began getting dressed. "Start explaining."

"There's something I want you to see."

"At this hour?" said Roosevelt suspiciously. "Where is it?"

"It's not far," said Hughes. "Perhaps a twenty-minute carriage ride away."

"What is it?"

"A body."

"And it couldn't wait until daylight?" asked Roosevelt.

Hughes shook his head. "If we don't have her in the morgue by daylight, there will be panic in the streets."

"I'm certainly glad you're not given to exaggeration," remarked Roosevelt sardonically.

"If anything," replied the small Englishman seriously, "that was an understatement."

"All right. Tell me about it."

"I would prefer that you saw it without any preconceptions."

"Except that it could cause a riot if seen in daylight."

"I said a panic, not a riot," answered Hughes, still without smiling.

Roosevelt buttoned his shirt and fiddled with his tie. "What time is it, anyway?"

"6:20 AM."

"The sun's not an early riser in London, is it?"

"Not at this time of year." Hughes shifted his weight awkwardly.

"Now what's the matter?"

"We have a crisis on our hands, Mr. Roosevelt. I realize that I have no legal right to enlist your help, but we are quite desperate."

"Enough hyperbole," muttered Roosevelt, slipping on his coat.

"You *really* hunted down those murderers in a blizzard?" said Hughes suddenly.

"The Winter of the Blue Snow," said Roosevelt, nodding his head briskly. "Doubtless exaggerated by every dime novelist in America."

"But you *did* bring them back, alone and unarmed," persisted the Englishman, as if Roosevelt's answer was the most important thing in his life.

"Yes...but I knew the territory, and I knew who and where the killers were. I don't know London, and I assume the identity of the killer you're after is unknown."

"So to speak."

"I don't understand," said Roosevelt, adjusting his hat in front of a mirror.

"We don't know who he is. All we know is that he calls himself Saucy Jack."

The two men approached the police line behind the Black Swan. The night fog had left the pavement damp, and there was a strong smell of human waste permeating the area. Chimneys spewed thick smoke into the dawn sky, and the sound of a horse's hooves and a cart's squeaking wheels could be heard in the distance.

"Sir?" asked one of the constables, looking from Hughes to Roosevelt.

"It's all right, Jamison," said Hughes. "This is Theodore Roosevelt, a colleague from America. He is the man who brought Billy the Kid and Jesse James to justice."

Constable Jamison stepped aside immediately, staring at the young American in awe.

"Now, why did you say that, John?" asked Roosevelt in low tones.

"It will establish respect and obedience much faster than if I told him you were an expert on birds."

The American sighed. "I see your point." He paused. "Just what am I supposed to be looking at?"

"It's back here," said Hughes, leading him behind the building to an area that had been temporarily lit by flaming torches.

They stopped when they were about ten feet away. There was a mound beneath a blood-drenched blanket.

"Steel yourself, Mr. Roosevelt," said Hughes.

"After all the monographs I've written on taxidermy, I don't imagine you can show me anything that can shock me," answered Roosevelt.

He was wrong.

The blanket was pulled back, revealing what was left of a middle-aged woman. Her throat had been slit so deeply that she was almost decapitated. A bloody handkerchief around her neck seemed to be the only thing that stopped her head from rolling away.

Her belly was carved open, and her innards were pulled out and set on the ground just above her right shoulder. Various internal organs were mutilated, others were simply missing.

"What kind of creature could do something like this?" said Roosevelt, resisting the urge to retch.

"I was hoping you might be able to tell *us*," said Hughes.

Roosevelt tore his horrified gaze from the corpse and turned to Hughes. "What makes you think I've ever encountered anything like this before?"

"I don't know, of course," said Hughes. "But you *have* lived in America's untamed West. You have traveled among the aboriginal savages. You have rubbed shoulders with frontier cowboys and shootists. Americans are a simpler, more brutal people—barbaric, in ways—and I had hoped…"

"I take it you've never been to America."

"No, I haven't."

"Then I shall ignore the insult, and only point out that Americans are the boldest, bravest, most innovative people on the face of the Earth."

"I assure you I meant no offense," said Hughes quickly. "It's just that we are under enormous pressure to bring Saucy Jack to justice. I had hoped that you might bring some fresh insight, some different methodology..."

"I'm not a detective," said Roosevelt, walking closer to the corpse. "There was never any question about the identities of the three killers I went after. As for *this* murder, there's not much I can tell you that you don't already know."

"Won't you try?" said Hughes, practically pleading.

Roosevelt squatted down next to the body. "She was killed from behind, of course. She probably never knew the murderer was there until she felt her jugular and windpipe being severed."

"Why from behind?"

"If I were trying to kill her from in front, I'd stab her in a straight-forward way—it would give her less time to raise her hand to deflect the blade. But the throat was slit, not punctured. And it had to be the first wound, because otherwise she would have screamed and some-one would have heard her."

"What makes you think someone didn't?"

Roosevelt pointed to the gaping hole in the woman's abdomen. "He wouldn't have had the leisure to do *that* unless he was sure no one had seen or heard the murder." The American stood up again. "But you know all that."

"Yes, we do," said Hughes. "Can you tell us anything we *don't* know?"

"Probably not. The only other obvious fact is that the killer had some knowledge of anatomy."

"This hardly looks like the work of a doctor, Mr. Roosevelt," said Hughes.

"I didn't say that it was. But it was done by someone who knew where the various internal organs belonged, or else he'd never have been able to remove them in the dark. Take a look. There's no sub-cutaneous fat on the ground, and he didn't waste his time mutilating muscle tissue."

"Interesting," said Hughes. "Now that *is* something we didn't know." He smiled. "I think we should be very grateful that you are a taxidermist as well as an ornithologist." He covered the corpse once more, then summoned another constable. "Have her taken to the morgue. Use the alleyways and discourage onlookers."

The constable saluted and gathered a team of policemen to move the body.

"I assume we're through here," said Roosevelt, grateful that he no longer had to stare at the corpse.

"Yes. Thank you for coming."

Roosevelt pulled his timepiece out of a vest pocket and opened it.

"No sense going back to sleep. Why don't you come back to the Savoy with me and I'll buy breakfast?"

"I've quite lost my appetite, but I will be happy to join you for a cup of tea and some conversation, Mr. Roosevelt."

"Call me Theodore." He shook his head. "Poor woman. I wonder who she was?"

Hughes pulled a notebook out of his pocket. "Her name was Annie Chapman. She was a Whitechapel prostitute."

"Whitechapel?"

"Whitechapel is the section of the city we are in."

Roosevelt looked around, truly seeing it for the first time, as the sun began burning away the fog. "I hope New York never has a slum like this!" he said devoutly.

"Wait until New York has been around as long as London, and it will have this and worse," Hughes assured him.

"Not if I have anything to say about it," said Roosevelt, his jaw jutting out pugnaciously as he looked up and down the street.

Hughes was surprised by the intensity of the young man's obvious belief in himself. As they stared at the broken and boarded windows, the drunks lying in doorways and on the street, the mangy dogs and spavined cats and fat, aggressive rats, the endless piles of excrement from cart horses, the Englishman found himself wondering what kind of man could view a woman's mutilated corpse with less distaste than he displayed toward surroundings that Hughes took for granted.

They climbed into Hughes' carriage, and the driver set off for the Savoy at a leisurely trot. Before long they were out of Whitechapel, and, Roosevelt noted, the air instantly seemed to smell fresher.

Roosevelt had eaten the last of his eggs, and was concentrating on his coffee when an officer entered the dining room and approached Hughes.

"I'm sorry to interrupt, sir," he said apologetically, "but they said at the Yard that this is of the utmost urgency."

He handed a small envelope to Hughes, who opened it and briefly looked at what it contained.

"Thank you," said Hughes.

"Will there be anything else, sir?" asked the officer. "Any reply?"

"No, that will be all."

The officer saluted, and when he left Hughes turned back to Roosevelt.

"What are your plans now, Theodore?"

"I have two more speeches to give on ornithology," answered Roosevelt, "and one on naval warfare, and then I board the boat for home on Friday."

"Let me tell you something about the murder you saw today," began Hughes.

"Thank you for letting me finish my breakfast first," said Roosevelt wryly.

"We have a madman loose in Whitechapel, Theodore," continued Hughes.

"That much is obvious."

"We knew that before today," said Hughes.

Roosevelt looked up. "This wasn't his first victim?"

"It was at least his second." Hughes paused. "It's possible that he's killed as many as five women."

"How can he still be at large?"

"We can't watch every Whitechapel prostitute every minute of the day and night."

"He only kills prostitutes?"

"Thus far."

"Were they all this brutally mutilated?"

"The last one—a girl named Polly Nichols—was. The first three suffered less grievous damage, which is why we cannot be sure they were all killed by the same hand."

"Well, you've got your work cut out for you," said Roosevelt. "I certainly don't envy you." He paused. "Have you any suspects so far?"

Hughes frowned. "Not really."

"What does that mean?"

"Nothing."

Roosevelt shrugged. "As you wish. But the subject of Saucy Jack is closed. Either you confide in me or I can't help."

Hughes looked around the half-empty dining room, then lowered his voice. "All right," he said in little more than a whisper. "But what I tell you must go no farther than this table. It is for you and you alone."

Roosevelt stared at him with open curiosity. "All right," he said. "I can keep a secret as well as the next man."

"I hope so."

"You sound like you're about to name Queen Victoria."

"This is not a joking matter!" whispered Hughes angrily. "I am convinced that the man who has been implicated is innocent, but if word were to get out..."

Roosevelt waited patiently.

"There are rumors, undoubtedly spread about by anarchists, that are little short of sedition," continued Hughes. "Scandalous behavior within one's own class is one thing—but murders such as you witnessed this morning...I simply cannot believe it!" He paused, started to speak, then stopped. Finally he looked around the room to make certain no one was listening. "I can't give you his name, Theodore. Without proof, that would be tantamount to treason." He lowered his voice even more. "He is a member of the Royal Family!"

"Every family's got its black sheep," said Roosevelt with a shrug.

Hughes stared at him, aghast. "Don't you understand what I'm telling you?"

"You think royalty can't go berserk just as easily as common men?"

"It's unthinkable!" snapped Hughes. He quickly glanced around the room and lowered his voice again. "This is not Rome, and our Royals are not Caligula and Nero." He struggled to regain his composure. "You simply do not comprehend the gravity of what I am confiding in you. If even a hint that we were investigating this slander were to get out, the government would collapse overnight."

"Do you really think so?" asked Roosevelt.

"Absolutely." The small, dapper policeman stared at Roosevelt. "I would like to enlist your aid in uncovering the *real* murderer before these vile rumors reach a member of the force who cannot keep his mouth shut."

"I don't believe you were listening to me," said Roosevelt. "My ship leaves on Friday morning."

"Without you, I'm afraid."

Roosevelt frowned. "What are you talking about?"

Hughes handed the envelope he'd been given across the table to Roosevelt.

"What is this?" demanded Roosevelt, reaching for his glasses.

"A telegram from your President Cleveland, offering us your services in the hunt for the madman."

Roosevelt read the telegram twice, then crumpled it up in a powerful fist and hurled it to the floor.

"Grover Cleveland doesn't give a tinker's damn about your murderer!" he exploded.

Hughes looked nervously around the room and gestured the American to keep his voice down.

"He just wants to keep me from campaigning for his Republican opponent!"

"Surely you will not disobey the request of your president!"

"I can if I choose to!" thundered Roosevelt. "He's my president, not my king, a difference that I gather was lost on you when you manipulated him into sending this!" He glowered at the telegram that lay on the floor. "I knew he was worried about Harrison, but this is beyond the pale!"

"I apologize," said Hughes. "I wanted a fresh outlook so badly, I seem to have overstepped my..."

"Oh, be quiet," Roosevelt interrupted him. "I'm staying."

"But I thought you said—"

"Americans rise to challenges. I'll rise to this one. I'm just annoyed at the way you went about securing my services." He frowned again. "I'll show that corrupt fool in the White House! I'll solve your murder *and* get back to the States in time to help Ben Harrison defeat him in the election!"

"You'll stay?" said Hughes. "I can't tell you what this means! And of course, I'll help you in any way I can."

"You can start by checking me out of this palace and finding me a room in Whitechapel."

"In *Whitechapel?*" repeated Hughes with obvious distaste. "My dear Theodore, it simply isn't done."

"Well, it's about to *get* done," said Roosevelt. "I saw the way the onlookers stared at you, as if you were the enemy, or at least a foreign power. If they're going learn to trust me, then I've got to live like they do. I can't look for a killer until dinnertime, then come back to the Savoy, don a tuxedo, and mingle with the rich and the powerful until the next morning."

"If you insist."

"I do. I just want time to send a wire to my wife Edith, explaining why I won't be on the ship when it docks."

"We can send for her, if—"

"American men do not put their wives in harm's way," said Roosevelt severely.

"No, of course not," said Hughes, getting hastily to his feet. "I'll send my carriage by for you in an hour. Is there any other way I can assist you?"

"Yes. Gather all the newspaper articles and anything else you have on these murders. Once I've got a room in Whitechapel, I'll want all the material sent there."

"You can have everything we've got on Saucy Jack."

"Some name!" snorted Roosevelt contemptuously.

"Well, he does seem to have acquired another one, though it's not clear yet whether he chose it himself or the press gave it to him."

"Oh?"

"Jack the Ripper."

"Much more fitting," said Roosevelt, nodding his head vigorously.

My Dearest Edith:

I'm having Mr. Carlson hand-deliver this letter to you, to explain why I'm not aboard the ship.

Let me first assure you that I'm in perfect health. My extended stay here is due to a pair of conscienceless culprits—the President of the United States and someone known only as Jack the Ripper.

The latter has embarked on a rampage of murder that would shock even our own Western shootists such as Doc Holliday and Johnny Ringo. You do not need to know the details, but believe me when I say that this fiend must be brought to justice.

An officer from Scotland Yard has read of my experiences in the Dakota Bad Lands and asked Grover Cleveland to "loan" me to the British until these murders have been solved—and Cleveland pounced on such an excuse to remove me from the upcoming campaign.

With luck, I'll have things sorted out and solved in time to see Ben Harrison give his victory speech in a little less than two months.

My best to Alice and little Ted.

Your Theodore

Roosevelt sat on a rickety wooden chair, his back to the window, thumbing through Hughes' files.

It was clear that Polly Nichols was a Ripper victim. He doubted that the three who preceded her—Emma Smith, Ada Wilson, and Martha Tabram—were. They'd been brutally murdered, but the *modus operandi* differed appreciably from the two most recent killings.

The files were very circumspect about the Royal who had come under suspicion, but Roosevelt deduced that it was Prince Eddy, more formally Albert Victor, son of the Prince of Wales and, quite possibly, the future King of England.

Roosevelt put the papers down, leaned back on his chair, and closed his eyes. It just didn't make any sense. It would be as if Grover Cleveland had walked into a Washington slum and killed a pair of women and no one had recognized him. It was true that Prince Eddy was a dissolute and depraved man, and Roosevelt held him in total contempt—but there was just no way he could walk fifty yards in any direction, in or out of Whitechapel, without being recognized.

He removed his spectacles, rubbed his eyes, and then stood up. It was time to stop hypothesizing and go out and meet the residents of the area. He needed to talk to them, get to know them, and learn *their* opinions, which, he was sure, would be worth more than the police's.

He walked over to a decrepit coat rack, then paused and smiled. He crossed the room to his steamer trunk, opened it, and a few moments later was dressed in the fringed buckskin he wore at his Dakota ranch. (It had been designed by his favorite New York haberdasher, since all the Dakotans were busily trying to look like New Yorkers.) He took off his shining black shoes and pulled on a pair of well-worn boots. Then he tucked a knife and a pistol into his belt.

He considered a coonskin hat, but decided to wear a stetson instead. He looked at himself in the fly-specked mirror and grinned in approval. As long as he was going to be identified as an American the moment he opened his mouth, he might as well dress like one.

He walked out the door of his shabby building and was immediately aware that he had become an object of notoriety. Every pedestrian within sight stopped to stare at him. Even horse-drawn carriages slowed down as they passed by.

He grinned at them, waved, and began making his way to the Black Swan, next to where Annie Chapman's body had been found. A number of curious onlookers had followed him, and most of them entered the tavern when he did.

He walked up to the bar, staring approvingly at his image in the mirror that faced him.

"I didn't know the circus had come to Whitechapel!" laughed a burly man who was standing a few feet away.

Roosevelt smiled and extended his hand. "Theodore Roosevelt. Pleased to meet you."

"Hey, you're a Yank!" said the man. "Ain't never met one before." He paused and frowned. "Don't rightly know if I like Yanks."

"Them the duds you fight Indians in, guv?" asked another.

"We don't fight Indians any more," answered Roosevelt.

"Killed 'em all, did you?"

"No. Now we live side by side with them."

"I heard they was all killers," said the burly man. "They go around cuttin' people's heads off."

"Most of them are pretty decent people," said Roosevelt, seeing an opportunity to bring up the subject he wanted to discuss. "And even the bad ones couldn't hold a candle to your Saucy Jack."

"Old Jack?" said the burly man with a shrug. "He's off the deep end, he is. Mad as a hatter and ten times as vicious."

"Has anyone here seen him?" asked Roosevelt.

"The only people what's seen him is lying in the morgue chopped up in bits and pieces," said a woman.

"They say he eats their innards," offered another, looking scared as she downed her drink.

"He only goes after women," added the burly man. "Men either fight too hard or don't taste so good."

"Maybe your women should go armed," suggested Roosevelt.

"What good would it do?" responded a woman. "If you're with a John, you don't need no weapon—and if you find you're with old Jack, you ain't got time to use it."

"That's muddled thinking," said Roosevelt.

"Who are you to come in here and tell us how to think?" said the burly man pugnaciously.

"I'm a friend who wants to help."

"Not if you don't live in Whitechapel, you ain't," said the man. "We ain't got no friends except for them what's stuck here."

"You didn't give me a chance to answer," said Roosevelt. "Yes, I live in Whitechapel."

"I ain't never seen you around," said a man from the back of the tavern.

"Me neither," chimed in another.

"I just arrived."

"This ain't a place where you 'arrive', Yank," said the burly man. "It's a place where you get dumped while the rest of London pisses on you."

"Bloody right!" said another of the women, "I'll bet the coppers are probably cheering for old Jack. Every time he strikes, there's less of us for them to worry about."

"If the police won't hunt him down, we'll have to do it ourselves," said Roosevelt.

"What do you mean—*ourselves?*" said the burly man. "You ain't one of us! What do you care?"

"All right-thinking men should care," responded Roosevelt. "There's a crazed killer out there. We have to protect society and bring him to the bar of justice."

"What kind of man dresses like a dandy and wants to hunt down Jack the Ripper? It just don't make no sense." He glared at the American. "You sure you ain't a writer for one of them magazines—them penny dreadfuls, here to make a hero out of old Jack?"

"I told you: I want to hunt him down."

"And when he jumps you, you'll point out that it's not fair to hit a man with spectacles!" guffawed the burly man.

Roosevelt removed his glasses, folded them carefully, and set them down on the bar.

"There are many things I don't need glasses for," he said, jutting out his chin. "You're one of them."

"Are you challenging me to a fight, yank?" said the burly man, surprised.

"Personally, I'd much rather fight the Ripper," said Roosevelt. "But it's up to you."

The man suddenly laughed and threw a huge arm around Roosevelt's shoulders. "I like your nerve, Yank! My name's Colin Shrank, and you and me are going to be great friends!"

Roosevelt grinned. "That suits me just fine. Let me buy you a drink."

"A pint of ale!" Shrank yelled to the bartender. He turned back to Roosevelt. "You're here too early, Yank. Old Jack, he only comes out at night."

"But I see a number of ladies here, and at least some of them must be prostitutes," said Roosevelt.

"They ain't hardly ladies," said Shrank with a laugh, "and they're here because he's got 'em too scared to work at night, which is the proper time for their particular business."

"Too bloody true!" chimed in one of the women. "You ain't gettin' *me* out after dark!"

"I don't even feel safe in the daylight," said another.

"Did anyone here know Polly Nichols or Annie Chapman?" asked Roosevelt.

"I knew Annie," said the bartender. "Came here near every night to find a new bloke. Nice lady, she was."

"Why would she go off with the Ripper?" asked Roosevelt.

"Well, she didn't know it was the Ripper, now did she?" answered the bartender.

Roosevelt shook his head. "Everyone in Whitechapel knows that prostitutes are at risk, so why would Annie go out with someone she didn't know?"

"There's thousands of men come here every night," answered one of the prostitutes. "Maybe tens of thousands. What're the odds any one of them is Jack the Ripper?"

"It ain't *our* fault," said another. "We're just out to make a living. It's the police and the press and all them others. They don't care what happens here. They'd burn Whitechapel down, and us with it, if they thought they could get away with it."

A heavyset woman entered the tavern, walked right up to the bar, and thumped it with her fist.

"Yeah, Irma," said the bartender. "What'll it be?"

"A pint," she said in a deep voice.

"Hard night?"

"Four of 'em." She shook her head disgustedly. "You'd think they'd learn. They never do."

"That's what they've got you for," said the bartender.

She grimaced and took her beer to a table.

"What was that all about?" asked Roosevelt.

"Irma, she's a midwife," answered Shrank.

"She delivered four babies last night?"

Shrank seemed amused. "She cut four of 'em out before they became a bother."

"A *midwife* performs abortions?" said Roosevelt, surprised. "Don't you have doctors for that?"

"Look around you, Yank. There's ten times as many rats as people down here. A gent's got to be as well-armed as you if he don't want to get robbed. Women are being sliced to bits by a monster and no one does nothing about it. So you tell me: why would a doctor work here if he could work anywhere else?"

"No one cares about Whitechapel," said Irma bitterly.

"Well, they'd better *start* caring," said Roosevelt. "Because if this butcher isn't caught, you're going to be so awash in blood that you might as well call it Redchapel."

"Redchapel," repeated Shrank. "I like that! Hell, if we change the name, maybe they'd finally pay attention to what's going on down here."

"Why do you think he's going to kill again?" asked the bartender.

"If his motive is to kill prostitutes, there are still hundreds of them left in Whitechapel."

"But everyone knows he's crazy," said Shrank. "So maybe he never had no motive at all."

"All the more reason for him to strike again," said Roosevelt. "If he had no reason to start, then he also has no reason to stop."

"Never thought of that," admitted Shrank. He gave Roosevelt a hearty slap on the back. "You got a head on your shoulders, Yank! What do you do back in America?"

"A little of everything," answered Roosevelt. "I've been a politician, a rancher, a Deputy Marshall, a naturalist, an ornithologist, a taxidermist, and an author."

"That's a hell of a list for such a young bloke."

"Well, I have one other accomplishment that I'm glad you didn't make me show off," said Roosevelt.

"What was that?"

Roosevelt picked his glasses up from the bar and flashed Shrank another grin. "I was lightweight boxing champion of my class at Harvard."

My Dearest Edith:

I must be a more formidable figure than I thought. No sooner do I agree to help apprehend Jack the Ripper than he immediately goes into hiding.

I have spent the past two weeks walking every foot of the shabby slum known as Whitechapel, speaking to everyone I meet, trying to get some information—any information—about this madman who is making headlines all over the world. It hasn't been productive—though in another way it has, for it has shown me how not to govern a municipality, and I suspect the day will come when that will prove very useful knowledge indeed.

I know America has its rich and its poor, its leaders and its followers, but any man can, through his own sweat and skills, climb to the top of whatever heap he covets. I find England's class system stifling, and I keep wondering where America would be if, for example, Abraham Lincoln had been forced to remain the penniless frontiersman he had been born. We have Negroes who were born into slavery who will someday hold positions of wealth and power, and while slavery is a shameful blot on our history, it was a system that men of good will and reason eventually destroyed. I see no such men attempting to bring about the necessary changes in British society.

I walk through Whitechapel, and I can envision what a handful of Americans, with American know-how and American values, could do to it in five years' time. And yet I fear it is doomed to remain exactly what it is until the buildings finally collapse of their own decrepitude.

I have made some friends among the residents, many of whom have been extremely hospitable to an alien. (Yes, I know I was well treated by the Royal Society, but I came there with a reputation as an expert. I came to Whitechapel only as an outsider. And yet I find I prefer to rub shoulders with the common man on this side of the ocean, even as I have always done at home.)

One special friend is a day laborer (who seems to labor as infrequently as possible) named Colin Shrank, who has been my guide down the fog-shrouded streets and filthy alleys of Whitechapel. As I say, we've discovered no useful information, but at least I now feel I have a reasonably thorough working knowledge of the geography of the place, a knowledge I will be only too happy to expunge the moment I return to our beloved Sagamore Hill.

My best to Alice and little Ted.
Your Theodore

Roosevelt opened a letter, tossing the envelope carelessly on the bar of the Black Swan.

"Another note from your pal Hughes?" asked Shrank.

Roosevelt nodded. "He's through asking who the Ripper is. Now he just wants to know if he's through killing women."

Shrank shrugged. "Could be."

Roosevelt shook his head. "I doubt it. I think he takes too much joy in killing and disemboweling helpless women."

"Up against a man with a knife like that, they're *all* helpless," offered Shrank.

"Not so, Colin." Roosevelt looked around the tavern, and his gaze came to rest on Irma, the burly midwife. "The women he's attacked have all been on the slender side. If he went after someone like Irma here, he might have a real battle on his hands."

"I'm no whore!" snapped Irma indignantly. "I honor the Bible and the Commandments!"

"No offense intended," said Roosevelt quickly. "I was just suggesting that perhaps being a prostitute is not the Ripper's sole criterion, that maybe he goes after women he knows he can dispatch quickly."

"Why quickly, if he's having such a good time?" asked the bartender.

"Secrecy is his ally," answered Roosevelt. "He can't butcher them unless he kills them before they can scream. That means they can't struggle for more than a second or two."

"Ever been anything like him in America?" asked Shrank.

"Not to my knowledge. Certainly not in our cities, where such crimes would not go unnoticed and unreported."

"They gets noticed and reported, all right," said a woman. "Just no one cares, is all."

Roosevelt looked out the window. "It's starting to get dark." He walked to the door. "Come on, Colin. It's time to make our rounds."

"You go alone tonight," said Shrank, taking a drink of his ale.

"Aren't you feeling well?"

"I feel fine. But I been walking those damned bloody streets with you every night since he chopped Annie Chapman. It's been raining all day, and the wind bites right through my clothes to my bones, so I'm staying here. If you spot him, give a holler and I'll join you."

"Stick around, Theodore," added the bartender. "He ain't out there. Hell, he's probably got his throat sliced on the waterfront."

Roosevelt shook his head. "If I can save a single life by patrolling the streets, then I have no choice but to do it."

"That's the coppers' job," insisted Shrank.

"It's the job of every civic-minded citizen who cares about the safety of Whitechapel," replied Roosevelt.

"That lets you out. You ain't no citizen."

"Enough talk," said Roosevelt, standing at the door, hands on hips. "You're sure you won't come with me?"

"I can't even keep up with you in *good* weather," said Shrank.

Roosevelt shrugged. "Well, I can't stand here talking all night."

He turned and walked out into the fog for another fruitless night of hunting for the Ripper.

Roosevelt felt a blunt object poking his shoulder. He sat up, swinging wildly at his unseen assailant.

"Stop, Theodore!" cried a familiar voice. "It's me—John Hughes."

Roosevelt swung his feet to the floor. "You're lucky I didn't floor you again."

"I learned my lesson the first time," said Hughes, displaying a broom. "The handle's two meters long."

"All right, I'm awake," said Roosevelt. "Why are you here?"

"Jack the Ripper has struck again."

"What?" yelled Roosevelt, leaping to his feet.

"You heard me."

"What time is it?" asked Roosevelt as he threw his clothes on.

"About 3:30 in the morning."

"It's Sunday, right?"

"That's correct."

"Damn! I only went to bed about half an hour ago! Where did it happen?"

"In a little court off Berner Street," said Hughes. "And this time he was interrupted."

"By whom?"

"We're not sure."

"That doesn't make sense."

"Come with me, and I'll explain."

Roosevelt finished dressing. "Let's go."

"There it is," said Hughes as he and Roosevelt stared at the woman's body. The head lay in a pool of blood. "He cut her throat and slashed her face, but there's no other damage. He'd pulled her dress up and was just about to cut her belly open when he was interrupted."

"What makes you think he was interrupted?" asked Roosevelt. "Why couldn't he just have stopped for some other reason?"

"Because those two gentlemen"—Hughes pointed at a pair of locals who were speaking with two officers—"heard the scuffle and approached from different directions. We don't know which one startled him—for all we know, he might have heard them both—but he suddenly took flight. They saw the body, realized what had happened, and gave chase."

"For how long?"

Hughes shrugged. "Three or four blocks, before they knew for sure they'd lost him."

"Did they get a glimpse of him?" persisted Roosevelt. "Any kind of description at all?"

Hughes shook his head. "But one of them, Mr. Packer, alerted us, and the body was still warm and bleeding when we found it. We couldn't have missed him by five minutes." He paused. "We've got a hundred men scouring every street and alley in Whitechapel. With a little luck we may find him."

"May I speak to the two witnesses?" asked Roosevelt.

"Certainly."

Hughes accompanied Roosevelt as the American approached the men. "This is Mr. Roosevelt," he announced. "Please answer his questions as freely as you would answer mine."

Roosevelt walked up to the taller of the two men. "I only have a couple of questions for you. The first is: how old are you?"

"34," said the man, surprised.

"And how long have you lived in Whitechapel?"

"All my life, guv."

"Thank you."

"That's all you want to know?" asked the man.

"That's all," said Roosevelt. He turned to the smaller man. "Could you answer the same two questions, please?"

"I'm 28. Ain't never been nowhere else." He paused. "Well, I took the missus to the zoo oncet."

"Thank you. I have no further questions." He shook the smaller man's hand, then walked back to look at the corpse again. "Have you identified her yet?"

Hughes nodded. "Elizabeth Stride. Long Liz, they called her."

"A prostitute, of course?"

"Yes."

"When was the last time anyone saw her alive?"

"She was seen at Bricklayers Tavern just before midnight," answered Hughes.

"With a customer?"

"Yes, but she'd already serviced him. He has an alibi for the time of the murder."

"Which was when?"

"About 45 minutes ago." Hughes looked off into the fog. "I wonder if he's still out there?"

"If he is, I'm sure that—"

He was interrupted by a woman's scream.

"Where did *that* come from?" demanded Hughes.

"I don't know, sir," said one of the policemen. "Either straight ahead or off to the left. It's difficult to tell."

He turned back to Roosevelt. "What do you...*Theodore!!!*"

But the American was already racing into the fog, gun in hand.

"Follow him!" shouted Hughes to his men.

"But—"

"He's a hunter! I trust his instincts!"

They fell into stride behind Roosevelt, who ran through the darkness until he reached Church Passage. He leaned forward in a gunfighter's crouch and peered into the fog.

"It came from somewhere near here," he whispered as Hughes finally caught up with him. "Where does this thing lead?" he asked, indicating the narrow passage.

"To Mitre Street."

"Let's go," said Roosevelt, moving forward silently. He traversed the passage, emerged on Mitre Street, spotted a bulky object in an open yard, and quickly ran over to it.

"Damn!" muttered Hughes as he joined the American. "Another one!"

"Post a man to watch the body and make sure no one touches anything," said Roosevelt. "The Ripper can't be more than a minute ahead of us."

He trotted off down Mitre Street. The police began using their whistles to identify each other, and soon the shrill noise became almost deafening. Roosevelt had gone a short distance when he heard a faint moaning coming from a recessed doorway. He approached the source warily, gun in hand.

"Who are you?" he demanded.

"Thank God it's you, sir!" said a familiar voice, and as he moved closer he realized that it was Irma, the midwife. He lit a match and saw a large bruise over her left temple.

"What happened?"

"I was coming back from Elsie Bayne's when I heard a woman scream. Then a bloke dressed all in black run down the street and bowled me over." She was overcome by a sudden dizziness.

"Did you see his features?"

"He had crazy eyes," said Irma. "The kind what gives you nightmares."

"What color were they?"

"I don't know," she said helplessly. "It's dark."

"How tall was he?"

"Taller than you, sir," she replied. "Much taller. And thin. Like a skeleton, he was!"

"Was there anything, however small, that you can remember?" demanded Roosevelt. "Think hard. It's important."

"All I know is he wore black gloves."

"No distinguishing marks?"

"Just the wound."

"Wound?" said Roosevelt, pouncing on the word. "What wound?"

"On his cheek. It was dripping blood, it was."

"Which cheek?"

"I don't remember."

"Please try."

She frowned as if trying to recall, then whimpered in pain. "I don't know, sir." She looked down the street, where some bobbies were approaching them. "He done sliced another one, didn't he, sir?"

The American nodded. "Not far from here."

"These poor women!" sobbed Irma, starting to cry. "When will it stop?"

Roosevelt stood up. "You're our only eyewitness," he said. "The police artist may want to speak to you later."

"But I done told you what I know!"

"Other details may come back to you. Try to cooperate with him."

She nodded her head while rubbing her tears away with a filthy coat sleeve, and Roosevelt turned to the nearest officer. "When she feels strong enough, take her to the nearest hospital." He turned and walked rapidly back to the latest victim.

"He really did a job on this one, sir," said one of the policemen, staring down at the corpse.

The woman's throat had been slit from ear to ear. The Ripper had then opened her up from neck to groin and gutted her like a fish. Each of her internal organs lay on the ground, neatly arranged in a seemingly meaningless pattern. A piece of her apron had been cut away; the Ripper had evidently use it to wipe his knife.

"Jesus!" said another officer, staring in fascination. "I never saw anyone sliced up like this!"

"You're the taxidermist, Theodore," said Hughes, joining them. "Can you tell if anything's missing?"

Roosevelt studied the organs. "A kidney, I think."

"I'll have the police surgeon make sure," said Hughes. He paused. "If you're right, then we have to ask the question: as crazy as he is, *why* would he steal her kidney?"

"I'd hate to know the answer to that one, sir," said one of the policemen.

"Does anyone know who she is?" asked Roosevelt.

"If she's got any identification on her, it's too blood-soaked to read it," replied Hughes. "We'll ask around. We should know by morning."

Roosevelt walked away from the corpse, then signaled Hughes to join him.

"What is it, Theodore?"

"I wanted to speak where we couldn't be overheard," replied Roosevelt. "I'm sure you'll be happy to know that we can definitely eliminate Prince Eddy from the list of suspects."

"I am, of course," said Hughes. "But how do you know?"

"I've met him," said Roosevelt. "He's a weak man, ravaged by disease. He could barely grip my hand."

"Are you saying he's too weak to have killed these women?" asked Hughes, looking unconvinced.

"Anyone can kill an unsuspecting victim with a knife," responded the American.

"Well, then?"

"Your two witnesses," said Roosevelt. "They were 28 and 34 years old, in the prime of life. They were healthy, and neither was carrying any excess weight. And they know their way around Whitechapel." Roosevelt paused. "How could such an ill man, especially one who doesn't know the area, outrun them? Remember, they said they chased him for three or four blocks. The Albert Victor I met couldn't have run for *one* block, let alone four."

"Thank you, Theodore," said Hughes, obviously relieved. "You've lifted an enormous burden from me."

"Forget about him, and concentrate on what we *do* know," said the American. "For example, we know that the Ripper has an intimate knowledge of Whitechapel or he couldn't have evaded his pursuers. In fact, he evaded pursuit twice in one night, because we couldn't have been 60 seconds behind him at the site of *this* murder, and he vanished like an Apache in the Arizona hills."

"He probably ducked into a building after he bumped into the midwife," said Hughes.

"How would he know which ones were unlocked if he didn't know the area like the back of his hand? Whatever else he may or may not be, the Ripper is a resident of Whitechapel."

"Blast!" muttered Hughes. "That probably clears a second suspect as well."

"Oh?"

"A Dr. Thomas Neill Cream. But he wouldn't know Whitechapel any better than Prince Eddy. Furthermore, he's quite fat. I doubt that he could have outrun *any*one."

Roosevelt stared off into the distance, frowning.

"Is something wrong, Theodore?"

"Of course something's wrong," said Roosevelt irritably. "That madman has butchered two more women right under our noses." He continued looking into the fog and frowning. "And I'm missing something."

"What?"

He frowned again. "I don't know. But it's something I *should* know, something I'm sure I've overlooked."

"Can I be of any assistance?" asked Hughes. Roosevelt remained motionless for another moment, then shrugged and shook his head.

The morgue wagon arrived, Hughes began supervising the removal of the corpse, and Roosevelt went back to his room where he replayed the events of the evening over and over in his mind, looking for the detail he had missed.

My Dearest Edith:

They identified the evening's second victim, a poor prostitute named Catherine Eddowes. I know I said I would be coming home shortly, but I cannot leave while this fiend remains at large.

There is no question that he will strike again, but when and where is almost impossible to predict. There seems to be no pattern

*to his murders until after he has dispatched his victim, and then
the pattern is one that I shall not distress you by describing.*

*There was absolutely nothing I could do to prevent the four
murders, but I have the uneasy feeling that I have the ability
right now to prevent any further killings, if I could but see the
tree rather than the forest. I am certain I know something that
might lead to his apprehension, yet I have no idea what that
knowledge may be.*

*Ah, well, there is no need to worry you with my problems. I
shall be on the first ship home after this dreadful affair has been
brought to a successful conclusion, hopefully in time to make
a speech or two on Ben Harrison's behalf, and then perhaps
we'll take Alice and little Ted on a vacation to Yosemite or the
Yellowstone.*

Your Theodore

"Where were you last night?" demanded Roosevelt when he
entered the Black Swan on the morning of October 1.

"Right here," answered Colin Shrank. "You think I sliced them
two women?"

"I just want to know what time you went home," said Roosevelt.

"Two o'clock or so."

"The first of them wasn't killed until almost three."

"Well, it weren't me!" snapped Shrank. "I didn't kill no bloody
women!"

"I never said you did," said Roosevelt.

"Then why all the questions?"

"Because the one night you didn't make the rounds with me, the
Ripper claimed two more victims. I think I should at least inquire
after your whereabouts."

"Where was *you?*" shot back Shrank.

"I was in bed when Elizabeth Stride was murdered, but I was
in Captain Hughes' company when Catherine Eddowes was killed,"
replied Roosevelt.

"So are you saying I done it or not?" said Shrank belligerently, his
hands balled into massive fists.

Roosevelt stared long and hard at the man, then sighed. "No, I'm not."

"Good!" said Shrank. "And just to show there's no hard feelings, I'll let you buy me a pint of ale."

Roosevelt nodded to the bartender. "And I'll take a cup of coffee."

"Ain't got no coffee, Mr. Roosevelt," said the bartender. "How about a cup of tea?"

"That'll do," said Roosevelt, walking over to a table and sitting down.

"Now we're friends again, what made you decide I *ain't* the Ripper?" asked Shrank.

"Your education."

"What education?" laughed Shrank. "I ain't never been to school in my life!"

"*That* education," said Roosevelt. "If you killed someone, could you find the spleen?"

"What's a spleen?"

"How about the pancreas?"

"Never heard of them."

"Point to where you think my lungs are."

Shrank pointed.

"There's your answer," said Roosevelt. "The Ripper knows where those organs are."

"How do you know I'm not lying?" said Shrank.

"Where would you have learned?"

"Maybe I read it in a book."

"Can you read?"

Suddenly Shrank laughed aloud. "Not a word!"

Roosevelt smiled. "One more reason why you're not the Ripper."

"One *more*?" repeated Shrank. "What was the first?"

"I've seen you get winded *walking* three blocks. The Ripper *ran* for at least half a mile last night and eluded some very fit pursuers."

"Then why'd you come in asking questions like that?"

"I'm just being thorough."

"I thunk we was friends—mates, you might say," said Shrank.

"We are. But if you were the Ripper, that wouldn't stop me from putting you away."

"At least you give a damn. I can't say as much for the rest of 'em."

"You mean the police?" responded Roosevelt. "You misjudge them. They've got hundreds of men working on the case."

"Only because the press keeps goading 'em," said Shrank. "But they don't care about us or Whitechapel. They'll catch the Ripper and then cross us off the map again."

"What do you think would make them do something about Whitechapel?" asked Roosevelt.

"It'll sound balmy—but as long as Saucy Jack's around, they pay attention to us. Maybe having him ain't such a bad thing after all." Shrank laughed bitterly. "He slices up another 40 or 50 women, they might clean this place up and turn it into Hyde Park."

"No," said the bartender with a smile. "Mayfair."

"You really think so?" asked Roosevelt.

"Nobody paid no attention to us before the Ripper, Mr. Roosevelt, and that's a fact," said the bartender.

"That's a very interesting outlook," said Roosevelt. "But I'll keep trying to catch him anyway."

"Maybe old Jack is really your pal Hughes," offered Shrank. "Y'know, he's always the first one at the body."

Roosevelt shook his head. "I was with him when the second woman was killed last night."

"It's a puzzle, all right."

"There are a *lot* of puzzles in this case," said Roosevelt.

"You mean, besides who is he?" said Shrank.

"Yes," said Roosevelt. He frowned again. *For example,* he thought, *why would he have walked off with Catherine Eddowes' kidney?*

It took 16 days for Roosevelt to get his answer. Then Hughes summoned him and showed him a crudely scrawled message that had been sent to George Lusk, the head of the Whitechapel Vigilance Committee.

"From Hell, Mr. Lusk—

Sir, I send you half the Kidne I took from one woman, prasarved it for you tother piece I fried and ate it was very nise I may send you the bloody knif that too it out if you only wate a whil longer signed Catch me when yu can Mishter Lusk"

—*Jack the Ripper*
October 16, 1888

"Well, at least now we know why the kidney was missing," said Hughes. A look of disgust crossed his face. "Do you really think he ate it?"

Roosevelt shrugged. "Who knows? He's certainly *capable* of eating it." He stared at the letter. "Does the handwriting match the previous messages?"

Hughes nodded. "It's the same man, all right."

Roosevelt lowered his head in thought for a moment. "All right," he said. "Here's what you must do. Make copies of that letter and give it to every newspaper in London."

"We can't do that, Theodore! There would be widespread panic."

"I hope so."

"I beg your pardon!" said Hughes heatedly.

"Try to understand, John," said Roosevelt. "Everyone in Whitechapel has been aware of the Ripper for more than a month. Prostitutes know that they're his quarry, and yet they continue to ply their trade and put themselves at risk. Maybe if they read this, if they get a brief peek into the mind of this madman, we can keep them off the streets until he's apprehended."

"Keep prostitutes off the streets?" laughed a nearby policeman. "You might as well try to keep the sun from rising."

"It's that, or prepare yourselves for more murders."

"It's not my decision to make," replied Hughes. "You've been working on this case at my request, and I've been your sole contact, so you can be forgiven for thinking that I'm in charge...but in point of fact we have more than 500 police officers working around the clock on the Ripper murders. I'll have to go through channels before we can get it published."

"What if I just took it to the papers, and said that I hadn't told you what I'd planned?"

"You'd be on the first ship back to America, and I doubt that your presence would ever be tolerated in England again."

That's no great loss in a land that worships royalty and allows some-thing like Whitechapel to exist, thought Roosevelt. Aloud he said, "All right, John—but hurry! The sooner this is made known to the press, the better."

Hughes picked up the letter and stared at it. "I'll do what I can," he said.

"So will we all," replied Roosevelt.

Nothing happened.

A day passed, then a week, then three. The police again began suggesting that the Ripper might have been killed by some other member of the criminal class—there were enough stabbings and bludgeonings in Whitechapel and on the waterfront to write *fini* to a dozen Rippers.

Even Roosevelt relaxed his guard. He spent a day birding in the Cotswolds. He made a speech to the Royal Zoological Society, and another to Parliament. He found the time to write three articles and more than one hundred letters.

And still, he couldn't rid himself of the nagging feeling that this was the calm before the storm, and that he possessed some small but vital piece of the puzzle that could help him prevent another murder.

On the evening of November 8, he sat down to write a letter to his wife.

My Dearest Edith:

It has been almost six weeks since the fiend last struck, and most of the authorities here have convinced themselves that he is dead, possibly by his own hand, possibly murdered. I don't agree. There was no pattern or regularity to his prior killings. The first and second were separated by nine days, the second and third by 22 days, the third and fourth by no more than an hour. Since there has been no pattern, I don't see how they can conclude that he's broken one.

As I mentioned in previous letters, some of the police still lean toward Prince Albert Victor, which is simply beyond the realm of possibility. All of their other suspects also seem to come from the upper classes: a doctor, a lawyer, a shipbuilder. They mean well, the London Metropolitan Police, but they simply lack American practicality as they go about this most important and onerous task.

I may not send this letter to you at all, because I do not want the details to cause you dismay, but I need to clarify my thinking by putting things down on paper.

I begin with the question: what do we know about Jack the Ripper?

It's true that there is an eyewitness account that makes him a head taller than myself, and thoroughly emaciated, but it was made by an hysterical woman whose veracity cannot be relied upon. Still, it's all the police have to go on, and that is the man they are searching for.

But that is all we know empirically. The rest comes from logic—or the science of deduction, to borrow from Sherlock Holmes, the fictional detective who has made such an impact here in the past year.

And what can I deduce?

First, he has at least a rudimentary knowledge of anatomy. The nature of the mutilations implies that he takes pleasure in removing certain internal organs—and he was able to tell a kidney from other organs in near-total darkness on the night of September 30.

Second, he is trying to delude us into thinking he is illiterate. That letter of his is a masterpiece of misdirection—for if he is a doctor, or if he has even studied medicine for a year, how could his spelling, diction and penmanship be so indicative of a barely literate man?

Third, he must possess an intimate knowledge of White-chapel. The only time he was seen he eluded his pursuers, and being unseen the other times also implies familiarity with his surroundings.

Fourth, these murders must be planned in advance—a theory I have not shared with the police, because none of them would accept such a notion. But damn it, he had to know when and where he would kill each of his victims! Because if he didn't, then how did he get fresh clothing, and without fresh clothing, how did this man, who must have been soaked in the blood of his victims, escape detection as he walked through the streets of Whitechapel on his way back to wherever he goes when his foul work is done? He must have had a clean set of clothes hidden within yards of his victim, and that implies premeditation.

Fifth, and this is the one that I cannot begin to answer: even though they have been alerted, even though they know the Ripper is lurking in the darkness, he is nonetheless able to approach his victims with complete impunity. Do they know him? Does he appear so wealthy that they feel it is worth the risk? What leads otherwise cautious women to allow this fiend to approach them? There has been no sign of a struggle at any of the murder scenes. No victim has tried to run from him.

Why?

Roosevelt pulled out his timepiece and opened it. It was 3:40 AM, and he realized that he had fallen asleep.

He looked at the letter, read it over, frowned, and began writing again.

Why? Why? Why?

Suddenly there was a pounding on his door.

"Theodore, wake up!" shouted Hughes. "He's struck again! It's the worst yet!"

Room #13, 26 Dorset Street, was a scene straight out of hell.

Marie Jeanette Kelly—or what remained of her—lay on a blood-soaked bed. Her throat has been slashed. Her abdomen was sliced open. Both her breasts were cut off. Her liver and entrails had been ripped out and placed between her feet. Flesh from her thighs and her breasts had been put on a nearby table. Her right hand was stuck in her belly.

"My God!" exclaimed Hughes, covering his mouth and nose with a handkerchief.

"He was crazy to begin with, but this is past all imagining," said another officer. "He didn't cut her organs out, like the others. He reached in and *pulled* them out with his hands!"

"He had to be drenched in blood," said Roosevelt. "Surely someone saw him, if not here, then walking the street, or trying to hide until he could change into a clean outfit."

"Nobody saw a thing, sir," said the officer.

"They *had* to!" exclaimed Roosevelt. "They couldn't have missed him." He frowned and muttered: "But why didn't it register?"

Roosevelt paused, motionless—and then, slowly, a grin crossed the American's face. The officer stared at him as if he might soon start running amuck.

The American turned and walked to the door.

"Where are you going, Theodore?" asked Hughes.

"Back to my room," answered Roosevelt. "There's nothing more to see here."

"I'll be seeing it in my nightmares for the next thirty years," said Hughes grimly.

Roosevelt went to his desk, opened a drawer, pulled out his pistol, filled it with cartridges, and put it in the pocket of his buckskin coat.

Then he took his pen out, and added a few lines to the letter he had been writing to Edith. *I curse my own blindness! I could have prevented this latest atrocity. I knew everything I had to know more than a month ago, but I didn't put it together until tonight.*

I am going out now, to make sure this fiend never kills again.

Roosevelt sat in the dark, his pistol on his lap, waiting.

Finally the knob turned, and a short, burly figure entered the room.

"Hello, Jack," said Roosevelt, pointing his pistol at the figure.

"Jack? Who's Jack?"

"We both know what I'm talking about," said Roosevelt calmly.

"I just come back from helping poor Liza Willoughby!"

"No," said Roosevelt, shaking his head. "You just got back from murdering Marie Jeanette Kelly."

"You're daft!"

"And you're Jack the Ripper."

"You've done lost your bloody mind!" yelled Irma the midwife, finally stepping out of the shadows.

"The Ripper had to live in Whitechapel," said Roosevelt, never lowering the pistol. "He had to know the area intimately. Who knows it better than a woman who lives and works here and makes dozens of house calls every week?"

He watched her reaction, then continued.

"The Ripper had to have some knowledge of anatomy. Not much —but enough to know one organ from another. Your letter fooled me for awhile. I thought *it* was the misdirection, but I was wrong: you need no formal schooling for your work." He paused. "Are you following me so far?"

She glared at him silently.

"There were two things that bothered me," continued Roosevelt. "Why would these women let the Ripper approach them when they knew he was killing prostitutes in Whitechapel? They'd been warned repeatedly to watch out for strange men. But then I realized that you're a trusted, even a necessary, member of the community. They were all looking for Jack, not Jane.

"The other thing I couldn't figure out," he said, "was how the Ripper could walk around in blood-spattered clothing without drawing everyone's attention. I made the false assumption that the killer had picked the spots for his murders and hidden fresh clothing nearby." Roosevelt grimaced. "I was wrong. Those murders were so deranged I should have known there couldn't be anything premeditated about them. Then, when I was at Marie Kelly's apartment tonight, I saw how you ripped out her intestines with your hands and I *knew* how much blood you had to have splashed on yourself, it occurred to me that I've never seen you when you *weren't* wearing blood-stained clothes. After all, you do nothing all day but deliver babies and perform abortions; there's nothing unusual about a midwife's clothing being bloody."

"So maybe a midwife killed all them women!" yelled Irma. "Do you know how many midwives there are in Whitechapel? Why pick on me?"

"That's what's been haunting me for six weeks," answered Roosevelt. "I knew everything I had to know right after you killed Catherine Eddowes, and yet I couldn't piece it together until I realized that a midwife was the likely killer. You made a major blunder, and it took me until tonight to realize what it was."

"What are you talking about?" demanded Irma, curiosity mingling with hatred on her chubby face.

"You told me you heard a woman scream, and then the Ripper knocked you over while he was escaping from the scene of the crime."

"He did!" said Irma. "He come running out of the darkness and—"

"You're lying," said Roosevelt. "I should have known it immediately."

"It's God's own truth!"

He shook his head. "I found you on the ground less than a minute after we heard Catherine Eddowes scream. The Ripper knocked you down just before I got there, right?"

"Yeah, right."

Roosevelt grinned in triumph. "*That's* what I missed. It would have taken the Ripper five minutes or more to disembowel poor Catherine and arrange her innards on the ground the way he did. Surely she couldn't have screamed four minutes into that. She was dead before he started." The grin vanished. "That was *you* screaming. What better way to escape from the scene of a murder than to have a solicitous policeman escort you to a hospital? If there were any contradictions in your statements, we would write it off to hysteria. After all, you'd just come face to face with Jack the Ripper."

She glared at him balefully.

"Before we put an end to this, perhaps you'll tell me why you did it?"

"I told you before," said the midwife. "I honor the commandments. *They* broke 'em all! They were all sinners, and God told me to rid the world of 'em!"

"Did God tell you to disembowel them, too?" asked Roosevelt. "Or was that your own idea?"

Suddenly a butcher knife appeared in her hand. She held it above her head, screamed something unintelligible, and leaped toward him. Roosevelt never flinched. He kept the pistol trained on her and pulled the trigger.

She fell backward, a new red blotch appearing on the front of her blood-stained dress.

She tried to get up, and he fired once more. This time she lay still.

My Dearest Edith:

Please destroy this letter after you have read it.
I have faked the symptoms of the malaria I contracted some years

ago on a trip to the Everglades, and have been relieved of my unofficial duties here. I will be put aboard the next ship to America (quite possibly on a stretcher if you can imagine that!) and within a very few days I will once again be able to hold you and the children in my arms. And I'm pleased to see that Harrison defeated that fool Cleveland without my help.

My work here is done. I would have preferred to arrest the fiend, but I was given no choice in the matter. Jack the Ripper is no more.

If I make that fact public, two things will happen. First, I will probably be arrested for murder. Second (and actually more important, for no jury would convict me once they have heard my story), Whitechapel will remain a blight upon the face of England. Whereas a conversation I had a few days ago has convinced me that as long as the British authorities think the madman is still at large, they might do something positive about eradicating Whitechapel's intolerable conditions. If that is so, then it may actually be serendipitous that only I (and now you) know that the Ripper is dead.

At least I hope that is the outcome. One would like to think that if one's life didn't count for much, at least one's death did—and if Whitechapel can either be cleansed or razed to the ground, then perhaps, just perhaps, these five unfortunate women did not die totally in vain.

Your Theodore

Theodore Roosevelt returned to London 22 years later, in 1910, on the way home from the year-long safari that followed his Presidency.

Whitechapel remained unchanged.

TWO HUNTERS IN MANHATTAN

This is my most recent Roosevelt story. It was written for Darrell Schweitzer's original anthology *The True History of Vampires*, and the conceit was to have real historical characters interact with vampires at various times and places.

Well, when it comes to real historical characters my first choice is always Teddy Roosevelt, and if there was a vampire in Manhattan in the mid-1890s, he was just the man to deal with it, as he was the city's Police Commissioner from 1895 to 1897.

Things had not been going well for New York's Commissioner of Police. He'd started like a house afire, cleaning up most of the more obvious crime within a year—but then he came to a stone wall. He'd never before met a problem that he couldn't overcome by the sheer force of his will, but although he had conquered the political world, the literary world, and what was left of the Wild West, Theodore Roosevelt had to admit that after making a good start, his efforts to conquer the criminal elements of his city had come to a dead halt.

He'd insisted that every policeman go armed. In their first three shoot-outs with wanted criminals, they'd killed two bystanders, wounded seven more, and totally missed their targets.

So he'd made target practice mandatory. When the city's budget couldn't accommodate the extra time required, almost a quarter of the force quit rather than practice for free.

He'd begun sleeping days and wandering the more dangerous areas by night—but everyone knew that Teddy Roosevelt wasn't a man to miss what he was aiming at, or to run away when confronted by superior numbers, so they just melted away when word went out (and it *always* went out) that he was on the prowl.

1896 drew to a close, and he realized he wasn't much closer to achieving his goal then he'd been at the end of 1895. He seriously considered resigning. After all, he and Edith had four children now, he had two books on the bestseller list, he'd been offered a post as Chief Naturalist at the American Museum, and he'd hardly been able to spend any time at his beloved Sagamore Hill since accepting the post as Commissioner. But every time he thought about it, his chin jutted forward, he inadvertently bared his teeth in a cross between a humorless smile and a snarl, and he knew that he wasn't going anywhere until the job was done. Americans didn't quit when things got rough; that was when they showed the courage and sense of purpose that differentiated them from Europeans.

But if he was to stay, he couldn't continue to depend on his police force to do the job. Men were quitting every day, and many of the ones who stayed did so only because they knew a corrupt cop could make more money than an honest businessman.

There had to be a way to tame the city—and then one day it came to him. Who knew the criminal element better than anyone else? The criminals themselves. Who knew their haunts and their habits, their leaders and their hideouts? Same answer.

Then, on a Tuesday evening in January, he had two members of the most notorious gang brought to his office. They glared at him with open hostility when they arrived.

"You got no right to pull us in here," said the taller of the two, a hard-looking man with a black eye-patch. "We didn't do nothing."

"No one said you did," answered Roosevelt.

The shorter man, who had shaved his head bald—Roosevelt suspected it was to rid himself of lice or worse—looked around. "This ain't no jail. What are we doing here?"

"I thought we might get to know each other better," said Roosevelt.

"You gonna beat us and then put us in jail?" demanded Eye-Patch.

"Why would I do something like that?" said Roosevelt. He turned to the officers who had brought them in. "You can leave us now."

"Are you sure, sir?" said one of them.

"Quite sure. Thank you for your efforts."

The officers looked at each other, shrugged, and walked out, closing the door behind them.

"You men look thirsty," said Roosevelt, producing a bottle and a pair of glasses from his desk drawer. "Why don't you help yourselves?"

"That's damned Christian of you, Mr. Roosevelt, sir," said Baldy. He poured himself a drink, lifted it to his lips, then froze.

"It's not poisoned," said Roosevelt.

"Then you drink it first," said Baldy.

"I don't like to imbibe," said Roosevelt, lifting the bottle to his lips and taking a swallow. "But I'll have enough to convince you that it's perfectly safe."

Baldy stood back, just in case Roosevelt was about to collapse, and when the Commissioner remained standing and flashed him a toothy smile, he downed his drink, and Eye-Patch followed suit a moment later.

"That's mighty good stuff, sir," said Baldy.

"I'm glad you like it," said Roosevelt.

"Maybe we was wrong about you," continued Baldy. "Maybe you ain't such a bad guy after all." He poured himself another drink.

"You still ain't told us what we're here for," said Eye- Patch. "You got to want *something* from us."

"Just the pleasure of your company," said Roosevelt. "I figure men who get to know each other are less likely to be enemies."

"That suits me fine," said Baldy. "You mind if I sit down?"

"That's what chairs are for," said Roosevelt. He picked up the bottle, walked over to each of them, and refilled their glasses.

"They say you spent some time out West as a cowboy, sir," said Baldy. "Maybe you'd like to tell us about it. I ain't never been west of the Hudson River."

"I'd be happy to," said Roosevelt. "But I wasn't a cowboy. I was a rancher, and I hunted bear and elk and buffalo, and I spent some time as a lawman."

"You ever run into Doc Holliday or Billy the Kid?" asked Eye-Patch.

Roosevelt shook his head. "No, I was in the Dakota Bad Lands and they were down in New Mexico and Arizona. But I did bring in three killers during the Winter of the Blue Snow."

He spent the next half hour telling them the story and making sure that their glasses stayed full. When he was done he walked to the door and opened it.

"This was most enjoyable, gentlemen," he said. "We must do it again very soon."

"Suits me fine," slurred Baldy. "You're an okay guy, Mr. Roosevelt, sir."

"That goes for me, too," said Eye-Patch.

Roosevelt put an arm around each of them. "Anyone care for one last drink?"

Both men smiled happily at the mention of more liquor, and just then a man stepped into the doorway. There was a loud pop! and a blinding flash of light.

"What the hell was that?" asked Eye-Patch, blinking his one functioning eye furiously.

"Oh, just a friend. Pay him no attention."

They had their final drink and staggered to the door.

"Boys," said Roosevelt, "you're in no condition to walk home, and I don't have a horse and buggy at my disposal. I suggest you spend the night right here. You won't be under arrest, your cell doors won't be locked or even closed, and you can leave first thing in the morning or sooner if you feel up to it."

"And you won't lock us in or keep us if we want to leave?" said Eye-Patch.

"You have my word on it."

"Well, they say you word is your bond..."

"I say we do it," said Baldy. "If we don't, I'm going to lay down and take a little nap right here."

"I'll summon a couple of men to take you to your quarters," said Roosevelt. He stepped into the corridor outside his office, waved his hand, and a moment later the two men were led to a pair of cells. True to his word, Roosevelt insisted that the doors be kept open.

When they woke up, Roosevelt was standing just outside the cells, staring at them.

"Good morning, gentlemen," he said. "I trust you slept well?"

"God, my head feels like there's an army trying to get out," moaned Baldy.

"We're free to go, right?" said Eye-Patch.

"Right," said Roosevelt. "But I thought we might have a little chat first."

"More stories about cowboy outlaws?"

"No, I thought we'd talk about New York City outlaws."

"Oh?" said Baldy, suddenly alert.

"The criminal element thinks it controls this city," answered Roosevelt. "And to be truthful, they are very close to being right. This is unacceptable. I will bring law and order to New York no matter what it takes." He paused, staring at each in turn through his spectacles. "I thought you two might like to help."

"I *knew* it!" said Baldy. He looked around. "Where's the rubber hoses?"

"Nobody's going to hurt you," said Roosevelt. "We're all friends, remember?"

"Sure we are."

"We *are*," insisted Roosevelt. "In fact, I have proof of it."

"What the hell are you talking about?" demanded Eye-Patch.

"This," said Roosevelt. He handed each of them a photograph, taken the night before. There was Roosevelt, throwing his massive arms around the two happy criminals.

"I don't understand," said Baldy.

"You're going to become my spies," said Roosevelt. "I've rented a room under a false name in the worst section of the Bowery. I'll be there every Monday and Thursday night, and twice a week you're going to report to me and tell me everything that's being planned, who's behind it, who is responsible for crimes that have already been committed, and where I can find the perpetrators."

"You must be crazy!" said Baldy.

"Oh, I don't think so. "There are more copies of that photo. If you *don't* agree to help me, the next time we capture a member from either of your gangs, that photo will be in every newspaper in the city, and the caption will say that it's a picture of me thanking you for informing on your friends."

"Oh, shit!" muttered Eye-Patch. "You'd do it, too, wouldn't you?"

"Absolutely. One way or another, I'm going to bring law and order to New York. Do we have an agreement?"

"We ain't got no choice," said Baldy.

"No, you don't," agreed Roosevelt.

"How long are you going to hold that photo like a rope over our heads?" asked Eye-Patch.

"As long as it takes to get some results."

"Are you open to a deal?"

"We just made one," said Roosevelt.

"A different one."

"Go ahead."

"We'll do what you want," said Eye-Patch. "We ain't got any choice. But there's a guy who can get everything you need a lot quicker than we can, and maybe put a few of the biggest crooks out of action for you. You don't know him—nobody on your side of the fence does—but if I can put you together with him and he's what I say he is, will you burn the pictures?"

"He'll never go for it," said Baldy.

"I might," said Roosevelt.

"I don't mean you, sir," said Baldy. "I'm talking about Big D. There's no place he can't go, and he ain't scared of nothing."

"Big D," Roosevelt frowned. "I've never heard of him."

"That's not surprising," said Eye-Patch. "He only comes around once a week or so, usually just before the bars close. But I've seen him talking and drinking with just about every man you want to nail. Yes, sir, if you'll go for my deal, we'll pass the word to Big D that you'd like to have a pow-wow with him."

Roosevelt pulled out a piece of paper and scribbled an address on it. "This is my room in the Bowery," he said, handing it to Eye-Patch. "Beneath it is the name I will be using while there. Tell him there's money involved if he accepts my offer."

"Then we have a deal?"

"Not until I meet him and decide if he's the man I need."

"And if he's not?" persisted Eye-Patch.

"Then you'll be no worse off than you are now," said Roosevelt.

"What happens to the photos if he kills you?" asked Baldy.

"You think he might?" asked Roosevelt.

"Anything's possible," said Baldy. "He's a strange one, that Big D." He paused uncomfortably. "So *if* he decides to kill you..." He let the sentence hang in the air.

"He'll find out what it's like to be up against a Harvard boxing champion," answered Roosevelt. "It's Wednesday morning. Can you get in touch with him in time for him to come to the room tomorrow night?"

"This town's got a pretty good grapevine," said Eye-Patch.

"Bully! The sooner we get the crusade under way, the better. Gentlemen, you're free to go."

Eye-Patch began walking toward the end of the cell block, but Baldy hung back for a moment.

"I don't figure I owe you nothing, the way you tricked us," he said to Roosevelt. He lowered his voice. "But watch yourself around him, sir." He made no attempt to hide the little shudder that ran through him. "I'm not kidding, sir. I ain't never been scared of nobody or nothing, but I'm scared of *him*."

Roosevelt went to his squalid Bowery room on Thursday night, laid his hat and a walking stick on a chair, and waited. He'd brought a book with him, in case this Big D character hadn't gotten the word or chose not to show up, and by midnight he was pretty sure he'd be reading straight through until dawn.

And then, at 2:30 AM, there was a knock at the door.

"Come," said Roosevelt, who was sitting on an oft-repaired wooden chair. He closed the book and put it on the ugly table that held the room's only lamp.

The door opened and a tall, skeletally thin man entered. He had wild black hair that seemed to have resisted all efforts to brush or comb it, piercing blue eyes, and very pale skin. He wore an expensively-tailored black suit that had seen better days.

"I understand you wish to speak to me," he said, articulating each word precisely.

"If you're Big D, I do," said Roosevelt.

A smile that Roosevelt thought seemed almost indistinguishable from a sneer briefly crossed the man's face. "I am the man you seek. But my name is not Big D."

"Oh?"

"They call me that because they are too uneducated to pronounce my real name. But you, Mr. Roosevelt, will have no difficulty with it."

"I didn't give my...ah...*representatives* permission to reveal my identity."

"They didn't," was the reply. "But you are a famous and easily-recognized man, sir. I have read many of your books, and seen your photograph in the newspapers."

"You still have the advantage of me," said Roosevelt. "If you are not to be called Big D..."

"You may call me Demosthenes."

"Like the ancient Greek?"

"Precisely," said Demosthenes.

"The Greeks are a swarthy race," said Roosevelt. "You don't look Mediterranean."

"I have been told that before."

"The hair seems right, though."

"Are we to discuss my looks or your proposition?" said Demosthenes.

"My proposition, by all means," said Roosevelt. He gestured toward a chair. "Have a seat."

"I prefer to stand."

"As you wish. But I must tell you that I am not intimidated by size."

Demosthenes smiled and sat down. "I like you already, Mr. Roosevelt. But from your books I knew I would. You take such pleasure in the slaughter of animals who want only to escape."

"I am a hunter and a sportsman, not a slaughterer," answered Roosevelt severely. "I shoot no animal that does not have a chance to escape."

"How inefficient," said Demosthenes. He cocked his head and read the spine of Roosevelt's book. "Jane Austen? I should have thought you were beyond a comedy of manners, Mr. Roosevelt."

"She has an exquisite felicity of expression which seems to have eluded you," said Roosevelt.

"Her felicity of expression is duly noted." Another cold smile. "It is manners that elude me."

"So I've noticed. Shall we get down to business?"

"Certainly," said Demosthenes. "Which particular criminal are you after?"

"What makes you think I'm after a criminal?" asked Roosevelt.

"Do not be obtuse, Mr. Roosevelt," said Demosthenes. "I move freely among the criminal element. Two lawbreakers have passed the word that you wished to meet with me. What other reason could you possibly have for this extravagant charade?"

"All right," said Roosevelt. "At present three men control seventy percent of the crime in Manhattan: William O'Brien, Antonio Pascale, and Israel Zuckerman. Thus far my men have been unable to ferret them out. I have been told that you have access to them and the ability to adapt to dangerous situations. The City of New York will pay you a one thousand dollar bounty for each one you deliver to my office."

"And you think this will end crime in Manhattan?" asked Demosthenes, amused.

"No, but we have to start somewhere, and I prefer starting at the top. Each of them will implicate dozens of others if it will get them lighter sentences." Roosevelt paused and stared at the tall man. "Can you do it?"

"Of course."

"*Will* you do it?"

"Yes."

"I'll expect you to keep this agreement confidential," said Roosevelt. "Say one word of it to anyone else and I will feel no obligation to fulfill my end of it."

"I will say nothing of it," answered Demosthenes. "It is comforting to note that even the remarkable Theodore Roosevelt breaks the law when it suits his purposes."

"Only to apprehend greater lawbreakers. I don't question your morality or methodology; I'll thank you not to question mine."

"O'Brien, Pascale, Zuckerman," said Demosthenes. "Have the money ready, Mr. Roosevelt."

"I'll be in my office every afternoon."

"*I* won't." Before Roosevelt could object, he held up a hand. "These men hide by day and come out at night. It is at night that I shall apprehend them."

He turned and walked out of the room without another word.

Roosevelt went back to his Manhattan apartment and slept most of the day on Friday. He arose in late afternoon, had a hearty meal, and walked to his office just after sunset—

—and found the body of Antonio Pascale on the floor.

Damn! thought Roosevelt. *I told him I wanted this man alive for questioning!*

He inspected the body more closely. It seemed even more pale than Demosthenes. Pascale had a blue silk scarf wrapped around his neck. Roosevelt moved it, and found that his throat had been ripped out.

Roosevelt wasn't sickened by the sight. He'd done too much taxidermy, spent too much time in the wilderness, to turn away in horror or disgust...but he *was* puzzled. Did Demosthenes keep a killer dog he hadn't mentioned? Roosevelt tried to reconstruct their meeting in his mind. Could Demosthenes possibly have misunderstood that Roosevelt wanted to get information from the gang leader?

Roosevelt summoned a team of policemen and had them take the body down to the morgue, then sat down heavily on his office chair. How could he get hold of Demosthenes before he killed another man with information Roosevelt needed?

He was still pondering the problem a few hours later when Demosthenes, his color a bit darker and richer than the previous evening, stepped through the doorway, lowering his head to avoid bumping it against the molding. "You owe me a thousand dollars, Mr. Roosevelt."

"You owe *me* an explanation!" snapped Roosevelt. "You knew I wanted this man alive, that he had vital information!"

"He put up a fight," said Demosthenes calmly. "I killed him in self-defense."

"Did you tear out his throat in self-defense too?" demanded Roosevelt.

"No," answered Demosthenes. "I tore out his throat because I wanted to."

"Was there any doubt in your mind that I wanted him alive, that I was not paying you to kill him?"

"None whatsoever."

Roosevelt pulled a small pistol out of his pocket. "Then I am arresting you for murder."

"Put that toy away before I become annoyed with you, Mr. Roosevelt," said Demosthenes, unperturbed. "I will withdraw my request for the thousand dollars, and we'll call it even."

"You don't seem to understand," said Roosevelt. "You killed a man, and now you're going to stand trial for it."

"If you persist in threatening me, I may have to take that gun from you and destroy it."

"I wouldn't advise it."

"When I want your advice, Mr. Roosevelt," said Demosthenes, taking a step toward him, "you may rest assured I shall ask for it."

"That's close enough," said Roosevelt ominously.

"I'll be the judge of that," said Demosthenes.

Roosevelt fired his pistol point-blank at the tall man's chest. He could hear the *thunk!* of the bullet as it struck its target, but Demosthenes paid it no attention. He advanced another step and Roosevelt shot him right between the eyes, again to no effect. Finally the tall man reached out, grabbed the pistol, and bent the barrel in half.

"Who the hell *are* you?" demanded Roosevelt, as he tried to comprehend what had happened.

"I am the man who is going to clean up your city for you," answered Demosthenes calmly. "I have been doing so privately since I arrived here last year. Now I shall do so at the instigation of the Commissioner of Police. Keep your money. I will extract my own form of payment from those criminals whose presence we will no longer tolerate."

"Don't use the word 'we' as if we were partners," said Roosevelt. "You killed a man, and you're going to stand trial for it."

"I think not, Mr. Roosevelt," said Demosthenes. "I sincerely think not."

He turned and walked out of the office. Roosevelt raced to the doorway, spotted a trio of cops at the far end of the corridor, and yelled to them. "Stop that man! Use any force necessary!"

The three men charged Demosthenes, who knocked them flying like ten-pins. Before they could gather themselves to resume the attack, he was gone.

"Who the hell was he, sir?" asked one of the cops, spitting out a bloody tooth.

"I wish I knew," answered Roosevelt, a troubled expression on his face.

All right, thought Roosevelt, sitting at his desk, where he had been for the two hours since Demosthenes had left. *He never saw my gun in the Bowery. Edith would have told me if we'd had a visitor at the apartment. The next time I saw him was right here, so he couldn't have disabled my weapon. He knew it worked, and he knew it wouldn't harm him.*

And what about the three officers who tried to stop him? He brushed them aside like they were insects buzzing around his face. Just what kind of a man am I dealing with here?

There's no precedent for this, and if any member of the force had seen him perform similar acts, word would certainly have reached me.

Yet he implied that he's been killing people for a year now. Probably the criminal element; those are the murders that no one bothers to report.

But what's going on here? It's easy to label him a madman, but he doesn't strike me as deranged.

Roosevelt stood up and began pacing his office. Suddenly he felt almost claustrophobic. It was time to breathe some fresh air, to walk off some of his nervous energy. Maybe just getting out and exercising, taking his mind off Demosthenes for a few minutes, might let him come back to the problem with fresh insights.

Suddenly he heard half a dozen gunshots and an agonized scream. He rushed down the stairs to the main entrance in time to see four of his policemen clustered together around a fifth, who lay motionless on the pavement. A few feet away was another body, as pale as Pascale had been.

"What's going on here?" he demanded, striding out into the open.

"I'll be damned if I know, Mr. Roosevelt, sir," said an officer. "Some tall guy, I mean *real* tall and skinny as a rail came out of nowhere and dumped that body in front of the building. We confronted him and demanded that he come inside to be interrogated, and he refused. Jacobs walked up and grabbed him by the arm, and he threw him against that lamppost. Jacobs weighed about 200 pounds, and the lamppost was twenty feet away." The officer paused. "I think he's dead, sir."

"The tall man?"

"Jacobs, sir. We drew our guns and demanded that the tall man surrender to us, and he just laughed and began walking away, so we opened fire. So help me, sir, we must have hit him four or five times, and he didn't even flinch."

"Let's take a look at the body he brought to us," said Roosevelt. He walked over to the corpse. "Do you recognize him?"

"It's Israel Zuckerman, the guy who runs the Jewish gang." The officer frowned. "At least I think it is."

"You're not sure?"

"I remember Zuckerman being darker, like he'd spent most of his life in the sun. Mediterranean, I think they call the type. This guy's so pale he looks like he's spent the last twenty years in jail."

"It's Zuckerman," said Roosevelt. "Leave that scarf around his neck until you move him inside."

"Whatever you say, sir."

Another officer approached them. "Jacobs is dead, sir."

"Do you have any explanation for what happened?" asked Roosevelt.

The officer shook his head. "It almost like something out of that crazy book everyone's reading."

"I don't know what you're talking about," said Roosevelt.

"It's some kind of thriller about, I don't know, this creature that kills people and drinks their blood."

"I don't read popular literature," said Roosevelt with an expression of distaste.

"Well, if you change your mind, sir," said the other officer, "it's called *Dracula*."

"I think I heard someone mention it once or twice," said Roosevelt with no show of interest.

"It's about this guy who can't be hurt, at least at night. He drinks people's blood..."

"Enough!" said a third officer, who was examining Zuckerman's corpse. "I'd like to eat dinner again sometime before I die."

"Sorry," said the officer.

"All right," said Roosevelt. "Let's get these men inside before the sun comes up and we attract a crowd. Take them both down to the morgue, find out what killed Zuckerman (though I can hazard a pretty good guess right now), and have someone contact Officer Jacobs' widow."

"Shouldn't that be *your* job, sir?"

"It should be, but we've got a killer on the loose, a killer that bullets don't stop. I've got to find out what *will* stop him." He paused. "I suppose we should put a guard around O'Brien, but it wouldn't stop this man, and I'm not going to lose any more officers before I find out how to defeat him."

He went back into the building, climbed the stairs, and retrieved his hat and his walking stick from the corner of his office. Then he went back outside. A few minutes later he was walking up Park Avenue. After a mile he turned onto 34th Street, then turned left on Lexington. He wandered the city, considering the problem, discarding one approach after another, and suddenly realized that it was daylight.

He stopped by a newsstand to pick up a paper, was pleased to see that neither murder had been reported yet, and saw a full-page ad for the hot new bestseller, *Dracula*—the same book his officers had been talking about. He waited until the library opened, walked inside, picked up a copy, and skimmed the first sixty or seventy pages.

It was a flight of fancy. Well-written, though the man couldn't hold a candle to Austen or the Brontes, or Americans such as Mark Twain or Walt Whitman. But the similarities between the fictional Dracula and the very real Demosthenes were striking, and finally he put the book back where he'd found it and began searching through the non-fiction section, trying to find the legends that Bram Stoker had used as his source material. It wasn't easy. There were references to a Nosferatu, and to Wampyres, and to other creatures, but they were so far-fetched that he couldn't see them being of any use. Still, they were *something*, and that was more than he could find anywhere else.

He carried a dozen source books to a table and began taking notes, researching the legend as meticulously as he researched ornithology or naval strategy. He created two columns. The first contained suppositions that three or more sources held in common. When he couldn't find at least three, or when they were contradicted by another source, they were moved to the second column.

By late afternoon he had only two items remaining in the first column. Sooner or later every other "fact", every supposition, had come into conflict with some other legend's or purported history's facts and suppositions.

It wasn't much to go on, but he decided he couldn't wait. Demosthenes wasn't going to stop killing, but once he delivered O'Brien—and that was *if* he delivered O'Brien; he knew that no payment would made—there was every chance that Roosevelt would never see him again.

It would take perhaps half an hour to prepare, but although the sun was low in the sky, he didn't really expect to see Demosthenes before midnight. His three other appearances had always been between midnight and dawn.

Roosevelt stopped by the apartment to have dinner with Edith. Then he finished his preparations, told Edith that he would probably be spending the night at the office, promised to find a cot and not sleep in his chair, and finally took his leave of her, after selecting a book to read, and stuffing a pile of personal correspondence that required answers into a leather case.

He reached the office at about 8:00 PM, told the policemen on duty to pass the word that if Demosthenes showed up, even if he was carrying a corpse, not to try to stop him. They looked at him as if he'd been drinking, but he was the Commissioner of Police and finally they all agreed.

Roosevelt entered his office, sat down at his desk, immediately pulled out and destroyed all existing copies of the photo of himself with Baldy and Eye-Patch. After all, he reasoned, they'd done their duty, even if no one had foreseen the consequences. An avid letterwriter, he spent the next three hours catching up on his correspondence. Then he picked up a copy of F. C. Selous' latest African memoir and began reading it. He was soon so caught up in it that he didn't realize he was no longer alone until he heard the thud of a body being dropped to the floor.

"O'Brien," announced Demosthenes, gesturing toward the pale corpse.

"Why do you keep bringing them to me?" asked Roosevelt. "Our agreement has been abrogated."

"I am bound by a different moral code than you."

"Clearly," said Roosevelt, barely glancing at the body. "I'd like you to tell me something."

"If I can."

"Did you kill Pericles and Sophocles too, or is this a recent aberration?"

A cold smile crossed the tall man's face. "Ah! You know! But of course you would. You are not like the others, Mr. Roosevelt."

"I most certainly am," said Roosevelt. "I am a man. It is *you* who are not like the others, Demosthenes."

"They are sheep."

"Or cattle?" suggested Roosevelt. "You have relatives that live on cattle, do you not?"

Another smile. "You have done your homework, Mr. Roosevelt."

"Yes, I have. Enough that I find it difficult to believe you ever suggested that the warrior who runs away will live to fight another day."

"A misattribution," said Demosthenes with a shrug. "I do not retreat—ever."

"I don't doubt it."

"It nevertheless would have been good advice for you," said Demosthenes. "I intuit that you think you know enough to harm me.

Do not believe everything you believe you have learned. For example, it is said that a vampire may not cross over water, and yet I crossed the Atlantic Ocean to find fresh feeding grounds. They say the sunlight will kill me, yet I have walked down Fifth Avenue at high noon. They say I cannot enter a building without being invited, but you know that no one has invited me here."

"All that is true," agreed Roosevelt. "And it is all irrelevant."

"I admire you, Mr. Roosevelt. Do not do anything foolish that will force me to harm you."

"You are not going to harm me," said Roosevelt, getting to his feet.

"I warn you..." said Demosthenes.

"Save your warnings for those who are afraid of animals," said Roosevelt. "I told you before: I am a hunter."

"We are both hunters, each in our own way," said Demosthenes. "Do you think to slay me with your fabled Winchester rifle?" he added with a contemptuous smirk.

"No," answered Roosevelt, picking up his weapon and positioning himself between Demosthenes and the door. "We both know that bullets have no effect on you."

"Ah!" said Demosthenes with a smile. "You expect to beat me to death with your walking stick?"

"I have a motto," said Roosevelt. "Thus far I've shared it with very few people, but someday I think I shall make it public, for it has served me well in the past and will serve me even better tonight." He paused. "It is: Speak softly and carry a big stick." He removed the metal tip from his wooden walking stick, revealing the sharp point that he had whittled earlier in the evening. "*This* is my big stick."

"So you've learned that much," said Demosthenes, unperturbed. "Has any of your research told you how to drive a wooden stake into the heart of a being with fifty times your strength?"

"Let's find out," said Roosevelt, advancing toward him.

Demosthenes reached out confidently and grabbed the walking stick with his right hand. An instant later he shrieked in agony and pulled his hand back as the flesh on it turned black and began bubbling.

"The wooden stake was not the only thing I learned this afternoon," said Roosevelt. "I took the liberty of rinsing my walking stick with holy water on the way here."

Demosthenes uttered a scream of rage and leaped forward. "If I die, I will not die alone!" he snarled as the point of the stick plunged deep into his chest and his hands reached out for Roosevelt's throat.

"Alone and unmourned," promised Roosevelt, standing his ground.

A minute later the creature named Demosthenes was no more.

It didn't take long for new kingpins to move into the positions vacated by Pascale, Zuckerman and O'Brien. Somehow, after Demosthenes, they didn't seem like the insurmountable problems they might have been a month earlier.

The Commissioner of Police looked forward to the challenge.

THE ROOSEVELT DISPATCHES

On the way home from the 1994 Worldcon in Winnipeg, Kevin Anderson approached me in the airport and asked me to write a story for his anthology, *War of the Worlds: Global Dispatches*. Each story in the book would proceed on the premise that H. G. Wells' Martian invasion had actually occurred, and various historical characters would have to react to it.

Of course I accepted, and of course I chose Teddy Roosevelt. I mean, it was set in 1898, and here a man who was a naturalist, a taxidermist, a politician, a hunter, and military leader who had just led his men in a successful charge up San Juan Hill. Who in all the world was better qualified to face the Martians?

Kevin gave me permission to place it with a magazine before the anthology appeared, and it ran in *F&SF*.

Excerpt from the Diary of Theodore Roosevelt (Volume 23):

July 9, 1898: Shot and killed a most unusual beast this afternoon. Letters of inquiry go off tomorrow to the various museums to see which of them would like the mounted specimen once I have finished studying it.

Tropical rain continues unabated. Many of the men are down with influenza, and in the case of poor Westmore, it looks like we shall lose him to pneumonia before the week is out.

Still awaiting orders, now that San Juan Hill and the surrounding countryside is secured. It may well be that we should remain here until we know that the island is totally free from any more of the creatures that I shot this afternoon.

It's quite late. Just time for a two-mile run and a chapter of Jane Austen, and then off to bed.

Letter from Theodore Roosevelt to F. C. Selous, July 12, 1898:
My Dear Selous:

I had the most remarkable experience this week, one that I feel compelled to share with you.

I had just led my Rough Riders in a victorious campaign in Cuba. We were still stationed there, awaiting orders to return home. With nothing better to do, I spent many happy hours bird-watching, and the event in question occurred late one afternoon when I was making my way through a riverine forest in search of the Long-billed Curlew.

Afternoon had just passed into twilight, and as I made my way through the dense vegetation I had the distinct feeling that I was no longer alone, that an entity at least as large as myself was lurking nearby. I couldn't imagine what it might be, for to the best of my knowledge the tapir and the jaguar do not inhabit the islands of the Caribbean.

I proceeded more cautiously, and in another twenty yards I came to a halt and found myself facing a *thing* the size of one of our American grizzlies. The only comparably-sized animal within your experience would probably be the mountain gorilla, but this creature was at least thirty percent larger than the largest of the silverbacks.

The head was round and was totally without a nose! The eyes were large, dark, and quite widely spread. The mouth was V-shaped and lipless and drooled constantly.

It was brown—not the brown of an impala or a koodoo, but rather the slick moist brown of a sea-slug, its body glistening as if greased. The thing had no arms as such, but it did have a number of long, sinewy tentacles, each seemingly the thickness and strength of an elephant's trunk.

It took one look at me, made a sound that was half-growl and half-roar, and charged. I had no idea of its offensive capabilities, but I didn't like the look of those tentacles, so I quickly raised my Winchester to my shoulder and fired at almost point-blank range.

I could hear the *smack!* of the bullet as it bounced off the trunk of the beast's body. The creature continued to approach me, and I hurled myself aside at the last instant, barely avoiding two of its outstretched tentacles.

I rolled as I hit the ground, and fired once more from a prone position, right into the open V of its mouth. This time there was a reaction and a violent one. The thing hooted noisily and began tearing up pieces of the turf, all the while shaking its head vigorously. Within seconds it was literally uprooting large bushes and shredding them as if they were no more than mere tissue paper.

I waited until it was facing in my direction again and put a bullet into its left eye. Again, the reaction was startling: the creature began ripping apart nearby trees and screaming at such a pitch that all the nearby bird life fled in terror.

By that point I must confess that I was looking for some means of retreat, for I know of no animal that could take a rifle bullet in the mouth and another in the eye and still remain not just standing but aggressive and formidable. I trained my rifle on the brute and began backing away.

My movement seemed to have caught its attention, for suddenly it ceased its ravings and turned to face me. Then it began advancing slowly and purposefully—and a moment later it did something that no animal anywhere in the world has ever done: it produced a weapon.

The thing looked like a sword, but when the creature pointed it at me, a beam of light shot out of it, missing me only by inches, and instantly setting the bush beside me ablaze. I jumped in the opposite direction as it fired its sword of heat again, and again the forest combusted in a blinding conflagration.

I turned and raced back the way I had come. After perhaps sixty yards I chanced a look back, and saw that the creature was following me. However, despite its many physical attributes, speed was not to be counted among them. I used that to my advantage, putting enough distance between us so that it lost sight of me. I then jumped into the nearby river, making sure that no water should invade my rifle. Here, at least, I felt safe from the indirect effects of the creature's heat weapon.

It came down the path some forty seconds later. Rather than shooting it immediately, I let it walk by while I studied it, looking for vulnerable areas. The thing bore no body armour as such, not even the type of body plating that our mutual friend Corbett describes on the Indian rhino, yet its skin seemed impervious to bullets. Its body, which I now could see in its entirety, was almost perfectly spherical except for the head and tentacles, and there were no discernable weak or thin spots where head and tentacles joined the trunk.

Still, I couldn't let it continue along the path, because sooner or later it would come upon my men, who were totally unprepared for it. I looked for an earhole, could not find one, and with only the back of its head to shoot at felt that I could not do it any damage. So I stood up, waist deep in the water, and yelled at it. It turned toward me, and as it did so I put two more bullets into its left eye.

Its reaction was the same as before but much shorter in duration. Then it regained control of itself, stared balefully at me through both eyes—the good one and the one that had taken three bullets—and began walking toward me, weapon in hand...and therein I thought I saw a way in which I might finally disable it.

I began walking backward in the water, and evidently the creature felt some doubt about the weapon's accuracy, because it entered the water and came after me. I stood motionless, my sights trained on the sword of heat. When the creature was perhaps thirty yards from me, it came to a halt and raised its weapon—and as it did so, I fired.

The sword of heat flew from the creature's hand, spraying its deadly light in all directions. Then it fell into the water, its muzzle— if that is the right word, and I very much suspect that it isn't—pointing at the creature. The water around it began boiling and hissing as steam rose, and the creature screeched once and sank beneath the surface of the river.

It took about five minutes before I felt safe in approaching it— after all, I had no idea how long it could hold its breath—but sure enough, as I had hoped, the beast was dead.

I have never before seen anything like it, and I will be stuffing and mounting this specimen for either the American Museum or the Smithsonian. I'll send you a copy of my notes, and hopefully a number of photographs taken at various stages of the post mortem examination and the mounting.

I realize that I was incredibly lucky to have survived. I don't know how many more such creatures exist here in the jungles of Cuba, but they are too malevolent to be allowed to survive and wreak their havoc on the innocent locals here. They must be eradicated, and I know of no hunter with whom I would rather share this expedition than yourself. I will put my gun and my men at your disposal, and hopefully we can rid the island of this most unlikely and lethal aberration.

Yours,
Roosevelt

Letter to Carl Akeley, hunter and taxidermist, c/o The American Museum of Natural History, July 13, 1898: Dear Carl:

Sorry to have missed you at the last annual banquet, but as you know, I've been preoccupied with matters here in Cuba.

Allow me to ask you a purely hypothetical question: could a life form exist that has no stomach or digestive tract? Let me further hypothesize that this life form ingests the blood of its prey—other living creatures—directly into its veins.

First, is it possible?

Second, could such a form of nourishment supply sufficient energy to power a body the size of, say, a grizzly bear?

I realize that you are a busy man, but while I cannot go into detail, I beg you to give these questions your most urgent attention.

Yours very truly,
Theodore Roosevelt

Letter to Dr. Charles Doolittle Walcott, Secretary of the Smithsonian Institution, July 13, 1898:

Dear Charles:

I have a strange but, please believe me, very serious question for you. Can a complex animal life form exist without gender? Could it possibly reproduce—don't laugh—by budding? Could a complex life form reproduce by splitting apart, as some of our single-celled animals do?

Please give me your answers soonest.

Yours very truly,
Theodore Roosevelt

Excerpts from monograph submitted by Theodore Roosevelt on July 14, 1898 for publication by the American Museum of Natural History:

...The epidermis is especially unique, not only in its thickness and pliability, but also in that there is no layer of subcutaneous fat, nor can I discern any likely source for the secretion of the oily liquid that covers the entire body surface of the creature.

One of the more unusual features is the total absence of a stomach, intestine, or any other internal organ that could be used for digestion. My own conclusion, which I hasten to add is not based on observation, is that nourishment is ingested directly into the bloodstream from the blood of other animals.

The V-shaped mouth was most puzzling, for what use can a mouth be to a life form that has no need of eating? But as I continued examining the creature, I concluded that I was guilty of a false assumption, based on the placement of the "mouth". The V-shaped opening is not a mouth at all, but rather a breathing orifice, which I shall not call a nose simply because it is also the source of the creature's vocalizations, if I may so term the growls and shrieks that emanate from it...

Perhaps the most interesting feature of the eye is not the multi-faceted pupil, nor even the purple-and-brown cornea, which doubtless distorts its ability to see colors as we do, but rather the bird-like nictitating membrane, (or haw, as this inner eyelid is called in dogs) which protects it from harm. Notice that although it could not possibly have known the purpose or effects of my rifle, it nonetheless managed to lower it quickly enough to shield the eye from the main force of my bullet. Indeed, as is apparent from even a cursory examination of the haw, the healing process is so incredibly rapid that although I shot it three times in the left eye, the three wounds are barely discernable, even though the bullets passed entirely through the haw and buried themselves at the back of the eye.

I cannot believe that the creature's color can possibly be considered protective coloration...but then, I do not accept the concept of protective coloration to begin with. Consider the zebra: were it brown or black, it would be no easier to spot at, say, a quarter mile, than a wildebeest or topi or prong-horned deer—but because God saw fit to give it black and white stripes, it stands out at more than half a mile, giving notice of its presence to all predators, thereby negating the notion of protective coloration, for the zebra's stripes are, if anything, anti-protective, and yet it is one of the most successful animals in Africa. Thus, while the creature I shot is indeed difficult to pick out in what I assume to be its natural forest surroundings, I feel that it is brown by chance rather than design.

...Field conditions are rather primitive here, but I counted more than one hundred separate muscles in the largest of the tentacles and must assume there are at least another two hundred that I was unable to discern. This is the only section of the body that seems criss-crossed with nerves, and it is conceivable that if the creature can be slowed by shock, a bullet placed in the cluster of nerves and blood vessels where the tentacle joins the trunk of the body will do the trick...

The brain was a surprise to me. It is actually three to four times larger and heavier, in proportion to the body, than a man's brain is in proportion to his body. This, plus the fact that the creature used a weapon (which, alas, was lost in the current of the river), leads me to the startling but inescapable conclusion that what we have here is a species of intelligence at least equal to, and probably greater than, our own.

Respectfully submitted on this 14th day of July, 1898, by
Theodore Roosevelt, Colonel
United States Armed Forces

Letter to Willis Maynard Crenshaw, of Winchester Rifles, July 14, 1898: Dear Mr. Crenshaw:

Enclosed you will find a sample of skin from a newly-discovered animal. The texture is such that it is much thicker than elephant or rhinoceros hide, though it in no way resembles the skin of either pachyderm.

However, I'm not asking you to analyze the skin, at least not scientifically. What I want you to do is come up with a rifle and a bullet that will penetrate the skin.

Just as importantly, I shall need stopping power. Assume the animal will weigh just under a ton, but has remarkable vitality. Given the terrain, I'll most likely be shooting from no more than twenty yards, so I probably won't have time for too many second shots. The first shot *must* bring it down from the force of the bullet, even if no vital organs are hit.

Please let me know when you have a prototype that I can test in the field, and please make no mention of this to anyone except the artisans who will be working on the project.

Thank you.

Yours very truly,
Theodore Roosevelt

Private hand-delivered message from Theodore Roosevelt to President William McKinley, July 17, 1898:

Dear Mr. President:

Certain facts have come to my attention that makes it imperative that you neither recall the Rough Riders from the Island of Cuba, nor disband them upon signing the Armistice with Spain.

There is something here, on this island, that is so evil, so powerful, so inimical to all men, that I do not believe I am exaggerating when I tell you that the entire human race is threatened by its very existence. I will make no attempt to describe it, for should said description fall into the wrong hands we could start a national panic if it is believed or become figures of public ridicule if it is not.

You will simply have to trust me that the threat is a very real one. Furthermore, I urge you not to recall *any* of our troops, for if my suspicions are correct we may need all of them and still more.

Col. Theodore Roosevelt
"The Rough Riders"

Letter to Secretary of War Daniel S. Lamont, July 20, 1898:

Dear Daniel:

McKinley is a fool! I warned him of perhaps the greatest threat yet to the people of America, and indeed to the world, and he has treated it as a joke.

Listen to me: it is essential that you cancel the recall order immediately and let my Rough Riders remain in Cuba. Furthermore, I want the entire army on standby notice, and if you're wise you'll transfer at least half of our forces to Florida, for that seems the likeliest spot for the invasion to begin.

I will be coming to Washington to speak to McKinley personally and try to convince him of the danger facing us. Anything you can do to pave the way will be appreciated.

Regards,
Roosevelt

Speech delivered from the balcony above the Columbia Restaurant, Tampa, Florida, August 3, 1898:

My fellow Americans:

It has lately come to your government's attention that there is a threat to the national security—indeed, to the security of the world— that currently lurks in the jungles of Cuba. I have seen it with my own eyes, and I assure you that no matter what you may hear in the days and weeks to come, the danger is real and cannot be underestimated.

Shortly after my Rough Riders took San Juan Hill, I encountered something in the nearby jungle so incredible that a description of it would only arouse your skepticism and your disbelief. It was a creature, quite probably intelligent, the likes of which has never before been seen on this Earth. I am, and always have been, a vociferous Darwinian, but despite my knowledge of the biological sciences, I cannot begin to hazard a guess concerning how this creature evolved.

What I *can* tell you is that it has developed the ability to create weapons unlike any we have seen, and that it has no compunction about using them against human beings. It is an evil and malevolent life form, and it must be eradicated before it can turn its hatred loose against innocent Americans.

I was fortunate enough to kill the one I encountered in Cuba, but where there is one there will certainly be more. The United States government was originally dubious about the veracity of my claim, but I gather than recent information forwarded to the White House and the State Department from England, where more of these creatures have appeared, has finally convinced them that I was telling the truth.

Thus far none of the creatures has been discovered in the United States, but I say to you that it would be foolhardy to wait until they are found before coming up with an appropriate response. Americans have always been willing to make sacrifices and take up arms to defend their country, and this will be no exception. These creatures may have had their momentary successes against Cuban peasants and an unprepared Great Britain, but I tell you confidently they have no chance against an army of motivated Americans, driven by the indomitable American spirit and displaying the unshakable courage of all true Americans.

To us as a people it has been granted to lay the foundations of our national life on a new continent. We are the heirs of the ages, and yet we have had to pay few of the penalties which in old countries are exacted by the bygone hand of a dead civilization. We have not been obliged to fight for our existence against any alien challenge—until now. I believe we are up to the challenge, and I am convinced that you believe so too.

I am leaving for Miami tomorrow, and from there I will be departing for Cuba two days later, to lead my men into battle against however many of these creatures exist in the dank rotting jungles of that tropical island. I urge every red-blooded, able-bodied American among you to join me on this greatest of adventures.

Letter to Kermit, Theodore Junior, Archie and Quentin Roosevelt, August 5, 1898:

Dear Boys:

Tomorrow I embark on a great and exciting safari. I'm sure the details will be wired back to the newspapers on a daily basis, but I promise that when I return, we'll sit around a campfire at Sagamore Hill, and I'll tell you all the stories that the press never reported. Not only that, but I will bring back a trophy for each and every one of you.

School will be starting before I return. I expect each of you to go to class prepared for his lessons and to apply your minds as vigorously as you apply your bodies to the games you play at home. Had I been slow of wit *or* of body, I would not have survived my initial encounter with the creatures I shall be hunting in the coming days and weeks. Always remember that *balance* is the key in all things.

Love,
Father

Letter (# 1,317) to Edith Carow Roosevelt, August 5, 1898:

My Dearest Edith:

My ship leaves tomorrow morning, so it will perhaps be some weeks before I have the opportunity to write to you again.

Shortly I shall be off on the greatest hunt of my life. Give my love to the children. I wish the boys were just a little bit older, so that I could take them along on what promises to be the most exciting endeavor of my life.

I am still trying to rid myself of the cold I picked up when I plunged into that river in Cuba, but other than that I feel fit as a bull moose. It will take a lot more than a strange beast and a runny nose to bring a true American to his knees. The coming days should be just bully!

Your Theodore

BULLY!

This was the first Teddy Roosevelt story I wrote. I had written a lot about Africa, and about distant worlds that were thinly disguised African analogs, and my observation—made very clear in all my stories and novels—was and still is that colonization has always had a deleterious effect on both the colonizers and the colonized.

One day I got a letter from a reader saying that he believed the fault lay with the Europeans, and that had America colonized Africa things would have worked out very differently. I had just finished reading all of Teddy's twenty-plus books, and I thought: Okay, let's let that greatest and most successful proponent of Americanism, Teddy Roosevelt, try his hand at it and see if things would have worked out any better.

I even found the exact historical moment for the story to begin—and to prove it, I began with two authentic quotes, and the date I started skewing history, a practice I would use in more than half my Roosevelt stories. I also got to use my second favorite historical character, a scalawag named John Boyes, whose two memoirs I was able to bring back into print in a series of classic African adventures I edited a few years ago.

Bully! was nominated for both the Hugo and the Nebula for Best Novella in 1991, and the Teddy Roosevelt stories were off and running.

1

"At midnight we had stopped at the station of Koba, where we were warmly received by the district commissioner, and where

we met half a dozen of the professional elephant hunters, who
for the most part make their money, at hazard of their lives,
by poaching ivory in the Congo. They are a hard-bit set, these
elephant poachers; there are few careers more adventurous, or
fraught with more peril, or which make heavier demands upon
the daring, the endurance, and the physical hardihood of those
who follow them. Elephant hunters face death at every turn,
from fever, from the assaults of warlike native tribes, from their
conflicts with their giant quarry; and the unending strain on
their health and strength is tremendous."

—Theodore Roosevelt

AFRICAN GAME TRAILS "...When we were all
assembled in my tent and champagne had been served out to
everyone except Roosevelt—who insisted on drinking non-
intoxicants, though his son Kermit joined us—he raised his
glass and gave the toast 'To the Elephant Poachers of the Lado
Enclave.' As we drank with him one or two of us laughingly
protested his bluntness, so he gravely amended his toast to 'The
Gentleman Adventurers of Central Africa', 'for,' he added,
'that is the title by which you would have been known in Queen
Elizabeth's time.'

"A real man, with the true outdoor spirit, the ex-President's
sympathy with and real envy of the life we were leading grew
visibly as the evening advanced; and he finally left us with
evident reluctance. I, for one, was shaken by the hand three times
as he made for the door on three separate occasions; but each
time, after hesitatingly listening to the beginning of some new
adventure by one of the boys, he again sat down to hear another
page from our every-day life. We even urged him to chuck all
his political work and come out like the great white man he
was, and join us. If he would do this, we promised to put a force
under his command to organize the hunting and pioneering
business of Central Africa, and perhaps make history. He was,
I believe, deeply moved by this offer; and long afterwards he
told a friend that no honor ever paid him had impressed and
tempted him like that which he received from the poachers of the
Lado Enclave."

—*John Boyes*
THE COMPANY OF ADVENTURERS

The date was January 8, 1910.

Roosevelt walked to the door of the tent, then paused and turned back to face Boyes.

"A force, you say?" he asked thoughtfully, as a lion coughed and a pair of hyenas laughed maniacally in the distance.

"That's right, Mr. President," said Boyes, getting to his feet. "I can promise you at least fifty men like ourselves. They may not be much to look at, but they'll be men who aren't afraid to work or to fight, and each and every one of them will be loyal to you, sir."

"Father, it's getting late," called Kermit from outside the tent.

"You go along," said Roosevelt distractedly. "I'll join you in a few minutes." He turned back to Boyes. "Fifty men?"

"That's right, Mr. President."

"Fifty men to tame the whole of Central Africa?" mused Roosevelt.

Boyes nodded. "That's right. There's seven of us right here; we could have the rest assembled inside of two weeks."

"It's very tempting," admitted Roosevelt, trying to suppress a guilty smile. "It would be a chance to be both a boy and a President again."

"The Congo would make one hell of a private hunting preserve, sir," said Boyes.

The American was silent for a moment, and finally shook his massive head. "It couldn't be done," he said at last. "Not with fifty men."

"No," said Boyes. "I suppose not."

"There are no roads, no telephones, no telegraph lines." Roosevelt paused, staring at the flickering lanterns that illuminated the interior of the tent. "And the railway ends in Uganda."

"No access to the sea, either," agreed Boyes pleasantly, as the lion coughed again and a herd of hippos started bellowing in the nearby river.

"No," said Roosevelt with finality. "It simply couldn't be done— not with fifty men, not with five thousand."

Boyes grinned. "Not a chance in the world."

"A man would have to be mad to consider it," said Roosevelt.

"I suppose so, Mr. President," said Boyes.

Roosevelt nodded his head for emphasis. "Totally, absolutely mad."

"No question about it," said Boyes, still grinning at the burly American. "When do we start?"

"Tomorrow morning," said Roosevelt, his teeth flashing as he finally returned Boyes' grin. "By God, it'll be bully!"

2

"Father?"

Roosevelt, sitting on a chair in front of his tent, continued staring through his binoculars.

"Kermit, you're standing in front of a lilac-breasted roller and a pair of crowned cranes."

Kermit didn't move, and finally Roosevelt put his binoculars down on a nearby table. He pulled a notebook out of his pocket and began scribbling furiously.

"Remarkable bird viewing here," he said as he added the roller and the cranes to his list. "That's 34 species I've seen today, and we haven't even had breakfast yet." He looked up at his son. "I love these chilly Ugandan nights and mornings. They remind me of the Yellowstone. I trust you slept well?"

"Yes, I did."

"Wonderful climate," said Roosevelt. "Just wonderful!"

"Father, I'd like to speak to you for a few moments, if I may."

Roosevelt carefully tucked the notebook back into his breast pocket. "Certainly," he replied. "What would you like to talk about?"

Kermit looked around, found another canvas chair, carried it over next to his father, and sat down on it.

"This entire enterprise seems ill-conceived, Father."

Roosevelt seemed amused. "That's your considered opinion, is it?"

"One man can't civilize a country half the size of the United States," continued Kermit. "Not even you."

"Kermit, when I was twelve years old, the best doctors in the world told me I'd always be underweight and sickly," said Roosevelt. "But when I was nineteen, I was the lightweight boxing champion of Harvard."

"I know, Father."

"Don't interrupt. People told me I couldn't write a proper sentence, but I've written twenty books, and four of them have been bestsellers. They told me that politics was no place for a young man, but when I was 24 I was Minority Leader of the New York State Legislature. They told me that law and order had no place in the West, but I went out and single-handedly captured three armed killers in the Dakota Bad Lands during the Winter of the Blue Snow." Roosevelt paused. "Even my Rough Riders said we couldn't take San Juan Hill; I took it." He stared at his son. "So don't tell me what I can't do, Kermit."

"But this isn't like anything else you've done," persisted Kermit.

"What better reason is there to do it?" said Roosevelt with a delighted grin.

"But—"

"Ex-Presidents are supposed to sit around in their rocking chairs and only come out for parades. Well, I'm 51 years old, and I'm not ready to retire yet. Another opportunity like this may never come along." Roosevelt gazed off to the west, toward the Congo. "Think of it, Kermit! More than half a million square miles, filled with nothing but animals and savages and a few missionaries. The British and French and Portugese and Belgians and Italians all have had their chance at this continent; Africa ought to have one country developed by someone who will bring them American know-how and American democracy and American values. We're a rustic, frontier race ourselves; who better to civilize yet another frontier?" He paused, envisioning a future that was as clear to him as the present. "And think of the natural resources! We'll turn it into a protectorate, and give it favored nation trading status. There's lumber here to build thirty million houses, and where we've cleared the forests away we'll create farms and cities. It will be America all over again—only this time there will be no slavery, no genocide practiced against an indigenous people, no slaughter of the buffalo. I'll use America not as a blueprint, but as a first draft, and I'll learn from our past mistakes."

"But it *isn't* another America, Father," said Kermit. "It's a harsh, savage country, filled with hundreds of tribes whose only experience with white men is slavery."

"Then they'll be happy to find a white man who is willing to redress the balance, won't they?" replied Roosevelt with a confident smile.

"What about the legalities involved?" persisted Kermit. "The Congo is a Belgian colony."

"They've had their chance, and they've muddled it badly." Roosevelt paused. "Suppose you let *me* worry about the Belgians."

Kermit seemed about to argue the point, then realized the fruitlessness of further debate. "All right," he said with a sigh.

"Was there anything else?"

"Yes," said Kermit. "What do you know about this man Boyes?"

"The man's a true pioneer," said Roosevelt admiringly. "He should have been an American."

Kermit shook his head. "The man's a scalawag."

"That's your conclusion after being wined and dined in his tent for a single evening?"

"No, Father. But while you were taking your morning walk and watching birds, I was talking to some of his companions about him. They thought they were bragging about him and telling me stories that would impress me—but what I heard gave me a true picture of the man."

"For example?" asked Roosevelt.

"He's always in trouble—with the law, with the British army, with the Colonial Office." Kermit paused. "They've tried to deport him from East Africa twice. Did you know that?"

"Certainly I know it," answered Roosevelt. Suddenly he grinned and pointed to a small book that was on the table next to his binoculars. "I spent most of the night reading his memoirs. Remarkable man!"

"Then you know that the British government arrested him for..." Kermit searched for the word.

"Dacoity?"

Kermit nodded. "Yes."

"Do you know what it means?" asked his father.

"No," admitted Kermit.

"In this particular case, it means that he signed a treaty with the Kikuyu and got them to open their land to white settlement, and some higher-up in the Colonial government felt that Mr. Boyes was usurping his authority." Roosevelt chuckled. "So they sent a squad of six men into Kikuyuland to arrest him, and they found him surrounded by five thousand armed warriors. And since none of the arresting officers cared very much for the odds, Mr. Boyes volunteered to march all the way to Mombasa on his own recognizance." Roosevelt paused and grinned. "When he walked into court with his five thousand Kikuyu, the case was immediately thrown out." He laughed. "Now, *that's* a story that could have come out of our own Wild West."

"There were other stories, too, Father," said Kermit. "Less savory stories."

"Good," said Roosevelt. "Then he and I will have something to talk about on the way to the Congo."

"You know, of course, that he's the so-called White King of the Kikuyu."

"And I'm an honorary Indian chief. We have a lot in common."

"You have nothing in common," protested Kermit. "You *helped* our Indians. Boyes became king through deceit and treachery."

"He walked into a savage kingdom that had never permitted a white man to enter it before, and within two years he became the king of the entire Kikuyu nation. That's just the kind of man I need for the work at hand."

"But Father—"

"This is a harsh, savage land, Kermit, and I'm embarking on an enterprise that is neither for the timid nor the weak," said Roosevelt with finality. "He's the man I want."

"You're certain that you won't reconsider?"

Roosevelt shook his head. "The subject is closed."

Kermit stared at his father for a long moment, then sighed in defeat.

"What shall I tell Mother?"

"Edith will understand," said Roosevelt. "She has always understood. Tell her I'll send for her as soon as I've got a proper place to house us all." Suddenly he grinned again. "Maybe we should send for your sister Alice immediately. If there's any native opposition, she can terrify them into submission, just the way she used to do with my Cabinet."

"I'm being serious, Father."

"So am I, Kermit. America's never had an empire, and doesn't want one—but I made us a world power, and if I can increase our influence on a continent where we've yet to gain a foothold, then it's my duty to do so."

"And it'll be such fun," suggested Kermit knowingly.

Roosevelt flashed his son another grin. "It will be absolutely bully!"

Kermit stared at his father for a moment. "If I can't talk you out of this enterprise, I wish you'd let me stay here with you."

Roosevelt shook his head. "Someone has to make sure all the trophies we've taken get to the American Museum on schedule. Besides, if we both stay here, the press will be sure I died during the safari. You've got to go back and tell them about the work I'm doing here." Suddenly he frowned. "Oh, and you'll have to see my editor at Scribner's and tell him that I'll be a little late on the safari manuscript. I'll start working on it as soon as we set up a permanent camp." He paused again. "Oh, yes. Before you woke up this morning, I gave a number of letters to Mr. Cunninghame, who will accompany you for the remainder of the journey. I want you to mail them when you get back to the States. The sooner we get some engineers and heavy equipment over here, the better."

"Heavy equipment?"

"Certainly. We've got a lot of land to clear and a railway to build." A superb starling walked boldly up to the mess tent, looking for scraps, and Roosevelt instantly withdrew his notebook and began scribbling again.

"The Congo's in the middle of the continent," Kermit pointed out. "It will be very difficult to bring in heavy equipment from the coast."

"Nonsense," scoffed Roosevelt. "The British disassembled their steamships, transported them in pieces, and then reassembled them on Lake Victoria and Lake Nyasa. Are you suggesting that Americans, who could build the Panama Canal and crisscross an entire continent with railroads, can't find a way to transport bulldozers and tractors to the Congo?" He paused. "You just see to it that those letters are delivered. The rest will take care of itself."

Just then Boyes approached them.

"Good morning, Mr. Boyes," said Roosevelt pleasantly. "Are we ready to leave?"

"We can break camp whenever you wish, Mr. President," said Boyes. "But one of our natives tells me there's a bull elephant carrying at least one hundred and thirty pounds a side not five miles from here."

"Really?" said Roosevelt, standing up excitedly. "Is he certain? I never saw ivory that large in Kenya."

"This particular boy's not wrong very often," answered Boyes. "He says this bull is surrounded by three or four *askaris*—young males—and that he's moving southeast. If we were to head off in *that* direction"—he pointed across the river to an expanse of dry, acacia-studded savannah—"we could probably catch up with him in a little less than three miles."

"Have we time?" asked Roosevelt, trying unsuccessfully to hide his eagerness.

Boyes smiled. "The Congo's been waiting for someone to civilize it for millions of years, Mr. President. I don't suppose another day will hurt."

Roosevelt turned to his son and shook his hand. "Have a safe trip, Kermit. If I bag this elephant, I'll have his tusks sent on after you."

"Good-bye, Father."

Roosevelt gave the young man a hug, and then went off to get his rifle.

"Don't worry, son," said Boyes, noting the young man's concern. "We'll take good care of your father. The next time you see him, he'll be the King of the Congo."

"President," Kermit corrected him.

"Whichever," said Boyes with a shrug.

3

It took Roosevelt six hours to catch up with his elephant, and the close stalk and kill took another hour. The rest of the day was spent removing the tusks and—at the ex-President's insistence—transporting almost three hundred pounds of elephant meat to the porters who had remained with Kermit.

It was too late to begin the trek to the Congo that day, but their little party was on the march shortly after sunrise the next morning. The savannah slowly changed to woodland, and finally, after six days, they came to the Mountains of the Moon.

"You're a remarkably fit man, Mr. President," remarked Boyes, as they made their first camp in a natural clearing by a small, clear stream at an altitude of about 6,000 feet.

"A healthy mind and a healthy body go hand-in-hand, John," replied Roosevelt. "It doesn't pay to ignore either of them."

"Still," continued Boyes, "once we cross the mountains, I think we'll try to find some blooded horses to ride."

"Blooded?" repeated Roosevelt.

"Horses that have already been bitten by the tsetse fly and survived," answered Boyes. "Once they've recovered from the disease, they're immune to it. Such animals are worth their weight in gold out here."

"Where will we find them, and how much will they cost?"

"Oh, the Belgian soldiers will have some," answered Boyes easily. "And they'll cost us two or three bullets."

"I don't understand."

Boyes grinned. "We'll kill a couple of elephants and trade the ivory for the horses."

"You're a resourceful man, Mr. Boyes," said Roosevelt with an appreciative grin.

"Out here a white man's either resourceful or he's dead," answered Boyes.

"I can well imagine," replied Roosevelt. He stared admiringly at the profusion of birds and monkeys that occupied the canopied forest that surrounded the clearing. "It's beautiful up here," he commented. "Pleasant days, brisk nights, fresh air, clear running water, game all around us. A man could spend his life right here."

"*Some* men could," said Boyes. "Not men like us."

"No," agreed Roosevelt with a sigh. "Not men like us."

"Still," continued Boyes, "there's no reason why we can't spend two or three days here. We'll be meeting our party on the other side of the mountains, but they probably won't arrive for another week to ten days. It will take time for word of our enterprise to circulate through the Lado."

"Good!" said Roosevelt. "It'll give me time to catch up on my writing." He paused. "By the way, where did you plan to pitch my tent?"

"Wherever you'd like it."

"As close to the stream as possible," answered Roosevelt. "It's really quite a lovely sight to wake up to."

"No reason why not," said Boyes. "I haven't seen any crocs or hippos about." He gave a brief command to the natives, and pointed to the spot Roosevelt had indicated.

"Please make sure the American flag is stationed in front of it," said Roosevelt. "Oh, and have my books placed inside it."

"You know," said Boyes, "we're using two boys just to carry your books, Mr. President. Perhaps we could leave some of them behind when we break camp and push inland."

Roosevelt shook his head. "That's out of the question: I'd be quite lost without access to literature. If we're short of manpower, we'll leave my rifle behind and have my gunbearer carry one of the book boxes."

Boyes smiled. "That won't be necessary, Mr. President. It was just a suggestion."

"Good," said Roosevelt with a smile. "Just between you and me, I'd feel almost as lost without my Winchester."

"You handle it very well."

"I'm just a talented amateur," answered Roosevelt. "I'm not in a class with you professional hunters."

Boyes laughed. "I'm no professional."

"You were hunting for ivory when we met."

"I was trying to increase my bank account," answered Boyes. "The ivory was just a means to an end. Karamojo Bell is a real hunter, or your friend Selous. I'm just an entrepreneur."

"Don't be so modest, John," said Roosevelt. "You managed to amass quite a pile of ivory. You couldn't do that if you weren't an expert hunter."

"Would you like to know how I actually went about collecting that ivory?" asked Boyes with a grin.

"Certainly."

"I don't know the first thing about tracking game, so I stopped at a British border post, explained that I was terrified of elephants, and slipped the border guards a few pounds to mark the major concentrations on a map of the Lado Enclave so I could avoid them."

Roosevelt laughed heartily. "Still, once you found the herds, you obviously knew what to do."

Boyes shrugged. "I just went where there was no competition."

"I thought the Enclave was filled with ivory hunters."

"Not in the shoulder-high grass," answered Boyes. "No way to sight your rifle, or to maneuver in case of a charge."

"How did you manage to hunt under such conditions?"

"I stood on my bearer's shoulders." Boyes chuckled at the memory. "The first few times I used a .475, but the recoil was so powerful that it knocked me off my perch each time I fired it, so in the end I wound up using a Lee-Enfield .303."

"You're a man of many talents, John."

A yellow-vented bulbul, bolder than its companions, suddenly landed in the clearing to more closely observe the pitching of the tents.

"Lovely bird, the bulbul," remarked Roosevelt, pulling out his notebook and entering the time and location where he had spotted it. "It has an absolutely beautiful voice, too."

"You're quite a birdwatcher, Mr. President," noted Boyes.

"Ornithology was my first love," answered Roosevelt. "I published my initial monograph on it when I was fourteen." He paused. "For the longest time, I thought my future would be in ornithology and taxidermy, but eventually I found men more interesting than animals." Suddenly he grinned. "Or at least, more in need of leadership."

"Well, we've come to the right place," replied Boyes. "I think the Congo is probably more in need of leadership than most places."

"That's what we're here for," agreed Roosevelt. "In fact, I think the time has come to begin formulating an approach to the problem. So far we've just been speaking in generalizations; we must have some definite plan to present to the men when we're fully assembled." He paused. "Let's take another look at that map."

Boyes withdrew a map from his pocket and unfolded it.

"This will never do," said Roosevelt, trying to study the map as the wind kept whipping through it. "Let's find a table."

Boyes ordered two of the natives to set up a table and a pair of chairs, and a moment later he and Roosevelt were sitting side by side, with the map laid out on the table and held in place by four small rocks.

"Where are we now?" asked Roosevelt.

"Right about here, sir," answered Boyes, pointing to their location. "The mountains are the dividing line between Uganda and the Congo. We'll have to concentrate our initial efforts in the eastern section."

"Why?" asked Roosevelt. "If we move *here*"—he pointed to a more centrally-located spot—"we'll have access to the Congo River."

"Not practical," answered Boyes. "Most of the tribes in the eastern quarter of the country understand Swahili, and that's the only native language most of our men will be able to speak. Once we get inland we'll run into more than two hundred dialects, and if they speak any civilized language at all, it'll be French, not English."

"I see," said Roosevelt. He paused to consider this information, then stared at the map again. "Now, where does the East African Railway terminate?"

"Over here," said Boyes, pointing. "In Kampala, about halfway through Uganda."

"So we'll have to extend the railway or build a road about 300 miles or more to reach a base in the eastern section of the Congo?"

"That's a very ambitious undertaking, Mr. President," said Boyes dubiously.

"Still, it will have to be done. There's no other way to bring in the equipment we'll need." Roosevelt turned to Boyes. "You look doubtful, John."

"It could take years. The East African Railway wasn't called the Lunatic Line without cause."

Roosevelt smiled confidently. "They called it the Lunatic Line because only a lunatic would spend one thousand pounds per mile of track. Well, if there's one thing Americans can build, it's railroads. We'll do it for a tenth of the cost in a fiftieth of the time."

"If you extend it from Kampala, you'll have to run it over the Mountains of the Moon," noted Boyes.

"We ran railroads over the Rocky Mountains almost half a century ago," said Roosevelt, dismissing the subject. "Now, are there any major cities in the eastern sector? Where's Stanleyville?"

"Stanleyville could be on a different planet, for all the commerce it has with the eastern Congo," replied Boyes. "In fact, most of the Belgian settlements are along the Congo River"—he pointed out the river—"which, as you can see, doesn't extend to the eastern section. There are no railways, no rivers, and no roads connecting the eastern sector to the settlements." He paused. "Initially, this may very well work to our advantage, as it could be months before news of anything we may do will reach them."

"Then what *is* in the east?"

Boyes shrugged. "Animals and savages."

"We'll leave the animals alone and elevate the savages," said Roosevelt. "What's the major tribe there?"

"The Mangbetu."

"Do you know anything about them?"

"Just that they're as warlike as the Maasai and the Zulu. They've conquered most of the other tribes." He paused. "And they're supposed to be cannibals."

"We'll have to put a stop to that," said Roosevelt. He flashed Boyes another grin. "We can't have them going around eating registered voters."

"Especially Republicans?" suggested Boyes with a chuckle.

"Especially Republicans," agreed Roosevelt. He paused. "Have they had much commerce with white men?"

"The Belgians leave them pretty much alone," answered Boyes. "They killed the first few civil servants who paid them a visit."

"Then it would be reasonable to assume that they will be unresponsive to our peaceful overtures?"

"I think you could say so, yes."

"Then perhaps we can draw upon your expertise, John," said Roosevelt. "After all, Kikuyuland was also hostile to white men when you first entered it."

"It was a different situation," explained Boyes. "They were warring among themselves, so I simply placed myself and my gun at the disposal of one of the weaker clans and made myself indispensable to them. Once word got out that I had sided with them and turned the tide of battle, they knew they'd be massacred if I left, so they begged me to stay, and one by one we began assimilating the other Kikuyu clans until we had unified the entire nation." He paused. "The Mangbetu are already united, and I very much doubt that they would appreciate any interference from us." He stared thoughtfully at Roosevelt. "And there's something else."

"What?"

"I didn't enter Kikuyuland to bring them the benefits of civilization. The East African Railway needed supplies for 25,000 coolie laborers, and all I wanted to do was find a cheap source of food that I could resell. I was just trying to make a living, not to change the way the Kikuyu lived." He paused. "African natives are a very peculiar lot. You can shoot their elephants, pull gold and diamonds out of their land, even buy their slaves, and they don't seem to give a damn. But once you start interfering with the way they live, you've got a real problem on your hands."

"There's an enormous difference between American democracy and European colonialism," said Roosevelt firmly.

"Let's hope the residents of the Congo agree, sir," said Boyes wryly.

"They will," said Roosevelt. "You know, John, this enterprise was initially your suggestion. If you feel this way, why have you volunteered to help me?"

"I've made and lost three fortunes on this continent," answered Boyes bluntly. "Some gut instinct tells me that there's another one to be made in the Congo. Besides," he added with a smile, "it sounds like a bully adventure."

Roosevelt laughed at Boyes' use of his favorite term. "Well, at least you're being honest, and I can't ask for more than that. Now let's get back to work." He paused, ordering his thoughts. "It seems to me that as long as the Mangbetu control the area, it makes sense to work through them, to use them as our surrogates until we can educate *all* the natives."

"I suppose so," said Boyes. "Still, we can't just walk in there, tell them that we're bringing them the advantages of civilization, and expect a friendly reception."

"Why not?" said Roosevelt confidently. "The direct approach is usually best."

"They're predisposed to dislike and distrust you, Mr. President."

"They're predisposed to dislike and distrust Belgians, John," answered Roosevelt. "They've never met an American before."

"I don't think they're inclined to differentiate between white men," said Boyes.

"You're viewing them as Democrats," said Roosevelt with a smile. "I prefer to think of them as uncommitted voters."

"I think you'd be better advised to think of them as hostile—and hungry."

"John, when I was President, I used to have a saying: Walk softly, but carry a big stick."

"I've heard it," acknowledged Boyes.

"Well, I intend to walk softly among the Mangbetu—but if worst comes to worst, we'll be carrying fifty big sticks with us."

"I wonder if fifty guns will be enough," said Boyes, frowning.

"We're not coming to slaughter them, John—merely to impress them."

"We might impress them more if we waited for some of your engineers and Rough Riders to show up."

"Time is a precious commodity," answered Roosevelt. "I have never believed in wasting it." He paused. "Bill Taft will almost certainly run for re-election in 1912. I'd like to make him a gift of the Congo as an American protectorate before he leaves office."

"You expect to civilize this whole country in six years?" asked Boyes in amused disbelief.

"Why not?" answered Roosevelt seriously. "God made the whole world in just six days, didn't He?"

4

They remained in camp for two days, with Roosevelt becoming more and more restless to begin his vast undertaking. Finally he convinced Boyes to trek across the mountain range, and a week later they set up a base camp on the eastern border of the Belgian Congo.

The ex-President was overflowing with energy. When Boyes would awaken at sunrise, Roosevelt had already written ten or twelve pages, and was undergoing his daily regimen of vigorous exercise. By nine in the morning he was too restless to remain in camp, and he would take a tracker and a bearer out to hunt some game for the pot. In the heat of the day, while Boyes and the porters slept in the shade, Roosevelt sat in a canvas chair beside his tent, reading from the 60-volume library that accompanied him everywhere. By late afternoon it was time for a long walk and an hour of serious bird-watching, followed by still more writing and then dinner. And always, as he sat beside the fire with Boyes and those poachers who had begun making their way to the base camp, he would speak for hours, firing them with his vision for the Congo and discussing how best to accomplish it. Then, somewhere between nine and ten at night, everyone would go off to bed, and while the others slept, Roosevelt's tent was always aglow with lantern light as he read for another hour.

Boyes decided that if Roosevelt weren't given something substantial to do he might spontaneously combust with nervous energy. Therefore, since 33 members of his little company had already arrived, he broke camp and assumed that the remaining 15 to 20 men would be able to follow their trail.

They spent two days tracking down a large bull elephant and his young *askaris*, came away with fourteen tusks, six of them quite large, and then marched them 20 miles north to a Belgian outpost. They traded the tusks for seven blooded horses, left three of their party behind to acquire more ivory and trade it for the necessary number of horses, and then headed south into Mangbetu country.

They were quite a group. There was Deaf Banks, who had lost his hearing from proximity to repeated elephant gun explosions, but had refused to quit Africa or even leave the bush, and had shot more than 500 elephants. There was Bill Buckley, a burly Englishman who had given up his gold mine in Rhodesia for the white gold he found further north. There was Mickey Norton, who had spent a grand total of three days in cities during the past twenty years. There was Charlie Ross, who had left his native Australia to become a Canadian Mountie, then decided that the life was too tame and emigrated to Africa. There was Billy Pickering, who had already served two sentences in Belgian jails for ivory poaching, and had his own notions concerning how to civilize the Congo. There were William and Richard Brittlebanks, brothers who had found hunting in the Klondike to be too cold for their taste, and had been poaching ivory in the Sudan for the better part of a decade. There was even an American, Yank Rogers, one of Roosevelt's former Rough Riders, who had no use for the British or the Belgians, but joined up the moment he heard that his beloved Teddy was looking for volunteers. Only the fabled Karamojo Bell, who had just killed his 962nd elephant and was eager to finally bag his thousandth, refused to leave the Lado.

It was understood from the start that Boyes was Roosevelt's lieutenant, and the few who choose to argue the point soon found out just how much strength and determination lay hidden within his scrawny, five foot two inch body. After a pair of fist fights and a threatened pistol duel, which Roosevelt himself had to break up, the chain of command was never again challenged.

They began marching south and west, moving further from the border and into more heavily forested territory as they sought out the Mangbetu. By the time a week had passed, eighteen more men had joined them.

On the eighth day they came to a large village. The huts were made of dried cattle dung with thatched roofs, and were clustered around a large central compound.

The inhabitants still spoke Swahili and explained that the Mangbetu territory was another two days' march to the south. Boyes had the Brittlebanks brothers shoot a couple of bushbuck and a duiker, and made a gift of the meat to the village. He promised to bring them still more meat upon their return, explaining to Roosevelt that this was a standard practice, as one never knew when one might need a friendly village while beating a hasty retreat.

Roosevelt was eager to meet the Mangbetu, and he got his wish two mornings later, shortly after sunrise, when they came upon a Mangbetu village in a large clearing by a river.

"I wonder how many white men they've seen before?" said Roosevelt as a couple of hundred painted Mangbetu, some of them wearing blankets and leopardskin cloaks in the cold morning air, gathered in the center of the village, brandishing their spears and staring at the approaching party.

"They've probably eaten their fair share of Belgians," replied Boyes. "At any rate, they'll know what a rifle is, so we'd better display them."

"They can see that we have them," answered Roosevelt. "That's enough."

"But sir—"

"We've come to befriend them, not decimate them, John. Keep the men back here so they don't feel that we're threatening them," ordered Roosevelt.

"Mr. President, sir," protested Mickey Norton, "please listen to me. I've had experience dealing with savages. We all have. You've got to show 'em who's boss."

"They're not savages, Mr. Norton," said Roosevelt.

"Then what *are* they?"

Roosevelt grinned. "Voters." He climbed down off his horse. "They're our constituents, and I think I'd like to meet them on equal footing."

"Then you'd better take off all your clothes and get a spear."

"That will be enough, Mr. Norton," said Roosevelt firmly.

One old man, wearing a headdress made of a lion's mane and ostrich feathers, seated himself on a stool outside the largest hut, and a number of warriors immediately positioned themselves in front of him.

"Would that be the chief?" asked Roosevelt.

"Probably," said Boyes. "Once in a while, you get a real smart chief who puts someone else on the throne and disguises himself as a warrior, just in case you're here to kill him. But since the Mangbetu rule this territory, I think we can assume that he's really the headman."

"Nice headdress," commented Roosevelt admiringly. He handed his rifle to Norton. "John, leave your gun behind and come with me. The rest of you men, wait here."

"Would you like us to fan out around the village, sir?" suggested Charlie Ross.

Roosevelt shook his head. "If they've seen rifles before, it won't be necessary, and if they haven't, then it wouldn't do any good."

"Is there anything we *can* do, sir?"

"Try smiling," answered Roosevelt. "Come on, John."

They began approaching the cluster of warriors. A dog raced up, barking furiously. Roosevelt ignored it, and when it saw that it had failed to intimidate them, it lay down in the dust with an almost human expression of disappointment on its face and watched the two men walk past.

The warriors began murmuring, softly at first, then louder, and someone began beating a primal rhythm on the drum.

"The Lado is looking better and better with every step we take," commented Boyes under his breath.

"They're just people, John," Roosevelt assured him.

"With very unusual dietary habits," muttered Boyes.

"If you're worried, I can always have Yank act as my interpreter."

"I'm not worried about dying," answered Boyes. "I just don't want to go down in the history books as the man who led Teddy Roosevelt into a Mangbetu cooking pot."

Roosevelt chuckled. "If it happens, there won't be any survivors to write about it. Now try to be a little more optimistic." He looked ahead at the assembled Mangbetu. "What do you suppose would happen if we walked right up to the chief?"

"He's got a couple of pretty mean-looking young bucks standing on each side of him," noted Boyes. "I wish we had our rifles."

"We won't need them, John," Roosevelt assured him. "I was always surrounded by the Secret Service when I was President—but they never interfered with my conduct of my office."

They were close enough now to smell the various oils that the Mangbetu had rubbed onto their bodies, and to see some of the patterns that had been tattooed onto their faces and torsos.

"Just keep smiling," answered Roosevelt. "We're unarmed, and our men are keeping their distance."

"Why do we have to smile?" asked Boyes.

"First, to show that we're happy to see them," said Roosevelt. "And second, to show them that we don't file our teeth."

The Mangbetu brandished their spears threateningly as Roosevelt reached them, but the old headman uttered a single command and they parted, allowing the two men a narrow path to the chief. When they got to within eight feet of him, however, four large bodyguards stepped forward and barred their way.

"John, tell him that I'm the King of America, and that I bring him greetings and felicitations."

Boyes translated Roosevelt's message. The chief stared impassively at him, and the four warriors did not relax their posture.

"Tell him that my country has no love for the Belgians."

Boyes uttered something in Swahili, and suddenly the old man seemed to show some interest. He nodded his head and responded.

"He says he's got no use for them either."

Roosevelt's smile broadened. "Tell him we're going to be great friends."

Boyes spoke to the chief again. "He wants to know why."

"Because I am going to bring him all the gifts of civilization, and I ask nothing in return except his friendship."

Another brief exchange followed. "He wants to know where the gifts of civilization are."

"Tell him they're too big for our small party of men to carry, but they're on their way."

The chief listened, finally flashed Roosevelt a smile, and turned to Boyes.

"He says any enemy of the Belgians is a friend of his."

Roosevelt stepped forward and extended his hand. The chief stared at for a moment, then hesitantly held out his own. Roosevelt took it and shook it vigorously. Two of the old man's bodyguards tensed and raised their spears again, but the chief said something to them and they immediately backed off.

"I think you startled them," offered Boyes.

"A good politician always likes to press the flesh, as we say back home," responded Roosevelt. "Tell him that we're going to bring democracy to the Congo."

"There's no word for democracy in Swahili."

"What's the closest approximation?"

"There isn't one."

The chief suddenly began speaking. Boyes listened for a moment, then turned to Roosevelt.

"He suggests that our men leave their weapons behind and come join him in a feast celebrating our friendship."

"What do you think?"

"Maybe he's as friendly as he seems, but I don't think it would be a good idea just yet."

"All right," responded Roosevelt, holding his hand up to his glasses as a breeze brought a cloud of dust with it. "Thank him, tell him that the men have already eaten, but that you and I will accept his gracious invitation while our men guard the village against the approach of any Belgians."

"He says there aren't any Belgians in the area."

"Tell him we didn't see any either, but one can't be too careful in these dangerous times, and that now that we are friends, our men are prepared to die defending his village from his Belgian oppressors."

The chief seemed somewhat mollified, and nodded his acquiescence.

"Did you ever drink *pombe*?" asked Boyes, as the chief arose and invited them into his hut.

"No," said Roosevelt. "What is it?"

"A native beer."

"You know I don't imbibe stimulants, John."

"Well, Mr. President, you're going to have to learn how to imbibe very fast, or you're going to offend our host."

"Nonsense, John," said Roosevelt. "This is a democracy. Every man is free to drink what he wants."

"Since when did it become a democracy?" asked Boyes wryly.

"Since you and I were invited to partake in dinner, rather than constitute it," said Roosevelt. "Now let's go explain all the wonders we're going to bring to the Congo."

"Has it occurred to you that you ought to be speaking to the *people* about democracy, rather than to the hereditary chief?" suggested Boyes wryly.

"You've never seen me charm the opposition, John," said Roosevelt with a confident smile. He walked to the door of the hut, then lowered his head and entered the darkened interior. "Give me three hours with him and he'll be our biggest supporter."

He was wrong. It only took 90 minutes.

5

They spent the next two weeks marching deeper into Mangbetu territory. News of their arrival always preceded them, transmitted by huge, eight-foot-drums, and their reception was always cordial, so much so that after the first four villages Roosevelt allowed all of his men to enter the villages.

By their eighth day in Mangbetu country the remainder of their party had caught up with them, bringing enough horses so that all 53 men were mounted. Boyes assigned rotating shifts to construct camps, cook, and hunt for meat, and Roosevelt spent every spare minute trying to master Swahili. He forbade anyone to speak to him in English, and within two weeks he was able to make himself understood to the Mangbetu, although it was another month before he could discuss his visions of a democratic Congo without the aid of a translator.

"A wonderful people!" he exclaimed one night as he, Boyes, Charlie Ross and Billy Pickering sat by one of the campfires, after having enlisted yet another two thousand Mangbetu to their cause. "Clean, bright, willing to listen to new ideas. I have high hopes for our crusade, John."

Boyes threw a stone at a pair of hyenas that had been attracted by the smell of the impala they had eaten for dinner, and they raced off into the darkness, yelping and giggling.

"I don't know," he replied. "Everything's gone smoothly so far, but..."

"But what?"

"These people don't have the slightest idea what you're talking about, Mr. President," said Boyes bluntly.

"I was going to mention that myself," put in Charlie Ross.

"Certainly they do," said Roosevelt. "I spent the entire afternoon with Matapoli—that was his name, wasn't it?—and his elders, explaining how we were going to bring democracy to the Congo. Didn't you see how enthused they all were?"

"There's still no word for *democracy* in Swahili," answered Boyes. "They probably think it's something to eat."

"You underestimate them, John."

"I've lived among blacks all my adult life," replied Boyes. "If anything, I tend to overestimate them."

Roosevelt shook his head. "The problem is cultural, not racial. In America, we have many Negroes who have become doctors, lawyers, scientists, even politicians. There is nothing a white man can do that a Negro can't do, given the proper training and opportunity."

"Maybe American blacks," said Billy Pickering. "But not Africans."

Roosevelt chuckled in amusement. "Just where do you think America's Negroes came from, Mr. Pickering?"

"Not from the Congo, that's for sure," said Pickering adamantly. "Maybe West African blacks are different."

"All men are pretty much the same, if they are given the same opportunities," said Roosevelt.

"I disagree," said Boyes. "I became the King of the Kikuyu, and you're probably going to become President of the Congo. You don't see any blacks becoming king or president of white countries, do you?"

"Give them time, John, and they will."

"I'll believe it when I see it."

"You may not live to see it, and I may not," said Roosevelt. "But one of these days it's going to happen. Take my word for it."

A lion coughed about a hundred yards away. Both men ignored it.

"Well, you're a very learned man, so if you say it's going to happen, then I suppose it is," said Boyes. "But I hope you're also right that I'll be dead and buried when that happy day occurs."

"You know," mused Roosevelt, "maybe I ought to urge some of our American Negroes to come over here. They could become the first generation of congressmen, so to speak."

"A bunch of your freed slaves set up shop in Liberia a few years back," noted Charlie Ross. "The first thing they did was to start rounding up all the native Liberians and sell them into slavery." He snorted contemptuously. "Some democracy."

"This will be different, Mr. Ross," responded Roosevelt. "These will be educated American politicians, who also just happen to be Negroes."

"Their heads would be decorating every village from here to the Sudan a week later," said Pickering with absolute certainty.

"The Belgians may be oppressing the natives now," added Boyes, "but as soon as they leave, it'll be back to tribal warfare as usual." He paused. "Your democracy is going to have exactly as many political parties as there are tribes, no more and no less, and no tribal member will ever vote for anyone other than a tribal brother."

"Nonsense!" scoffed Roosevelt. "If that philosophy held true, I'd never have won a single vote outside of my home state of New York."

"We're not in America, Mr. President," responded Boyes.

"I obviously have more faith in these people than you do, John."

"Maybe that's because I know them better."

Suddenly Roosevelt grinned. "Well, it wouldn't be any fun if it was too easy, would it?"

Boyes smiled wryly. "I think you're in for a little more fun than you bargained for."

"God put us here to meet challenges."

"Oh," said Charlie Ross. "I was *wondering* why He put us here."

"That's blasphemy, Mr. Ross," said Roosevelt sternly. "I won't hear any more of it."

The men fell silent, and a few moments later, when the fire started dying down, Roosevelt went off to his tent to read.

"He's biting off more than he can chew, John," said Billy Pickering when the ex-President was out of earshot.

"Maybe," said Boyes noncommittally.

"There's no maybe about it," said Pickering. "He hasn't lived with Africans. *We* have. You know what they're like."

"There's another problem, too, John," added Ross.

"Oh?" said Boyes.

"I have a feeling he thinks of us as the Rough Riders, all in for the long haul. But the long rains are coming in a couple of months, and I've got to get my ivory to Mombasa before then. So do a lot of the others."

"You're making a big mistake, Charlie," said Boyes. "He's offering us a whole country. There's not just ivory here; there's gold and silver and copper as well, and *somebody* is going to have to administer it. If you leave now, we may not let you come back."

"You'd stop me?" asked Ross, amused.

"I've got no use for deserters," answered Boyes seriously.

"I never signed any enlistment papers. How can I be a deserter?"

"You can be a deserter by leaving the President when he needs every man he can get."

"Look, John," said Ross. "If I thought there was one chance in a hundred that he could pull this off, I'd stay, no question about it. But we've all managed to accumulate some ivory, and we've had a fine time together, and we haven't had to fight the Belgians yet. Maybe it's time to think about pulling out, while we're still ahead of the game."

Boyes shook his head. "He's a great man, Charlie, and he's capable of great things."

"Even if he does what he says he's going to do, do you really want to live in the Congo forever?"

"I'll live anywhere the pickings are easy," answered Boyes. "And if you're smart, so will you."

"I'll have to think about it, John," said Ross, getting up and heading off toward his tent.

"How about you, Billy?" asked Boyes.

"I came here for just one reason," answered Pickering. "To kill Belgians. We haven't seen any yet, so I guess I'll stick around a little longer." Then he, too, got up and walked away.

The little Yorkshireman remained by the dying embers for a few more minutes, wondering how just much time Roosevelt had before everything fell apart.

6

Two months into what Roosevelt termed their "bully undertaking" they finally ran into some organized resistance. To nobody's great surprise, it came not from the various tribes they had been enlisting in their project, but from the Belgian colonial government.

Despite the imminent arrival of the long rains, Roosevelt's entire party was still in the Congo, due mostly to the threats, pleadings, and promise of riches that Boyes had made when the ex-President was out of earshot.

They had made their way through a dense forest and were now camped by a winding, crocodile-infested river. A dozen of the men were out hunting for ivory, and Pickering was scouting about thirty miles to the west with a Mangbetu guide, seeking a location for their next campsite. Three more members of the party were visiting large Mangbetu villages, scheduling visits from the "King of America" and arranging for word to be passed to the leaders of the smaller villages, most of whom wanted to come and listen to him speak of the wonders he planned to bring to the Congo.

Roosevelt was sitting on a canvas chair in front of his tent, his binoculars hung around his neck and a sheaf of papers laid out on a table before him, editing what he had written that morning, when

Yank Rogers, clad in his trademark stovepipe chaps and cowboy stetson, approached him.

"We got company, Teddy," he announced in his gentle Texas drawl. "Oh?"

Rogers nodded. "Belgians—and they look like they're ready to declare war before lunch."

"Mr. Pickering will be heartbroken when he finds out," remarked Roosevelt wryly. He wiped some sweat from his face with a handkerchief. "Send them away, and tell them we'll only speak to the man in charge."

"In charge of what?" asked Rogers, puzzled.

"The Congo," answered Roosevelt. "We're going to have to meet him sooner or later. Why should we march all the way Stanleyville?"

"What if they insist?"

"How big is their party?" asked Roosevelt.

"One guy in a suit, six in uniforms," said Rogers.

"Take twenty of our men with you, and make sure they're all carrying their rifles. The Belgians won't insist."

"Right, Teddy."

"Oh, and Yank?"

The American stopped. "Yes?"

"Tell Mr. Boyes not to remove their wallets before they leave."

Rogers grinned. "That little bastard could find an angle on a baseball. You know he's taking ten percent off the top on all the ivory our men shoot?"

"No, I didn't know. Has anyone objected?"

"Not since he went up against Big Bill Buckley and gave him a whipping," laughed Wallace. "I think he's got notions of taking a percentage of every tusk that's shipped out of the Congo from now til Doomsday." He paused. "Well, I'd better round up a posse and go have a pow-wow with our visitors."

"Do that," said Roosevelt, spotting an insect that was crawling across his papers and flicking it to the ground. "And send Mr. Boyes over here. I think I'd better have a talk with him."

"If you're going fight him, I think I can get three to one on you," said Rogers. "The rest of 'em never saw you take out that machine gun nest single-handed at San Juan Hill; *I* did. Want me to put a little something down for you, Teddy?"

Roosevelt chuckled at the thought. "Maybe a pound or two, if it comes to that. Which," he added seriously, "it won't."

Rogers went off to gather some of the men, and a few minutes later Boyes approached Roosevelt's tent.

"You wanted to see me, Mr. President?" he asked.

"Yes, I did, John."

"Is it anything to do with the Belgians? Yank Rogers said you were sending them away."

"They'll be back," said Roosevelt, wiping his face once again and wondering if he'd ever experienced this much humidity anywhere in America. "Pull up a chair, John."

Boyes did so, and sat down opposite Roosevelt.

"John, Yank tells me that you've got a healthy little business going on here."

"You mean the ivory?" asked Boyes, making no attempt to conceal it.

Roosevelt nodded. "We're not here to get rich, John. We're here to turn the Congo into a democracy."

"There's no law against doing both," said Boyes.

"I strongly disapprove of it, John. It's profiteering."

"I'm not making a single shilling off the natives, Mr. President," protested Boyes. "How can that be profiteering?"

"You're making it off our own people," said Roosevelt. "That's just as bad."

"I was afraid you were going to look at it like that," said Boyes with a sigh. "Look, Mr. President, we're all for civilizing the Congo—but we're grown men, and we've got to make a living. Now, for most of them, that means ivory hunting when we're not busy befriending the natives. Believe me when I tell you that if you were to forbid it, eighty percent of the men would leave."

"I believe you, John," said Roosevelt. "And I haven't stopped them from hunting ivory whenever they've had the time."

"Well, I haven't got any spare time, between running the camp and acting as your second-in-command," continued Boyes, "so if I'm to make any money, it can't be by spending long days in the bush, hunting for ivory. So unless you see fit to pay me a salary, this seems like the most reasonable way of earning some money. It doesn't cost you anything, it doesn't cost the natives anything, and every one of our men knew the conditions before they signed on."

Roosevelt considered Boyes' argument for a moment, then nodded his consent.

"All right, John. Far be it from me to stand in the way of a entrepreneur." He paused for a moment. "But I want you to promise me one thing."

"What?"

"You'll let me know before you indulge in any other plans to get rich."

"Oh, I'm never without plans, Mr. President," Boyes assured him.

"Would you care to confide in me, then?"

"Why not?" replied Boyes with a shrug. "I've got nothing to hide." He leaned forward in his chair. "Once you start putting your railroad through here, you're going to need about ten thousand laborers. Now, I don't know if you're going to draft some workers from the local tribes, or hire a bunch of coolies from British East, or import all your labor from America—but I *do* know that ten thousand men eat a lot of food. I thought I'd set up a little trading company to deal with some of the tribes; you know, give them things they want in exchange for bags of flour and other edibles." He paused. "It'll be the same thing I did with the Kikuyu when they built the Lunatic Line, and I kept 25,000 coolies fed for the better part of two years."

"I don't want you fleecing the same people we're trying to befriend," said Roosevelt. "We're here to liberate this country, not plunder it."

"If they don't like what I have to trade, they don't have to part with their goods," said Boyes. "And if they *do* like it, I'll undersell any competitor by fifty percent, which will save your fledgling treasury a lot of money."

Roosevelt stared at him for a long moment.

"Well?" said Boyes at last.

"John, if you can save us that much money without cheating the natives, get as rich as you like."

Boyes smiled. "I don't mind if I do, Mr. President."

"You're a remarkable man, John."

Boyes shook his head. "I'm just a skinny little guy who had to learn to use his head to survive with all these brawny white hunters."

"I understand you gave one of them quite a lesson in fisticuffs," remarked Roosevelt.

"You mean Buckley? I had no choice in the matter," answered Boyes. "If I'd let him get away with it, by next week they'd all be backing out on their bargain." Suddenly he smiled again. "I gave him a bottle of gin and helped him finish it, and by the next morning we were good friends again."

"You're in the wrong profession, John," said Roosevelt. "You should have been a politician."

"Not enough money in it," answered Boyes bluntly. "But while we're on the subject of politics, why did we run the Belgians off? Sooner or later we're going to have to deal with them."

"It's simply a matter of practicality," answered Roosevelt. "I think we gave them enough of an insult that the governor of the Congo will have to come here in person to prove that we can't get away with such behavior—and the sooner we meet with him, the sooner we can present our demands."

"What, exactly, do we plan to demand?"

"We're going to demand their complete withdrawal from the Congo, and we're going to stipulate that they must make a public statement in the world press that they no longer have any colonial ambitions in Africa."

"You're not asking for much, are you?" said Boyes sardonically.

"The Belgians have no use for it, and it costs them a fortune to administer it." Roosevelt paused. "King Albert can go find another hunting reserve. We've got a nation to build here."

Boyes laughed in amusement. "And you think they're going to turn it over to a force of 53 men?"

"Certainly not," said Roosevelt. "They're going to turn it over to the natives who live here."

Boyes stared intently at Roosevelt. "You're serious, aren't you?"

"That *is* what we've come here for, isn't it?"

"Yes, but—"

"We have a job to do, John, and time is the one irreplaceable commodity in this world. We can't afford to waste it."

"Are you sure you're not being a little premature about this, Mr. President?" asked Boyes. "I thought we'd spend a year building a native army, and—"

"We can't win a war with the Belgians, John."

"Then what kind of pressure can you bring to bear on them?" asked Boyes, puzzled.

"We can threaten to *lose* a war with them."

Boyes frowned. "I don't think I quite understand, sir."

"You will, John," said Roosevelt confidently. "You will."

7

It took the Assistant Governor of the Congo exactly seven weeks to hear of Roosevelt's summary dismissal of his district representative and to trek from Stanleyville to the American's base camp, by which time the rains had come and gone, and the ex-President had enlisted not only the entire Mangbetu nation to his cause, but seven lesser tribes as well.

Word of the Belgians' impending arrival reached camp a full week before they actually showed up—"God, I love those drums!" was Roosevelt's only comment—and Yank Rogers and the Brittlebanks brothers were sent out to greet the party and escort them back to camp.

Roosevelt ordered Boyes to send five of their men out on a two-week hunting expedition. When the little Yorkshireman asked what they were supposed to be hunting for, Roosevelt replied that he didn't much care, as long as they were totally out of communication for at least fourteen days. Boyes shrugged, scratched his head, and finally selected five of his companions at random and suggested they do a little ivory hunting far to the south for the two weeks. Since they had virtually shot out the immediate area, he received no objections.

When the Belgian party finally reached the camp, Roosevelt was waiting for them. He had had his men construct a huge table, some thirty feet long and five feet wide, and the moment they dismounted he invited them to join him and his men for lunch. The Assistant Governor, a tall, lean, ambitious man named Gerard Silva, seemed somewhat taken aback by the American's hospitality, but allowed himself and his twenty armed soldiers to be escorted to the table, where a truly magnificent feast of warthog, bushbuck, and guinea fowl awaited them.

Roosevelt's men, such as could fit on one side of the table, sat facing the west, and the Belgian soldiers were seated opposite them. The American sat at the head of the table, and Silva sat at the foot of it, thirty feet away. Under such an arrangement, private discussions between the two leaders was impossible, and Roosevelt encouraged his men to discuss their hunting and exploring adventures, though not more than half a dozen of the Belgian soldiers could speak or understand English.

Finally, after almost two hours, the meal was concluded, and Roosevelt's men—except for Boyes—left the table one by one. Silva nodded to a young lieutenant, and the Belgian soldiers followed suit, clustering awkwardly around their horses. Then Silva stood up, walked down to Roosevelt's end of the table, and seated himself next to the American.

"I hope you enjoyed your meal, Mr. Silva," said Roosevelt, sipping a cup of tea.

"It was quite excellent, Mr...?" Silva paused. "What would you prefer that I call you?"

"Colonel Roosevelt, Mr. Roosevelt, or Mr. President, as you prefer," said Roosevelt expansively.

"It was an excellent meal, Mr. Roosevelt," said Silva in precise, heavily-accented English. He withdrew a cigar and offered one to Roosevelt, who refused it. "A wise decision," he said. "The tobacco we grow here is decidedly inferior."

"You must be anxious to return to Belgium, then," suggested Roosevelt.

"As you must be anxious to return to America," responded Silva.

"Actually, I like it here," said Roosevelt. "But then, I don't smoke."

"A nasty habit," admitted Silva. "But then, so is trespassing."

"*Am* I trespassing?" asked Roosevelt innocently.

"Do not be coy with me, Mr. Roosevelt," said Silva. "It is most unbecoming. You have brought a force of men into Belgian territory for reasons that have not been made clear to us. You have no hunting permit, no visa, no permission to be here at all."

"Are you telling us to leave?"

"I am simply trying to discover your purpose here," said Silva. "If you have come solely for sport, I will personally present you with papers that will allow you to go anywhere you wish within the Congo. If you have come for some other reason, I demand to know what it is."

"I would rather discuss that with the governor himself," responded Roosevelt.

"He is quite ill with malaria, and may not be able to leave Stanleyville for another month."

Roosevelt considered the statement for a moment, then shook his head. "No, we've wasted enough time already. I suppose you'll simply have to take my message to him." He paused. "I suppose it doesn't make much difference. The only thing he'll do is transmit my message to King Albert."

"And what is the gist of your message, Mr. Roosevelt?" asked Silva, leaning forward intently.

"My men and I don't consider ourselves to be in Belgian territory."

Silva smiled humorlessly. "Perhaps you would like me to pinpoint your position on a map. You are indeed within the legal boundaries of the Belgian Congo."

"We know where we are, and we fully agree that we are inside the border of the Congo," answered Roosevelt. "But we don't recognize your authority here."

"Here? You mean right where we are sitting?"

"I mean anywhere in the Congo."

"The Congo is Belgian territory, Mr. Roosevelt."

Roosevelt shook his head. "The Congo belongs to its inhabitants. It's time they began determining their own future."

"That is the most ridiculous thing I have ever heard," said Silva. "It has been acknowledged by all the great powers that the Congo is our colony."

"All but one," said Roosevelt.

"America acknowledges our right to the Congo."

"America has a history of opposing imperialism wherever we find it," replied Roosevelt. "We threw the British out of our own country, and we're fully prepared to throw the Belgians out of the Congo."

"Just as, when you were President, you threw the Panamanians out of Panama?" asked Silva sardonically.

"America has no imperial claim to Panama. The Panamanians have their own government and we recognize it." Roosevelt paused. "However, we're not talking about Panama, but about the Congo."

Silva stared at Roosevelt. "For whom do you speak, Mr. Roosevelt?" asked Silva. "You are no longer President, so surely you do not speak for America."

"I speak for the citizens of the Congo."

Silva laughed contemptuously. "They are a bunch of savages who have no interest whatsoever in who rules them."

"Would you care to put that to a vote?" asked Roosevelt with a smile.

"So they vote now?"

"Not yet," answered Roosevelt. "But they will as soon as they are free to do so."

"And who will set them free?"

"*We* will," interjected Boyes from his seat halfway down the table.

"*You* will?" repeated Silva, turning to face Boyes. "I've heard about you, John Boyes. You have been in trouble with every government from South Africa to Abyssinia."

"I don't get along well with colonial governments," replied Boyes.

"You don't get along well with native governments, either," said Silva. He turned to Roosevelt. "Did you know that your companion talked the ignorant natives who proclaimed him their king into selling him Mount Kenya for the enormous price of four goats?"

"Six," Boyes corrected him with a smile. "I wouldn't want it said that I was cheap."

"This is ridiculous!" said Silva in exasperation. "I cannot believe I am hearing this! Do you really propose to conquer the Belgian Congo with a force of 53 men?"

"Absolutely not," said Roosevelt pleasantly.

"Well, then?"

"First," said Roosevelt, "it is the Congo, not the Belgian Congo. Second, we don't propose to conquer it, but to liberate it. And third, your intelligence is wrong. There are only 48 men in my party."

"48, 53—what is the difference?"

"Oh, there is a difference, Mr. Silva," said Roosevelt. He paused. "The other five are halfway to Nairobi by now."

"What do they propose to do once they get there?" asked Silva suspiciously.

"They propose to tell the American press that Teddy Roosevelt—who is, in all immodesty, the most popular and influential American of the past half century—is under military attack by the Belgian government. His brave little force is standing firm, but he can't hold out much longer without help, and if he should die while trying to free the citizens of the Congo from the yoke of Belgian tyranny, he wants America to know that he died at the hands of King Albert, who, I believe, has more than enough problems in Europe without adding this to his burden."

"You are mad!" exclaimed Silva. "Do you really think anyone will care what happens here?"

"That is probably just what the Mahdi said to Chinese Gordon at the fall of Khartoum," said Roosevelt easily. "Read your history books and you'll see what happened when the British people learned of his death."

"You are bluffing!"

"You are welcome to think so," replied Roosevelt calmly. "But in two months' time, 50,000 Americans will be standing in line to fight at my side in the Congo—and if you kill me, you can multiply that number by one hundred, and most of them will want to take the battle right to Belgium."

"This is the most preposterous thing I have ever heard!" exclaimed Silva.

Roosevelt reached into a pocket of his hunting jacket and pulled out a thick, official-looking document he had written the previous day.

"It's all here in black and white, Mr. Silva. I suggest that you deliver it to your superior as quickly as possible, because he'll want to send it on to Belgium, and I know how long these things take." He paused. "We'd like you out of the Congo in six months, so you can see that there's no time to waste."

"We are going nowhere!"

Roosevelt sighed deeply. "I'm afraid you are up against an historic inevitability," he said. "You have 20 armed men. I have 47, not counting myself. It would be suicidal for you to attack us here and now, and by the time you return from Stanleyville, I'll have a force of more than 30,000 Mangbetu plus a number of other tribes, who will not be denied their independence any longer."

"My men are a trained military force," said Silva. "Yours are a ragtag band of outcasts and poachers."

"But good shots," said Roosevelt with a confident grin. He paused again and the grin vanished. "Besides, if you succeed in killing me, you'll be the man who precipitated a war with the United States. Are you quite certain you want that responsibility?"

Silva was silent for a moment. Finally he spoke.

"I will return to Stanleyville," he announced. "But I will be back. This I promise you."

"We won't be here," answered Roosevelt.

"Where will you be?"

"I have no idea—but I have every intention of remaining alive until news of what's happening here gets back to America." Roosevelt paused and smiled. "The Congo is a large country, Mr. Silva. I plan to make many more friends here while awaiting Belgium's decision."

Silva got abruptly to his feet. "With this paper," he said, holding up the document, "you have signed not only your own death warrant, but the death warrant of every man who follows you."

Boyes laughed from his position halfway down the table. "Do you know how many death warrants have been issued on me? I'll just add this one to my collection." He paused, amused. "I've never had one written in French before."

"You are both mad!" snapped Silva, stalking off toward his men.

Roosevelt watched the assistant governor mount his horse and gallop off, followed by his twenty soldiers.

"I suppose we should have invited him to stay for dinner," he remarked pleasantly.

"You don't really think this is going to work, do you?" asked Boyes.

"Certainly."

"It's a lot of fancy talk, but it boils down to the fact that we're still only 53 men," said Boyes. "You'll never get the natives to go to war with the Belgians. They haven't any guns, and even if they did, we can't prepare them to fight a modern war in just six months' time."

"John, you know Africa and you know hunting," answered Roosevelt seriously, "but I know politics and I know history. The Congo is an embarrassment to the Belgians; Leopold wasted so much money here that his own government took it away from him two years ago. Furthermore, Europe is heading hell for leather for a war such as it has never seen before. The last thing they need is a battle with America over a piece of territory they didn't really want to begin with."

"They must want it or they wouldn't be here," said Boyes stubbornly.

Roosevelt shook his head. "They just didn't want anyone else to have it. When Africa was divided among the great powers in 1885, Belgium would have lost face if it hadn't insisted on its right to colonize the Congo, but it's been an expensive investment that has been a financial drain and a political embarrassment for more than two decades." He paused. "And what I said about General Gordon was true. He refused to leave Khartoum, and his death eventually forced the British government to take over the Sudan when the public demanded that they avenge him." Suddenly Roosevelt grinned. "A lot more people voted for me than ever even heard of Gordon. Believe me, John, the Belgian government will bluster and threaten for a month or two, and then they'll start negotiating."

"Well, it all sounds logical," said Boyes. "But I still can't believe that a force of 53 men can take over an entire country. It's just not possible."

"Once and for all, John, we are *not* a force of 53 men," said Roosevelt. "We are a *potential* force of a million outraged Americans."

"So you keep saying. But still—"

"John, I trust you implicitly when we're stalking an elephant or a lion. Try to have an equal degree of trust in me when we're doing what *I* do best."

"I wish I could," said Boyes. "But it just *can't* be this easy."

On December 3, 1910, five months and 27 days later after receiving Roosevelt's demands, the Belgian government officially relinquished all claims to the Congo, and began withdrawing their nationals.

8

"*Damn* that Taft!"

Roosevelt crumpled the telegram, which had been delivered by runner from Stanleyville, in his massive hand and threw it to the ground. The sound of his angry, high-pitched voice combined with the violence of his gesture frightened a number of birds which had been searching for insects on the sprawling lawn, and they flew, squawking and screeching, to sanctuary in a cluster of nearby trees.

"Bad news, Mr. President?" asked Boyes.

They were staying at the house of M. Beauregard de Vincennes, a French plantation owner, some fifteen miles west of Stanleyville, on the shores of the Congo River. Three dozen of Roosevelt's men were camped out on the grounds, while the remainder were alternately hunting ivory and preparing the Lulua and Baluba, two of the major tribes in the area, for visits from Roosevelt himself.

"The man has no gratitude, no gratitude at all!" snapped Roosevelt. "I gave him the Presidency, handed it to him as a gift, and now I've offered to give him a foothold in Africa as well, and he has the unmitigated gall to tell me that he can't afford to send me the men and the money I've requested!"

"Is he sending anything at all?" asked Boyes.

"I requested ten thousand men, and he's sending six hundred!" said Roosevelt furiously. "I told him I needed at least twenty million dollars to build roads and extend the railroad from Uganda, and he's offered three million. Three million dollars for a country a third the size of the United States! *Damn* the man! J. P. Morgan may be a scoundrel and a brigand, but *he* would recognize an opportunity like this and pounce on it, I'll guarantee you that!" He paused and suddenly nodded his head vigorously. "By God, that's what I'll do! I'll wire Morgan this afternoon!"

"I thought he was your mortal enemy," remarked Boyes. "At least, that's the way it sounds whenever you mention him."

"Nonsense!" said Roosevelt. "We were on different sides of the political fence, but he's a competent man, which is more than I can say for the idiot sitting in the White House." Roosevelt grinned. "And he loves railroads. Yes, I'll wire him this afternoon."

"Are we refusing President Taft's offer, then?"

"Certainly not. We need all the manpower and money we can get. I'll wire our acceptance, and send off some telegrams to a few sympathetic newspaper publishers telling them what short shrift we're getting from Washington. I can't put any more pressure on Taft from here, but perhaps *they* can." Roosevelt shook his head sadly. "It serves me right for putting a fool in the White House. I tell you, John, if I didn't have a job to do right here, I'd go back to the States and take the nomination away from him in 1912. The man doesn't deserve to run a second time."

Roosevelt ranted against the "fat fool" in the White House for another fifteen minutes, then retired to his room to draft his telegrams. When he emerged an hour later for lunch, he was once again his usual pleasant, vigorous, optimistic self. Boyes, Bill Buckley, Mickey Norton, Yank Rogers, and Deaf Banks were sitting at a table beneath an ancient tree, and all of them except Banks, who hadn't heard the ex-President's approach, stood up as he joined them.

"Please be seated, gentlemen," said Roosevelt, pulling up a chair. "What's on the menu for this afternoon?"

"Salad and cold guinea hen in some kind of sauce," answered Norton. "Or that's what Madame Vincennes told me, anyway."

"I love guinea fowl," enthused Roosevelt. "That will be just bully!" He paused. "Good people, Monsieur and Madame Vincennes. I'm delighted that they offered to be our hosts." He paused. "This is much more pleasant than being cooped up in those airless little government buildings in Stanleyville."

"I hear we got some bad news from your pal Bill Taft," ventured Rogers.

"It's all taken care of," answered Roosevelt, confidently tapping the pocket that held his telegrams. "The men he's sending will arrive during the rainy season, anyway—and by the time the rains are over, we'll have more than enough manpower." He looked around the table. "It's time we considered some more immediate problems, gentlemen."

"What problems did you have in mind, sir?" asked Buckley, as six black servants approached the table, bearing trays of salad and drinks.

"We've had this country for two months now," answered Roosevelt. "It's time we began doing something with it—besides decimating its elephant population, that is," he added harshly.

"Well, we could decimate the Belgians that have stayed behind," said Buckley with an amused smile. "Billy Pickering would like that."

"I'm being serious, Mr. Buckley," said Roosevelt, taking a small crust of bread from his plate and tossing it to a nearby starling, which immediately picked it up and pranced off with it. "What's the purpose of making the Belgians leave if we don't improve the lot of the inhabitants? Everywhere we've gone we've promised to bring the benefits of democracy to the Congo. I think it's time we started delivering on that promise. The people deserve no less."

"Boy!" said Norton to one of the servants. "This coffee's cold. Go heat it up."

The servant nodded, bowed, put the coffee pot back on the tray, and walked toward the kitchen building.

"I don't know how you're going to civilize them when they can't remember from one day to the next that coffee's suppose to be served hot and not warm," said Norton. "And look at the way he's loafing: it could be hot when he gets it and cold by the time he brings it here."

"The natives don't drink coffee, so it can hardly be considered important to them," answered Roosevelt.

"They don't vote, or hold trial by jury, either," offered Buckley.

"Well, if we're to introduce them to the amenities of civilization, I think that voting and jury trials come well ahead of coffee drinking, Mr. Buckley."

"They can't even read," said Buckley. "How are you going to teach them to vote?"

"I plan to set up a public school system throughout the country," said Roosevelt. "The Belgian missionaries made a start, but they were undermanned and under-financed. In my pocket is a telegram that will appear in more than a thousand American newspapers, an open appeal to teachers and missionaries to come to the Congo and help educate the populace."

"That could take years, sir," noted Boyes.

"Ten at the most," answered Roosevelt confidently.

"How will you pay 'em, Teddy?" asked Rogers. "Hell, you can't even pay *us*."

"The missionaries will be paid by their churches, of course," said Roosevelt. "As for the teachers, I suppose we'll have to pay them with land initially."

"That might not sit too well with the people whose land we're giving away," noted Rogers.

"Yank, if there's one thing the Congo abounds in, besides insects and humidity, it's land."

"You say it'll take ten years to educate them," continued Rogers. "How will you hold elections in the meantime?"

"By voice," answered Roosevelt. "Every man and woman will enter the polling place and state his or her preference. As a matter of fact, there will probably be a lot less vote fraud that way."

"Did I hear you say that women are going to vote too, Teddy?" asked Yank Rogers.

"They're citizens of the Congo, aren't they?"

"But they don't even vote back home!"

"That's going to change," said Roosevelt firmly. "Our founding fathers were wrong not to give women the right to vote, and there's no reason to make the same mistake here. They're human beings, the same as us, and they deserve the same rights and privileges." Suddenly he grinned. "I pity the man who has to tell my Alice that she can't cast her vote at the polls. There won't be enough of him left to bury!"

"You know, we could raise money with a hut tax," suggested Buckley. "That's what the British have done wherever they've had an African colony."

"A hut tax?" asked Roosevelt.

Buckley nodded. "Tax every native ten or twenty shillings a year for each hut he erects. It not only raises money for the treasury, but it forces them to be something more than subsistence farmers, since they need money to pay the tax."

Roosevelt shook his head adamantly. "We're supposed to be freeing them, Mr. Buckley, not enslaving them."

"Besides," added Boyes, "it never worked that well in British East. If they didn't pay their hut tax, the government threw them into jail." He turned to Roosevelt and smiled. "You know what the Kikuyu and Wakamba called the jail in Nairobi? The King Georgi Hoteli. It was the only place they knew of where they could get three square meals a day and a free roof over their heads." He chuckled at the memory. "Once word of it got out, they were lining up to get thrown in jail."

"Well, there will be no such attempt to exploit the natives of the Congo," said Roosevelt. "We must always remember that this is *their* country and that our duty is to teach them the ways of democracy."

"That may be easier said than done," said Rogers.

"Why should you think so, Yank?" asked Roosevelt.

"Democracy's a pretty alien concept to them," answered Rogers. "It's going to take some getting used to."

"It was an alien concept to young Booker T. Washington and George Washington Carver, too," said Roosevelt, "but they seem to have adapted to it readily enough. It's never difficult to get used to freedom."

"We ain't talking freedom, Teddy," said Rogers. "They were free for thousands of years before the Belgians showed up, but they ain't never had a democracy. Their tribes are ruled by chiefs and witch doctors, not congressmen."

"And now that the Belgians are clearing out," added Norton, "our biggest problem is going to be to stop them from killing each other long enough to get to the polls."

"All of you keep predicting the most dire consequences," said Roosevelt irritably, "and yet you ignore the enormous strides the American Negro has taken since the Emancipation Proclamation. I tell you, gentleman, that freedom has no color and democracy is not the special province of one race."

Boyes smiled, and Buckley turned to him.

"What are you looking so amused about, John? You've been here long enough to know everything we've said is the truth."

"You all think you're discouraging Mr. Roosevelt, and that if you tell him enough stories about how savage the natives are, maybe you'll convince him to join you long enough to kill every last elephant in the Congo and then go back to Nairobi." Boyes paused. "But I know him a little better than you do, and if there's one thing he can't resist, it's a challenge." He turned to Roosevelt. "Am I right, sir?"

Roosevelt grinned back at him. "Absolutely, Mr. Boyes." He looked around at his companions. "Gentlemen," he announced, "I've heard enough doomsaying for one day. It's time to roll up our sleeves and get to work."

9

Roosevelt stared at his image in the full-length ornate gilt mirror that adorned the parlor of the state house at Stanleyville, and adjusted the tie of his morning suit.

"Good thing that little German tailor decided not to leave," he remarked to Boyes, who was similarly clad, "or we'd be conducting matters of state in our safari clothes."

"I'd be a damned sight more comfortable in them," replied Boyes, checking his appearance in the mirror, and deciding that his hair needed more combing.

"Nonsense, John," said Roosevelt. "We've got reporters and photographers from all over the world here."

"Personally, I'd much rather face a charging elephant," said Boyes, looking out the window. "I don't like crowds."

Roosevelt smiled. "I'd forgotten just how much I *miss* them." He put on his top hat and walked to the door. "Well, we might as well begin."

Boyes, unhappy and uncomfortable, and feeling quite naked without his pistol and rifle, followed the American out the front door to the raised wooden platform that had been constructed in front of the state house the previous day. The press was there, as Roosevelt had said: reporters and photographers from America, Belgium, England, France, Italy, Portugal, Kenya, and even a pair of Orientals had made the long, arduous trek to Stanleyville to hear this speech and record the moment for posterity. Seated on the front row of chairs, in a section reserved for VIPs and dignitaries, were the paramount chiefs of the Mangbetu, the Simba, the Mongo, the Luba, the Bwaka, the Zande, and the Kongo (which centuries ago had given the country its name). There was even a pair of pygmy chiefs, one who whom was completely naked except for a loincloth, a pair of earrings, and a necklace made of leopards' claws, while the other wore a suit that could have been tailored on Saville Row.

The crowd, some six hundred strong, and divided almost equally between whites and black Africans, immediately ceased its chattering when Roosevelt mounted the platform and waited in polite expectation while he walked to a podium and pulled some notes out of his pocket.

"Good morning, ladies and gentlemen. I thank you for your attendance and patience. I realize that, with our transportation system not yet constructed, you may have had some slight difficulty in reaching Stanleyville"—he paused for the good- natured laughter that he knew would follow—"but you're here now, and we're delighted to have you as the guests of our new nation."

He paused, pulled a brand-new handkerchief out of his pocket, and wiped away the sweat that had begun pouring down his face.

"We are here to proclaim the sovereignty of this beautiful land. Some years ago it was known as the Congo Free State. At the time, that was a misnomer, for it was anything but free. Today it is no longer a misnomer, and so it shall once again be known as the Congo Free State, an independent nation dedicated to the preservation of human dignity and the celebration of human endeavor."

A pair of blue turracoes began shrieking in a nearby tree, and he smiled and waited a few seconds until the noise had subsided.

"What's past is past," he continued, "and the Congo Free State begins life with a clean slate. It bears no rancor toward any person or any nation that may have exploited its resources and its people in the past. But"—and here Roosevelt's chin jutted out pugnaciously—"this land will never be plundered or exploited again." He stared darkly out at his audience. "Never again will a privileged minority impose its will upon the majority. Never again will one tribe bear arms against another. Never again will women do most of the work and reap none of the benefits. And never again will the dreadful spectres of ignorance, poverty and disease run rampant in what Henry Stanley termed Darkest Africa." He raised his voice dramatically. "From this day forward, we shall illuminate the Congo Free State with the light of democracy, and turn it into the exemplar of Brightest Africa!"

Roosevelt paused long enough for his words to be translated, then smiled and nodded as the row of chiefs rose to their feet and cheered wildly, followed, somewhat less enthusiastically, by the Europeans.

"Thank you, my friends," he continued when the chiefs finally sat down. "We who have been fortunate enough to help in the birth of the Congo Free State have great plans for its future." He smiled triumphantly. "Great plans, indeed!" he repeated emphatically.

"Within two years, we will extend the East African Railway from its present terminus in Uganda all the way to Stanleyville, and within another year to Leopoldville. This will give us access to the Indian Ocean, as the Congo River gives us access to the Atlantic, and with the modern farming methods we plan to introduce, we will shortly be shipping exports in great quantity to both coasts."

There was more applause, a little less rabid this time, as most of the chiefs had only the haziest understanding of an economy that extended beyond their own tribes.

"We will construct public schools throughout the country," Roosevelt added. "Our goal is nothing less than 100% literacy by the year 1930."

This time the applause came only from the chiefs, as the whites in the audience looked openly skeptical.

"We will soon begin the construction of modern hospitals in every major city in the Congo Free State," continued Roosevelt, "and no citizen shall ever again want for medical care. American engineers will build dams the length of the Congo River, so that we can generate all the electricity that a modern nation will need. While leaving vast tracts of land untouched as national parks and game reserves, we will nonetheless criss-cross the country with a network of roads, so that no village, no matter how remote, remains inaccessible."

He paused and glared at the disbelieving white faces in his audience.

"We will do everything I have said," he concluded. "And we will do it sooner than you think!"

The assembled chiefs began cheering and jumping around in their enthusiasm, and the remainder of the audience, sensing that he had concluded the major part of his address, applauded politely. "And now, ladies and gentlemen, if you will all rise, we will, for the very first time, raise the flag of the Congo Free State." He turned to Boyes. "Mr. Boyes?"

Boyes withdrew the folded flag that he had been carrying inside his morning coat, waited for an honor guard of khaki-clad native soldiers to approach, and solemnly handed the flag over to their leader. The soldiers then marched to a recently-erected flagpole near the platform, and began raising a banner that depicted the colorful shields of twenty of the major tribes arranged in a pattern on a field of green, while Yank Rogers, who had been unable to create a national anthem on two days notice, played a military march on his ancient bugle. Roosevelt stood at attention and saluted, Boyes and the chiefs followed suit, and the reporters, politicians, and dignitaries were quick to rise to their feet as well.

When the flag had been raised and the rope secured at the base of the flagpole, Roosevelt faced the crowd once more.

"I have been selected, by the unanimous consent of the tribes that are represented here today, to draft and implement a democratic constitution for the Congo Free State. During this time I shall hold the office of Chief Administrator, an office that will be abolished when the first national election is held one year from today. At that time all the people of the Congo Free State, regardless of race or gender, will choose their own President and legislature, and their destiny will finally be in their own hands."

He stared out at the audience.

"I thank you for your attendance at this historic ceremony. Lunch will be provided for everyone on the lawn, and I will be available for interviews throughout the afternoon."

He climbed down from the platform to one last round of applause, finally allowed them a look at the famed Roosevelt grin, waited for Boyes to join him, and disappeared into the interior of the state house.

"How was I, John?" he asked anxiously.

"I thought you were excellent, Mr. President," answered Boyes truthfully.

"Mr. Chief Administrator, you mean," Roosevelt corrected him. Suddenly he smiled. "Although by this time you certainly know me well enough to call me Teddy. Everyone else does."

"I think I prefer Mr. President," replied Boyes. "I'm used to it."

Roosevelt shrugged, then looked out the window as the crowd began lining up at the long buffet tables.

"They don't think I can do it, do they, John?"

"No, sir, they don't," answered Boyes honestly.

"Well, they'd be correct if I applied their outmoded methods," said Roosevelt. He drew himself up to his full height. "However, this is a new century. We have new technologies, new methods, and new outlooks."

"But this is an old country," said Boyes.

"What is that supposed to mean, John?"

"Just that it might not be ready for your new approach, Mr. President."

"You saw the chiefs out there, John," said Roosevelt. "They're my strongest supporters."

"It's in their best interest to be," said Boyes. "After all, you've promised them the moon."

"And I'll deliver it," said Roosevelt resolutely.

10

Boyes walked into the state house and was ushered into Roosevelt's office.

"Where have you been, John?" asked Roosevelt. "I expected you back three days ago."

"It took a little longer than I thought to set up my trading company," answered Boyes. "But if your laborers ever arrive, at least they won't starve to death. I've got commitments for flour and meat."

"What are you trading for them?"

"Iodine," answered Boyes. "That's what took me so long. My shipment was late arriving from Nairobi."

"Iodine?" repeated Roosevelt, curious.

Boyes smiled. "There are some infections even a witch doctor can't cure." He sat down in a leather chair opposite Roosevelt's desk, looking quite pleased with himself. "An ounce of iodine for thirty pounds of flour or one hundred pounds of meat."

"That's immoral, John. Those people *need* that medication."

"Our people will need that food," answered Boyes.

"My hospitals will put you out of business," said Roosevelt sternly. "We will never withhold treatment despite a patient's inability to pay for it."

"When you build your hospitals, I'll find something else to trade them," said Boyes with a shrug. He decided to change the subject. "I hear you held your first local election while I was gone. How did it go?"

"I would call it a limited success."

"Oh?"

"It was a trial run, so to speak," said Roosevelt. "We selected a district at random and tried to show them how an election works." He paused. "We had a turnout of almost ninety percent, which is certainly very promising."

"Let me guess about the unpromising part," said Boyes. "Your candidates didn't get a single crossover vote."

Roosevelt nodded his head grimly. "The vote went one hundred percent along tribal lines."

"I hope you're not surprised."

"No, but I *am* disappointed." Roosevelt sighed. "I'll simply have to keep explaining to them that they are supposed to vote on the issues and not the tribal connections until they finally understand the principle involved."

For the first time since they had met, Boyes felt sorry for the American.

"Not guilty?" repeated Roosevelt. "How in the name of pluperfect hell could they come in with a verdict of not guilty?"

He had turned the local theater into a court room, and had spent the better part of a week instructing the members of the Luba and Zande tribes in the intricacies of the jury system. Then he himself had acted as the presiding judge at the Congo Free State's very first trial by jury, and he was now in his makeshift chambers, barely able to control his fury.

"It was a unanimous decision," said Charlie Ross, who had acted as bailiff.

"I know it was a unanimous decision, Mr. Ross!" thundered Roosevelt. "What I don't know is how, in the face of all the evidence, they could come up with it?"

"Why don't you ask them?" suggested Ross.

"By God, that's exactly what I'll do!" said Roosevelt. "Bring them in here, one at a time."

Ross left the room for about five minutes, during which time Roosevelt tried unsuccessfully to compose himself.

"Sir," said Ross, re-entering in the company of a tall, slender black man, "this is Tambika, one of the jurors."

"Thank you, Mr. Ross," said Roosevelt. He turned to the African. "Mr. Tambika," he said in heavily-accented Swahili, "I wonder if you could explain your decision to me."

"Explain it, King Teddy?" asked Tambika, bewildered.

"Please call me Mr. Chief Administrator," said Roosevelt uncomfortably. He paused. "The man, Toma, was accused of stealing six cows. Four eyewitnesses claimed to see him driving the cows back toward his own home, and Mr. Kalimi showed you a bill of sale he received when he purchased the cows from Toma. There is no question that the cows bore the mark, or brand, of the plaintiff, Mr. Salamaki. Can you please tell me why you found him innocent?"

"Ah, now I understand," said Tambika with a large smile. "Toma owes me money. How can he pay me if he is in jail?"

"But he broke the law."

"True," agreed Tambika.

"Then you must find him guilty."

"But if I had found him guilty, he would never be able to pay me what he owes me," protested Tambika. "That is not justice, King Teddy."

Roosevelt argued with Tambika for another few minutes, then dismissed him and had Ross bring in the next juror, an old man named Begoni. After reciting the evidence again, he put the question to the old man.

"It is very clear," answered Begoni. "Toma is a Luba, as am I. Salamaki is a Zande. It is impossible for the Luba to commit a crime against the Zande."

"But that is precisely what he did, Mr. Begoni," said Roosevelt.

The old man shook his head. "The Zande have been stealing our cattle and our women since God created the world. It is our right to steal them back."

"The law says otherwise," Roosevelt pointed out.

"Whose law?" asked the old man, staring at him with no show of fear or awe. "Yours or God's?"

"If Mr. Toma were a Zande, would you have found him guilty?"

"Certainly," answered Begoni, as if the question were too ridiculous to consider.

"If Mr. Toma were a Zande and you knew for a fact that he had *not* stolen the cattle, would you have found him innocent?" asked Roosevelt.

"No."

"Why?" asked Roosevelt in exasperation.

"There are too many Zande in the world."

"That will be all, Mr. Begoni."

"Thank you, Mr. Teddy," said the old man, walking to the door. He paused for a moment just before leaving. "I like jury trials," he announced. "It saves much bloodshed."

"I can't believe it!" said Roosevelt, getting to his feet and stalking back and forth across the room after the door had closed behind Begoni. "I spent an entire week with these people, explaining how the system works!"

"Are you ready for the next one, sir?" asked Ross.

"No!" snapped Roosevelt. "I already know what he'll say. Toma's a tribal brother. Toma can't pay the bride price for his daughter if we throw him in jail. If a document, such as a bill of sale, implicates a Luba, then it must have been cursed by a Zande witch doctor and cannot be believed." Roosevelt stopped and turned to Ross. "What is the matter with these people, Charlie? Don't they understand what I'm trying to do for them?"

"They have their own system of justice, Mr. President," answered Ross gently.

"I've seen that system in action," said Roosevelt contemptuously. "A witch doctor touches a hot iron to the accused's tongue. If he cries out, he's guilty; if he doesn't, he's innocent. What kind of system is that, I ask you?"

"One they believe in," said Ross.

"Well, that's that," said Roosevelt grimly, after opening the weekly mail. "Morgan isn't interested in investing in a railroad."

"Is there anyone else you can ask?" inquired Boyes.

"Bill Taft is mismanaging the economy. I have a feeling that the people who can afford to invest are feeling exceptionally conservative this year."

Nevertheless, he wrote another thirty letters that afternoon, each soliciting funds, and mailed them the next morning. He expressed great confidence that the money would soon be forthcoming, but he began making contingency plans for the day, not far off, when construction of the Trans-Congo Railway would be forced to come to a halt.

"What do you mean, you have no more supplies?" demanded Roosevelt. "You had ample track for another five miles, Mr. Brody."

Brody, a burly American, stood uncomfortably before Roosevelt's desk, fidgeting with his pith helmet, which he held awkwardly in his huge hands.

"Yes, we did, Mr. Roosevelt."

"Well?"

"Its the natives, sir," said Brody. "They keep stealing it."

"Rubbish! What possible use could they have for steel track?"

"You wouldn't believe the uses they put it to, sir," answered Brody. "They use it to support their huts, and to make pens for their goats and cattle, and they melt it down for spearheads."

"Well, then, take it back."

"We were expressly instructed not to harm any of the natives, sir, and whenever we've tried to retrieve our tracks we've been threatened with spears, and occasionally even guns. If we can't take them back by force, they're going to stay right where they are until they rust."

"Who's the headman in your area, Mr. Brody?" asked Roosevelt.

"A Mangbetu named Matapoli."

"I know him personally," said Roosevelt, his expression brightening. "Bring him here and perhaps we can get this situation resolved."

"That could take six weeks, sir—and that's assuming he'll come with me."

Roosevelt shook his head. "That won't do, Mr. Brody. I can't pay your men to sit on their hands for six weeks." He paused, then nodded to himself, his decision made. "I'll return with you. It's time I got out among the people again, anyway."

He summoned Yank Rogers while Brody was getting lunch at a small restaurant down the street.

"What can I do for you, Teddy?" asked the American.

"I'm going to have to go to Mangbetu country, Yank," answered Roosevelt. "I want you and Mr. Buckley to remain in Stanleyville and keep an eye on things here while I'm gone."

"What about Boyes?" asked Rogers. "Isn't that his job?"

"John will be accompanying me," answered Roosevelt. "The Mangbetu seem to be very fond of him."

"They're equally fond of you, Teddy."

"I enjoy his company," said Roosevelt. He smiled wryly. "I'll also find it comforting to know that the state house hasn't been sold to the highest bidder in my absence."

"John," remarked Roosevelt, as he and Boyes sat beside a campfire, "have you noticed that we haven't seen any elephant sign in more than a week now?"

The horses started whinnying as the wind brought the scent of lion and hyena to them.

"Perhaps they've migrated to the west," said Boyes.

"Come on, John," said Roosevelt. "I'm not as old a hand at this as you are, but I know when an area's been shot out."

"We've shipped a lot of ivory to Mombasa and Zanzibar during the past year," said Boyes.

"I didn't mind our men making a little money on the side, John, but I won't have them decimating the herds."

"They've been more than a year without a paycheck," answered Boyes seriously. "If you tell them they have to stop hunting ivory, I doubt that more than a dozen of them will stay in the Congo."

"Then we'll have to make do without their services," said Roosevelt. "The elephants belong to the people of the Congo Free State now. We've got to start a game department and charge for hunting licenses while there's still something left to hunt."

"If you say so," replied Boyes.

Roosevelt stared long and hard at him. "Will *you* be one of the ones who leaves, John?"

Boyes shook his head. "I'm the one who talked you into this in the first place, Mr. President," he answered. "I'll stay as long as you do." He paused thoughtfully. "I've made more than my share of money off the ivory anyway, and I suppose we really ought to stop while there are still some elephants left. I was just pointing out the consequences of abolishing poaching."

"Then start passing the word as soon as we get back," said Roosevelt. Suddenly he frowned. "That's funny."

"What is, sir?"

"I felt very dizzy for just a moment there." He shrugged. "I'm sure it will pass."

But it didn't, and that night the ex-President came down with malaria. Boyes tended to him and nursed him back to health, but another week had been wasted, and Roosevelt had the distinct feeling that he didn't have too many of them left to put the country on the right track.

"Ah, my friend Johnny—and King Teddy!" Matapoli greeted them with a huge smile of welcome. "You honor my village with your presence."

"Your village has changed since the last time we were here," noted Boyes wryly.

Matapoli pointed proudly to the five railroad coach cars that his men had dragged miles through the bush over a period of months, and which now housed his immediate family and the families of four of the tribe's elders.

"Oh, yes," he said happily. "King Teddy promised us democracy, and he kept his promise." He pointed to one of the cars. "*My* democracy is the finest of all! Come join me inside it."

Roosevelt and Boyes exchanged ironic glances and followed Matapoli into the coach car, which was filled with some twenty or so of his children.

"King Teddy has returned!" enthused the Mangbetu chief. "We must have a hunt in the forest and have a feast in your honor."

"That's very thoughtful of you, Matapoli," said Roosevelt. "But it has been many months since we last saw each other. Let us talk together first."

"Yes, that would be very good," agreed Matapoli, puffing out his chest as the children recognized the two visitors and raced off to inform the rest of the village.

"Just how many children do you have?" asked Roosevelt.

Matapoli paused in thought for a moment. "Ten, and ten more, and then seven," he answered.

"And how many wives?"

"Five."

The puritanical American tried without success to hide his disapproval. "That's a very large family, Matapoli."

"Should be more, should be more," admitted the Mangbetu. "But it took many months to bring the democracies here."

"Had you left them on the track, you could have traveled all across the country on them," Boyes pointed out.

Matapoli threw back his head and laughed. "Why should I want to go to Lulua or Bwaka country?" he asked. "They would just kill me and take my democracies for themselves."

"Please try to understand, Matapoli," said Roosevelt. "There are no longer Mangbetu or Lulua or Bwaka countries. There is just the Congo Free State, and you all live in it."

"You are king of all the countries, King Teddy," answered Matapoli. "You need have no fear. If the Bwaka say that you are not, then we shall kill them."

Roosevelt spent the next ten minutes trying to explain the Congo Free State to Matapoli, who was no closer to comprehending it at the end of the discussion than at the beginning.

"All right," said the American with a sigh of resignation. "Let's get back to talking about the trains."

"Trains?" repeated Matapoli.

"The democracies, and the steel logs they rolled upon," interjected Boyes.

"Another gift from King Teddy," said Matapoli enthusiastically. "No longer can the leopards and the hyenas break through the thorns and kill my cattle. Now I use the metal thorns, and my animals are safe."

"The metal thorns were built so that you and the other Mangbetu could travel many miles without having to walk," said Roosevelt.

"Why should we wish to go many miles?" asked Matapoli, honestly puzzled. "The river runs beside the village, and the forest and its game are just a short walk away."

"You might wish to visit another tribe."

Matapoli smiled. "How could we sneak up on our enemies in the democracies? They are too large, and they would make too much noise when they rolled upon the iron thorns." He shook his head. "No, King Teddy, they are much better right here, where we can put them to use."

Long after the feast was over and Roosevelt and Boyes were riding their horses back toward Stanleyville, Roosevelt, who had been replaying the frustrating day over and over in his mind, finally sighed and muttered: "By God, that probably *is* the best use they could have been put to!"

Boyes found the remark highly amusing, and burst into laughter. A moment later Roosevelt joined him with a hearty laugh of his own, and that was the official end of the Trans-Congo Railway.

They came to a newly-paved road when they were fifteen miles out of Stanleyville and, glad to finally be free of the bush and the forest, they veered their mounts onto it. As they continued their journey, they passed dozens of men and women walking alongside the road.

"Why don't they walk *on* it, John?" asked Roosevelt curiously. "There can't be fifteen trucks in the whole of the Congo. Until we import some more, we might as well put the roads to some use."

"They're barefoot," Boyes pointed out.

"So what? The road is a lot smoother than the rocks alongside it."

"It's also a lot hotter," answered Boyes. "By high noon you could fry an egg on it."

"You mean we've spent a million dollars on roads for which there not only aren't any cars and trucks, but that the people can't even walk on?"

"This isn't America, sir."

"A point that is being driven home daily," muttered Roosevelt wearily.

11

Roosevelt sat at his desk, staring at a number of letters and documents that lay stacked neatly in front of him. To his left was a photograph of Edith and his children, to his right a picture of himself delivering a State of the Union address to the United States Congress, and behind him, on an ornate brass stand, was the flag of the Congo Free State.

Finally, with a sigh, he opened the final letter, read it quickly, and, frowning, placed it atop the stack.

"Bad news, Mr. President?" asked Boyes, who was sitting in the leather chair on the opposite side of the desk.

"No worse than the rest of them," answered Roosevelt. "That was from Mr. Bennigan, our chief engineer on the Stanley Falls Bridge. He sends his regrets, but his men haven't been paid in three weeks, and he's going to have to pull out." He stared at the letter. "There's no postmark, of course, but I would guess that it took at least two weeks to get here."

"We didn't need him anyway," said Boyes, dismissing the matter with a shrug. "What's the sense of building a bridge over the falls if we don't have any trains or cars?"

"Because someday we'll have them, John, and when we do, they're going to need roads and tracks and bridges."

"When that happy day arrives, I'm sure we'll have enough money to complete work on the bridge," replied Boyes.

Roosevelt sighed. "It's not as devastating a blow as losing the teachers. How many of them have left?"

"Just about all."

"Damn!" muttered Roosevelt. "How can we educate the populace if there's no one to teach them?"

"With all due respect, sir, they don't need Western educations," said Boyes. "You're trying to turn them into Americans, and they're not. Reading and writing are no more important to them than railroads are."

Roosevelt stared at him for a long moment. "What do *you* think is important to them, John?"

"You're talking about a primitive society," answered Boyes. "They need to learn crop rotation and hygiene and basic medicine far more than they need roads that they'll never use and railroad cars that they think are simply huts on wheels."

"You're wrong, John," said Roosevelt adamantly. "A little black African baby is no different than a little black American baby—or a little white American baby, for that matter. If we can get them young enough, and educate them thoroughly enough…"

"I don't like to contradict you, sir," interrupted Boyes, "but you're wrong. What's the point of having ten thousand college graduates if they all have to go home to their huts every night because there aren't two hundred jobs for educated men in the whole country?

If you want to have a revolution on your hands, raise their expectations, prepare them to live and function in London or New York—and then make them stay in the Congo."

Roosevelt shook his head vigorously. "If we did things your way, these people would stay in ignorance and poverty forever. I told you when we began this enterprise that I wasn't coming here to turn the Congo into my private hunting preserve." He paused. "I haven't found the key yet, but if anyone can bring the Congo into the 20th Century, I can."

"Has it occurred to you that perhaps no one can?" suggested Boyes gently.

"Not for a moment," responded Roosevelt firmly.

"I'll stay as long as you do, sir," said Boyes. "You know that. But if you don't come up with some answers pretty soon, we may be the last two white men in this country, except for the missionaries and some of the Belgian planters who stayed behind. Almost half our original party has already left."

"They were just here for ivory or adventure," said Roosevelt dismissively. "We need people who care about this country more than we need people who are here merely to plunder it." Suddenly he stared out the window at some fixed point in space.

"Are you all right, sir?" asked Boyes after Roosevelt had remained motionless for almost a minute.

"Never better," answered the American suddenly. "You know, John, I see now that I've been going about this the wrong way. No one cares as much for the future of the Congo as the people themselves. I was wrong to try to bring in help from outside; in the long run, any progress we make here will be much more meaningful if it's accomplished by our own efforts."

"Ours?" repeated Boyes, puzzled. "You mean yours and mine?"

"I mean the citizens of the Congo Free State," answered Roosevelt. "I've been telling you and the engineers and the teachers and the missionaries what they need. I think it's about time I told the people and rallied them to their own cause."

"We've already promised them democracy," said Boyes. "And there's at least one Mangbetu village that will swear we delivered it to them," he added with a smile.

"Those were politicians' promises, designed to get our foot in the door," said Roosevelt. "Democracy may be a right, but it isn't a gift. It requires effort and sacrifice. They've got to understand that."

"First they've got to understand what democracy means."

"They will, once I've explained it to them," answered Roosevelt.

"You mean in person?" asked Boyes.

"That's right," said Roosevelt. "I'll start in the eastern section of the country, now that my Swahili has become fluent, and as I move west I'll use translators. But I'm going to go out among the people myself. I'm certainly not doing any good sitting here in Stanleyville; it's time to go out on the stump and get my message across to the only people who really need to understand it." He paused. "I'd love to have your company, John, but there are so few of us left that I think it would be better for you to remain here and keep an eye on things."

"Whatever you say, Mr. President," replied Boyes. "When will you leave?"

"Tomorrow," said Roosevelt. He paused. "No. This afternoon. There's nothing more important to do, and we've no time to waste."

He went among the people for five weeks, and everywhere he stopped, the drums had anticipated his arrival and the tribes flocked to see him.

He took his time, avoided any hint of jingoism, and carefully explained the principles of democracy to them. He pointed out the necessity of education, the importance of modern farming methods, the need to end all forms of tribalism, and the advantages of a monied economy. At the end of each "town meeting", as he called them, he held a prolonged question-and-answer session, and then he moved on to the next major village and repeated the entire procedure again.

During the morning of his thirty-sixth day on the stump, he was joined by Yank Rogers, who rode down from Stanleyville to see him.

"Hello, Yank!" cried Roosevelt enthusiastically as he saw the American riding up to his tent, which had been pitched just outside of a Lulua village.

"Hi, Teddy," said Rogers, pulling up his horse and dismounting. "You're looking good. Getting out in the bush seems to agree with you."

"I feel as fit as a bull moose," replied Roosevelt with a smile. "How's John doing?"

"Getting rich, as usual," said Rogers, not without a hint of admiration for the enterprising Yorkshireman. "I thought he was going to be stuck with about a million pounds of flour when all the construction people pulled out, but he heard that there was a famine in Portugese Angola, so he traded the flour for ivory, and then had Buckley and the Brittlebanks brothers cart it to Mombasa when they decided to call it quits, in exchange for half the profits."

"That sounds like John, all right," agreed Roosevelt. "I'm sorry to hear that we've lost Buckley and the others, though."

Rogers shrugged. "They're just Brits. What the hell do they know about democracy? They'd slit your throat in two seconds flat if someone told them that it would get 'em an audience with the King." He paused. "All except Boyes, anyway. He'd find some way to put the King on display and charge money for it."

Roosevelt chuckled heartily. "You know, I do believe you're right."

"So much for Mr. Boyes," said Rogers, "How's your campaign going?"

"Just bully," answered Roosevelt. "The response has been wildly enthusiastic." He paused. "I'm surprised news of it hasn't reached you."

"How could it?" asked Rogers. "There aren't any radios or newspapers—and even if there were, these people speak 300 different languages and none of 'em can read or write."

"Still," said Roosevelt, "I've made a start."

"I don't doubt it, sir."

"I'm drawing almost five hundred natives a day," continued Roosevelt. "That's more than 15,000 converts in just over a month."

"If they stay converted."

"They will."

"Just another six million to go," said Rogers with a chuckle.

"I'm sure they're passing the word."

"To their fellow tribesmen, maybe," answered Rogers. "I wouldn't bet on their talking to anyone else."

"You sound like a pessimist, Yank," said Roosevelt.

"Pessimism and realism are next-door neighbors on this continent, Teddy," said Rogers.

"And yet you stay," noted Roosevelt.

Rogers smiled. "I figure if anyone can whip this country into shape, it's you—and if you do, I want to be able to laugh at all those Brits who gave up and left."

"Well, stick around," said Roosevelt. "I'm just getting warmed up."

"Sounds like fun," said Rogers. "I haven't heard you rile up a crowd since you ran for Governor of New York. I was in Africa before you ran for President." Suddenly he reached into his shirt pocket and withdrew an envelope. "I almost forgot why I rode all this way," he said, handing it to Roosevelt.

"What is it?"

"A letter from Boyes," answered Rogers. "He said to deliver it to you personally."

Roosevelt opened the letter, read it twice, then crumpled it into a ball and stuffed it into a pocket.

"I'm afraid you're not going to be able to hear me giving any speeches this week, Yank," he announced. "I've got to return to Stanleyville."

"Something wrong?"

Roosevelt nodded. "It seems that Billy Pickering found four Belgian soldiers in a remote area in the southwest, men who had never received word that the Belgians had withdrawn from the Congo, and shot them dead."

"You mean he had me ride all the way here just for that?" demanded Rogers.

"It's a matter of vital importance, Yank."

"What's so important about four dead men?" asked Rogers. "Life is cheap in Africa."

"The Belgian government is demanding reparation."

"Yeah, I see where *that* can make it a little more expensive," admitted Rogers.

12

"I wasn't sure how you wanted to handle it," Boyes said, staring across the desk at Roosevelt, who had just returned to Stanleyville less than an hour ago.

"You were right to summon me, John."

"So far they haven't made any threats, but we're receiving diplomatic communiques every other day."

"What's the gist of them?"

"Reparation, as I mentioned in my note to you."

Roosevelt shook his head. "They know we don't have any money," he answered. "They want something else."

"Pickering's head on a platter, I should think," suggested Boyes.

"They don't care any more about their soldiers than *he* did," said Roosevelt. "Let me see those communiques."

Boyes handed over a sheaf of papers, and Roosevelt spent the next few minutes reading through them.

"Well?" asked Boyes when the American had set the papers down.

"I don't have sufficient information," answered Roosevelt. "Have they gone to the world press with this?"

"If they have, we won't know it for months," said Boyes. "The most recent paper I've seen is a ten-week-old copy of the *East African Standard*." He paused. "Why would going to the press make a difference?"

"Because if they've gone public, then they're positioning themselves to try to take the Congo back from us, by proving that we can't protect European nationals."

"But they weren't nationals," said Boyes. "They were soldiers."

"That just makes our position worse," replied Roosevelt. "If we can't protect a group of armed men who know the Congo, how can we protect anyone else?"

"Then what do you want to do about Pickering?" inquired Boyes.

"Where is he now?"

"In the jail at Leopoldville. Charlie Ross brought him in dead drunk, and locked him away."

"The proper decision," said Roosevelt, nodding approvingly. "I must remember to commend him for it."

"I'm afraid you won't be able to, Mr. President," said Boyes. "He's back in Kenya."

"Charlie?" said Roosevelt, surprised. "I'd have thought he'd be just about the last one to leave."

Boyes paused and stared uncomfortably across the desk at Roosevelt.

"Except for Yank Rogers and me, he was."

"They're *all* gone?"

"Yes, sir." Boyes cleared his throat and continued: "You did your best, sir, but everything's coming unraveled. Most of them stuck it out for better than two years, but we always knew that sooner or later they'd leave. They're not bureaucrats and administrators, they're hunters and adventurers."

"I know, John," said Roosevelt, suddenly feeling his years. "And I don't hold it against them. They helped us more than we had any right to expect." He paused and sighed deeply. "I had rather hoped we'd have a bureaucracy in place by this time."

"I know, sir."

"I wonder if it would have done much good," Roosevelt mused aloud. He looked across at Boyes. "That trip I just returned from—I wasted my time, didn't I?"

"Yes, sir, you did."

"We needed more teachers," said Roosevelt. "One man can't educate them overnight. We needed more teachers, and more money, and more time."

Boyes shook his head. "You needed a different country, Mr. President."

"Let's have no more talk about the inferiority of the African race, John," said Roosevelt. "I'm not up to it today."

"I've never said they were inferior, Mr. President," said Boyes, surprised.

"Certainly you have, John—and frequently, too."

"That's not so, sir," insisted Boyes. "No matter what you may think, I have no contempt or hatred for the Africans—which is why I've always been able to function in their countries." He paused. "I understand them—as much as any white man can. They're not inferior, but they *are* different. The things that are important to us are of no consequence to them, and the things they care about seem almost meaningless to us—and because of that, you simply can't turn them into Americans in two short years, or even twenty."

"We did it in America," said Roosevelt stubbornly.

"That's because your blacks were being assimilated into a dominant society that already existed and was in possession of the country," answered Boyes. "The whites here are just passing through, and the Africans know it, even if the whites don't. They may have to put up with us temporarily, but we won't have any lasting effect on their culture." He paused as Roosevelt considered his words, then continued: "When all is said and done, it's their country and their continent, and one of these days they're going to throw us all out. But what follows us won't look anything like a Western society; it'll be an African society, shaped by and for the Africans." He smiled wryly. "I wish them well, but personally I wouldn't care to be part of it."

"I've said it before, John: You're a very interesting man," said Roosevelt, a strange expression on his face. "Please continue."

"Continue?" repeated Boyes, puzzled.

"Tell me why you wouldn't care to be part of an African nation based on African principles and beliefs."

"For the same reason that they have no desire to become Americans or Europeans, once we stop bribing them to pretend otherwise," answered Boyes. "Their culture is alien to my beliefs." He paused. "Democracy, and the Christian virtues, and the joys of literature, and a reverence for life, all these things work for you, sir, because you have a deep and abiding belief in them. They won't work here because the people of the Congo *don't* believe in them. They believe in witch doctors, and tribalism, and polygamy, and rituals that seem barbaric to me even after a quarter century of being exposed to them. We couldn't adapt to their beliefs any more than they can adapt to ours."

"Go on, John," said Roosevelt, his enthusiasm mounting.

Boyes stared at him curiously. "You've got that look about you, Mr. President."

"What look?"

"The same one I saw that first night we met in the Lado Enclave," said Boyes.

"How would you describe it?" asked Roosevelt, amused.

"I'd call it the look of a crusader."

Roosevelt chuckled with delight. "You're a very perceptive man, John," he said. "By God, I wish I were a drinking man! I'd celebrate with a drink right now!"

"I'll be happy to have two drinks, one for each of us, if you'll tell me what you're so excited about, Mr. President," said Boyes.

"I finally understand what I've been doing wrong," said Roosevelt.

"And what is that, sir?" asked Boyes cautiously.

"Everything!" said Roosevelt with a hearty laugh. "Lord knows I've had enough discussions on the subject with you and the others, but I've always proceeded on the assumption that I was part of the solution. Well, I'm not." He paused, delighted with his sudden inside. "I'm part of the problem! So are you, John. So are the British and the French and the Portugese and the Belgians and everyone else who has tried to impose their culture on this continent. That's what you and Mickey Norton and Charlie Ross and all the others have been telling me, but none of you could properly articulate your position or carry it

through to its logical conclusion." He paused again, barely able to sit still. "*Now* I finally see what we have to do, John!"

"Are you suggesting we leave?" asked Boyes.

Roosevelt shook his head. "It's not that simple, John. Eventually we'll have to, but if we leave now, the Belgians will just move back in and nothing will have changed. It's our duty—our holy mission, if you will—to make sure that doesn't happen, and that the Congo is allowed to develop free from all external influences, including ours."

"That's a mighty tall order, sir," said Boyes. "For instance, what will you do about the missionaries?"

"If they've made converts, they're here at the will of the people, and they've become part of the process," answered Roosevelt after some consideration. "If they haven't, eventually they'll give up and go home."

"All right," said Boyes. "Then what about—?"

"All in good time, John," interrupted Roosevelt. "We'll have to work out thousands of details, but I feel in my bones that after two years of false starts, we're finally on the proper course." He paused thoughtfully. "Our first problem is what to do with Billy Pickering."

"If you're worried about the Belgians, we can't give him a trial by jury," said Boyes. "These people have hated the Belgians for decades. They'll find him innocent of anything more serious than eliminating vermin, and probably vote him into the Presidency."

"No, we can't have a jury trial," agreed Roosevelt. "But not for the reason you suggest."

"Oh?"

"We can't have it because it's a Western institution, and that's what we're going to eradicate—unless and until it evolves naturally."

"Then do you want to execute him?" asked Boyes. "That might satisfy the Belgians."

Roosevelt shook his head vigorously. "We're not in the business of satisfying the Belgians, John." He paused thoughtfully. "Have Yank Rogers escort him to the nearest border and tell him never to return to the Congo. If the Belgians want him, let *them* get him."

Having summarily eliminated the system of justice that he had imposed on the country, Roosevelt spent the remainder of the week eagerly dismantling the rest of the democracy that he had brought to the Congo.

13

Roosevelt was sitting beneath the shade of an ancient baobob tree, composing his weekly letter to Edith. It had been almost three weeks since he had embraced his new vision for the future of the Congo, and he was discussing it enthusiastically, in between queries about Kermit, Quentin, Alice, and the other children.

Boyes sat some distance away, engrossed in Frederick Selous' latest memoirs, which had been personally inscribed to Roosevelt, whose safari he had arranged some three years earlier.

Suddenly Yank Rogers walked up the broad lawn of the state house and approached Roosevelt.

"What is it, Yank?"

"Company," he said with a contemptuous expression on his face.

"Oh?"

"Our old pal, Silva," said Rogers. "You want me to bring him to your office?"

Roosevelt shook his head. "It's too beautiful a day to go inside, Yank. I'll talk to him right here."

Rogers shrugged, walked around to the front of the building, and returned a moment later with Gerard Silva.

"Hello, Mr. Silva," said Roosevelt, getting to his feet and extending his hand.

"*Ambassador* Silva," replied Silva, shaking his hand briefly.

"I wasn't aware that Belgium had sent an Ambassador to the Congo Free State."

"My official title is Ambassador-at-Large," said Silva.

"Well, you seem to have come a long way since you were an Assistant Governor of an unprofitable colony," said Roosevelt easily.

"And *you* have come an equally long way since you promised to turn the Congo into a second America," answered Silva coldly. "All of it downhill."

"It's all a matter of perspective," said Roosevelt.

There was an uneasy silence.

"I have come to Stanleyville for two reasons, Mr. Roosevelt," said Silva at last.

"I was certain that you wouldn't come all this way without a reason," replied Roosevelt.

"First, I have come to inquire about the man, Pickering."

"Mr. Pickering was deported as an undesirable some 19 days ago," answered Roosevelt promptly.

"Deported?" demanded Silva. "He killed four Belgian soldiers!"

"That was hearsay evidence, Mr. Silva," responded Roosevelt. "We could find no eyewitnesses to confirm it."

"Pickering himself admitted it!"

"That was why he was deported," said Roosevelt. "Though there was insufficient evidence to convict him, we felt that there was every possibility that he was telling the truth. This made him an undesirable alien, and he was escorted to the border and told never to return."

"You let him go!"

"We deported him."

"This is totally unacceptable."

"We are a free and independent nation, Mr. Silva," said Roosevelt, a hint of anger in his high-pitched voice. "Are you presuming to tell us how to run our internal affairs?"

"I am telling you that this action is totally unacceptable to the government of Belgium," said Silva harshly.

"Then should Mr. Pickering ever confess to committing a murder within the borders of Belgium, I am sure that your government will deal with it in a manner that it more acceptable to you." Roosevelt paused, as Boyes tried not to laugh aloud. "You had a second reason for coming to Stanleyville, I believe?"

Silva nodded. "Yes, I have, Mr. Roosevelt. I bring an offer from my government."

"The same government that is furious with me for deporting Mr. Pickering?" said Roosevelt. "Well, by all means, let me hear it."

"Your experiment has been a dismal failure, Mr. Roosevelt," said Silva, taking an inordinate amount of pleasure in each word he uttered. "Your treasury is bankrupt, your railroads and highways will never be completed, your bridges and canals do not exist. You have failed to hold the national election that was promised to the international community. Even the small handful of men who accompanied you at the onset of this disastrous misadventure have deserted you." Silva paused and smiled. "You must admit that you are in an unenviable position, Mr. Roosevelt."

"Get to the point, Mr. Silva."

"The government of Belgium is willing to put our differences behind us."

"How considerate of them," remarked Roosevelt dryly.

"If you will publicly request our assistance," continued Silva, "we would be willing to once again assume the responsibility of governing the Congo." He smiled again. "You really have no choice, Mr. Roosevelt. With every day that passes, the Congo retreats further and further into insolvency and barbarism."

Roosevelt laughed harshly. "Your government has a truly remarkable sense of humor, Mr. Silva."

"Are you rejecting our offer?"

"Of course I am," said Roosevelt. "And you're lucky I don't pick you up by the scruff of the neck and throw you clear back to Brussels."

"Need I point out that should my government decide that the Congo's vital interests require our presence, you have no standing army that can prevent our doing what must be done?"

Roosevelt glanced at his wristwatch. "Mr. Silva," he said, "I'm going to give you exactly sixty seconds to say good-bye and take your leave of us. If you're still here at that time, I'm going to have Mr. Boyes escort you to the nearest form of transportation available and point you toward Belgium."

"That is your final word?" demanded Silva, his face flushing beneath his deep tan.

"My final word is for King Albert," said Roosevelt heatedly. "But since I am a Christian and a gentleman, I can't utter it. Now get out of my sight."

Silva glared at him, then turned on his heel and left.

Roosevelt turned to Boyes, who was still sitting in his chair, book in hand. "You heard?" he asked.

"Every word of it." Boyes paused and smiled. "I wish he'd have stayed another forty seconds." He got to his feet and approached Roosevelt. "What do you plan to do about the Belgians?"

"We certainly can't allow them back into the country, that much is clear," said Roosevelt.

"How do you propose to stop them?"

Roosevelt lowered his head in thought for a moment, then looked up. "There's only one way, John."

"Raise an army?"

Roosevelt smiled and shook his head. "What would we pay them with?" He paused. "Besides, we don't want a war. We just want to make sure that the Congo is allowed to develop in its own way, free from all outside influences."

"What do you plan to do?" asked Boyes.

"I'm going to return to America and run for the Presidency again," announced Roosevelt. "Bill Taft is a fat fool, and I made a mistake by turning the country over to him. I'll run on a platform of making the Congo a United States Protectorate. *That* ought to make the Belgians think twice before trying to march in here again!" He nodded his head vigorously. "That's what I'll have to do, if these people are ever to develop their own culture in their own way." His eyes reflected his eagerness. "In fact, I'll leave this afternoon! I'll take Yank with me; I'm sure I can find a place for him in Washington."

"You realize what will happen if you lose?" said Boyes. "The Belgians will march in here five minutes later."

"Then there's no time to waste, is there?" said Roosevelt. "You're welcome to come along, John."

Boyes shook his head. "Thank you for the offer, Mr. President, but there's still a few shillings to be made here in Africa." He paused. "I'll stay in Stanleyville until you return, or until I hear that you've lost the election."

"A little more optimism, John," said Roosevelt with a grin. "The word 'lose' is not in our lexicon."

Boyes stared at him for a long moment. "You mean it, don't you?" he said at last, as the fact of it finally hit home. "You're really going to run for the Presidency again."

"Of course I mean it."

"Don't you ever get tired of challenges?" asked Boyes.

"Do you ever get tired of breathing?" replied Roosevelt, his face aglow as he considered the future and began enumerating the obstacles he faced. "First the election, then Protectorate status for the Congo, and then we'll see just what direction its social evolution takes." He paused. "This is a wonderful experiment we're embarking upon, John."

"It'll be interesting," commented Boyes.

"More than that," said Roosevelt enthusiastically. "It'll be bully—just bully!"

The date was April 17, 1912.

14

After returning home from the Congo, Theodore Roosevelt was denied the Republican nomination for President in 1912. Undaunted, he formed the Bull Moose party, ran as its presidential candidate, and was believed to be ahead in the polls when he was shot in the chest by a fanatic named John Chrank on October 14. Although he recovered from the wound, he was physically unable to campaign further and lost the election to Woodrow Wilson, though finishing well ahead of the seated Republican President, William Howard Taft. He lost what remained of his health in 1914 while exploring and mapping the River of Doubt (later renamed the Rio Teodoro) at the behest of the Brazilian government, and never returned to Africa. He died at his home in Sagamore Hill, New York, on January 6, 1919.

John Boyes made and lost three more fortunes in British East Africa, spent his final days driving a horse-drawn milk wagon in Nairobi, and died in 1951.

The Belgian Congo (later renamed Zaire) was granted its independence in 1960, and held the first and only free election in its history. This was followed by three years of the most savage inter-tribal bloodletting in the history of the continent.

THE BULL MOOSE AT BAY

This was written for the anthology *Alternate Presidents*, in which each author was told to reverse a presidential election, make one of the losers a winner, and see how his presidency would have fared. And since I was the editor, no one but me was going to write the story of Teddy Roosevelt's 1912 presidency.

Roosevelt was always a populist and a progressive, far ahead of his time on certain issues—including the one in this story that stands a fair chance of costing him his bid for re-election. There's one thing I know about Teddy—once he knew he was right he wouldn't back off of a position one millimeter, even if it meant defeat.

The editor (me) thoughtfully allowed the author (me) to sell it to *Asimov's* prior to the anthology's publication.

I don't care what may be his politics, I don't care what may be his religion, I don't care what may be his color. I don't care who he is. So long as he is honest, he shall be served by me.
—*Theodore Roosevelt*
Speech at Cooper Union Hall,
New York, N.Y., October 15, 1886

Personally I feel that it is exactly as much a "right" of women as of men to vote. I always favored woman's suffrage, but only tepidly, until my association with women like Jane Addams and Frances Kellor changed me into a zealous instead of a lukewarm adherent to the cause.
—*Theodore Roosevelt*
Autobiography (1913)

The date was October 27, 1916.

It was a birthday party, but it resembled a wake.

The President had invited only his family and a few close friends to his retreat at Sagamore Hill on this, his 58th birthday. He walked from room to room in the huge old mansion, greeting them, trying to joke with them, but unable to keep a dark scowl from periodically crossing his face. Even Alice, his oldest daughter, who had distracted her share of cabinet meetings and press conferences, seemed unable to distract him tonight.

"Well?" demanded the President at last.

"Well, what, Theodore?" asked his wife.

"Why is everyone tiptoeing around me?" he demanded. "I'm not dead yet. There are worse things than taking an enforced vacation." He paused. "Maybe I'll go back to Africa again, or explore that river the Brazilian government has been asking me to map for them."

"What are you talking about, Mr. President?" said Elihu Root. "You're going to spend the next four years in the White House."

"This isn't a political rally, Elihu," answered Roosevelt. "It's a quiet party, and you're among friends." He sighed deeply. "You've seen the papers, you've heard what the pundits say: I'll be lucky to win six states."

"I believe in you, Mr. President," insisted Root.

"You're my Secretary of War," said Roosevelt, managing one of his famous grins. "You're *supposed* to believe in me." The grin vanished, to be replaced by a frown. "I wish I could say the same of the Republican Party."

"They're still angry at you for running and winning as a Bull Moose four years ago," said Edith, standing in front of her husband and stroking his hair lovingly. "Some of them probably wish that fanatic who tried to shoot you in Milwaukee had been a better shot. But when they're faced with a choice between you and Mr. Wilson, they'll do what's right."

Roosevelt shook his head. "If I can't win the Congress to my cause, how can I expect to win the people?" He strode restlessly across the parlor. "The choice isn't between me and Mr. Wilson; if it was that simple, I'd have no fear of the outcome. It's a choice between their principles and their prejudices, and given the splendid example of the Congress"—he spat out the word—"it would appear that their prejudices are going to win, hands down."

"I just can't believe it," said Gifford Pinchot.

"Gifford, you're a good man and a loyal man," said Roosevelt, "and I thank you for the sentiment." He paused. "But you're my Director of National Parks, and trees don't vote. What do you know about it?"

"I know that you came into office as the most popular American since Abraham Lincoln—probably since Jefferson, in fact—and that you managed to win the war with Germany in less than a year. We've become a true world power, the economy's never been stronger, and there aren't any more trusts left to bust. How in God's name can they vote you out of office? I simply refuse to believe the polls."

"Believe them, Gifford," said Roosevelt. "You've got less than three months to find employment elsewhere."

"I've spoken to Hughes, and he thinks you're going to win," persisted Pinchot.

"Charlie Hughes is my running mate. It's in his best interest to believe we're going to win." Roosevelt paused. "That's one thing I'm especially sorry about. Charlie is a good man, and he would have made an excellent President in 1920. A lot better than that fat fool from Ohio," he added, grimacing at the thought of William Howard Taft, who had succeeded him the first time he had left office.

"Speaking of Charlie," said Root, surveying the room, "I don't see him here tonight."

"This is a birthday party, for my friends and my family," answered Roosevelt. "I'm sick of politicians."

"*I'm* a politician, Theodore," said Root.

"And if that's all you were, you wouldn't be here," answered the President.

"What about *him*?" asked Root, nodding toward a tall, well-dressed young man who seemed uncomfortable in his surroundings, and viewed the world through an elegant *pince-nez*.

Roosevelt sighed. "He's family."

"He's also a Democrat."

"At least he's still speaking to me," said Roosevelt. "That's more than I can say for a lot of Republicans."

"He's too busy looking down his nose to speak to anyone," commented Pinchot.

"He's young," answered Roosevelt. "He'll learn. And he's got a good wife to teach him."

A tall, grizzled man clad in buckskins entered the room. Everyone stared at him for a moment, then went back to their drinks and conversations, and he walked across the parlor to where the President was standing.

"'Evening, Teddy," said Frank McCoy.

"Good evening, Frank," said Roosevelt. "I'm glad you could come."

"Brought some of the stuff you asked me to hunt up," said McCoy.

"Oh?"

McCoy nodded, and pulled a wrinkled folder out of his rumpled jacket. "Two hundred thousand acres adjoining the Yellowstone, a couple of lakes, nice little river flowing through it, even got some buf and grizzly left, and yours for the asking."

"You don't say?" replied Roosevelt, his eyes alight with interest.

"And I found another one, out by Medora in the Dakota Bad Lands, right near where you used to own a ranch."

"Medora," repeated Roosevelt, a wistful smile crossing his face. "It's been a long time since I've thought of Medora." He paused. "Stick around when the party is over, Frank. I'd like to go over these brochures with you."

"I won't hear of it!" snapped Pinchot. "You're going to be the President of the United States for four more years!"

"So who says the President can't own a ranch out near the Yellowstone?" asked McCoy.

"You should be out campaigning for him, not finding retirement homes," continued Pinchot angrily.

"Gifford, I've always been a realist," said Roosevelt. "I'm going to lose. It's time to start planning the next phase of my life."

"I won't hear of it!" said Pinchot.

"I admire your loyalty, but I question your grasp of politics," said Roosevelt gently. "The people will speak one week from today, and neither you nor I are going to like what they have to say—but we're going to have to abide by it, and I'm going to have to find something to do with myself."

"But you're *right*!" said Pinchot. "Can't they see it?"

"Evidently not," answered Roosevelt.

"If it wasn't for that bastard Morgan..." began Root.

"It isn't J. P. Morgan's fault," said Roosevelt. "He's opposed me for years, and I've always beaten him. No, you can lay the blame for this at the doorstep of the Republican Party. They're still bitter than I ran as a Bull Moose and beat Bill Taft—but they're slitting their own throats to have their revenge on me, and I can't seem to make them understand it." He sighed again. "Or maybe it's my own fault."

"You're not backing off what you've been fighting for, are you, Teddy?" asked McCoy, arching a bushy eyebrow.

"No, of course not," answered Roosevelt. "But obviously I didn't get my message across to the people who count—to the voters."

"How could you?" asked Root, taking a drink from a liveried servant as he passed through the room with a large tray. "The Republicans own three-quarters of the newspapers, and the rest think that God speaks directly to Woodrow Wilson."

"I should have realized that it was in their best interest to oppose me and gone out on the stump and spoken to the people directly. I've done it often enough before." The President shook his head. "What I can't understand is why the Democrats didn't grab this issue and wave it like a flag once the Republicans wouldn't have anything to do with it."

Root snorted contemptuously. "Because they're Democrats."

"And maybe they were afraid if they took *it*, they'd have to take *you*, too," added McCoy with an amused grin.

"It could turn their party around," said Roosevelt seriously. He looked across the room at the tall, well-dressed young man who was carefully inserting a cigarette into its holder. "Look at my cousin," he said, lowering his voice. "An effete blue-blooded snob, who dabbles in politics the way some men dabble in stamps and coins. Yet if he came down on the right side of this single issue, he could be in the White House fifteen or twenty years from now."

"God forbid!" laughed Pinchot in mock horror.

"Mark my words," said Roosevelt. "This is an issue that isn't going to go away. You and I may wind up in history's ashcan but not what we fought for. It's as inevitable as the stars in their courses, and I can't seem to make a single Republican Senator or Congressman see it!"

An almost animal growl of anger came forth from the President's lips, and Edith immediately approached him, bringing him a soft drink, straightening his tie, smoothing his hair.

"You must try to control yourself, my dear," she said soothingly.

"What for?" demanded Roosevelt. "I thought I was supposed to be among friends tonight, not politicians. If a man can't express disgust for the Congress to his friends, then who *can* he express it to?"

"Please, Theodore," said Edith. "You don't want to make a scene."

"Why not?" he said irritably. "A President has the right to make a scene if he wants to."

Edith shrugged. "He's all yours, gentlemen," she said to Root, McCoy and Pinchot. "I can't do a thing with him when he's like this."

She walked off to supervise the butler and servants.

"What is everyone staring at?" demanded Roosevelt, for all talk had stopped when Edith had approached him. "Isn't a beaten candidate allowed his tantrums?"

"You're not beaten yet, Father," said Alice.

Roosevelt shook his head impatiently. "Of course I am," he said, addressing the room at large. "But that's not the issue. *I'm* not important. I've put in eleven years at this job. It's time I moved on to other things: I've still got books to write and distant lands to see. The important thing is what's going to happen to the country." The President's voice rose in anger. "You can't simply disenfranchise sixty percent of it and expect things to run as they've always run."

"My cousin, the Samaritan," muttered the tall man with the *pince-nez* and the cigarette holder, and a number of people around him chuckled in amusement.

"Laugh all you want!" thundered Roosevelt. "That's what the Congress did, too. You want to vote me out of office? Go ahead, that's your right—*if* you happen to be a male of the Caucasian race." He glared at them. "Doesn't it bother you that more than half the people in this room *can't* vote me out of office no matter how much they disagree with me?"

"It bothers *me*, Cousin Theodore," said a plain-looking woman, who had been standing unobtrusively in a corner, reading some of the framed letters from other heads of state that were displayed on the wall.

"Well, it ought to bother *all* of you," said Roosevelt. "How can we build a country based on the principle that all men are created equal, and then refuse to give women the vote? We freed the slaves more than half a century ago—and we've erected so many barriers that more Negroes voted *before* the Civil War than vote now!" He paused. "How can I be President of all the people when six out of every ten of them can't vote for me or against me?"

"I believe we've heard this song before," said one of the guests, a one-time hunting companion from the Rockies.

"Well, *I* don't believe you've heard a word of it!" snapped Roosevelt. "What makes someone an American, anyway?"

"I don't think I understand you," said the hunter.

"You heard me—what makes you an American?"

"I...ah..."

"You were born here and you're breathing!" said Roosevelt. "Does anyone know of any other qualification?" He glared pugnaciously around the room. "All right, now. What do you think makes you better than any other American?"

"I consider that an insulting question, Mr. President."

"You'd consider it a lot more insulting if you were a woman, or a Negro, or an immigrant who received his citizenship papers but can't pass a literacy test at the polls—a test that nine out of ten college graduates couldn't pass!"

Roosevelt paused for breath. "Don't any of you understand? We're not living in a Utopia here. We haven't reached a plateau of excellence from which we will never budge. America is a living, growing experiment in democracy, and sooner or later, whether you like it or not, women *are* going to get the vote, and Negroes are *not* going to be harassed at the polls, and immigrants are going to be *welcomed* into a political party."

"If it's inevitable, why are you so worked up about it?" asked a distant relative. "Why did you let it cost you the presidency?"

"He hasn't lost anything!" snarled a younger man. "Those are fighting words! Step outside and—"

"He's right," interrupted Roosevelt. "It did cost me the election."

"But Mr. President—"

"That's a fact," continued Roosevelt. "And facts can be many things, pleasant and unpleasant, but the one thing they always are is true."

"Then I repeat—why did you let it cost you the presidency?"

"Because I believe in the principles of the Republican Party," answered Roosevelt.

"The Republicans voted almost ten-to-one against your proposals, and it took you six ballots to win the nomination once you decided to merge your Bull Moosers party with them," continued the man. "What makes you think this has anything to do with the Republican Party?"

"Please!" said Edith, coming back into the parlor. "We didn't invite you here to fight. This is supposed to be a birthday party."

"It's all right, Edith," said Roosevelt. "It's a fair question; it deserves an answer." He turned to his questioner. "I believe in the Republican Party," he said, "and I tell you that the party will rise or fall on this single issue. It's as simple as that."

"How can you say such a thing?" demanded the man incredulously.

"How can you not see it?" retorted Roosevelt. "How can *they* not see it, those fools in the Congress? It's only a matter of a few years, a decade at most, before women get the vote, before we stop harassing our minorities at the polls. Can't anyone else see that the party that fights most vigorously for their rights will count them among their numbers? Can't anyone else understand that an influx of voters greater than the number that already exist will totally change the balance of political power in this country?" He paused, and his chin jutted out pugnaciously. "No matter what you think, I haven't been waging this war for myself —though I pity the man who has to tell my Alice that she can't vote for her father on election day. I'm waging it because it's the right thing to do, whether I win or lose—and because if the Republicans don't realize what the future holds, then sooner or later the Democrats will, and we will permanently become the nation's minority party."

"Calm yourself, Theodore," said Root, laying a hand on his shoulder. "We can't have the President dying of a stroke a week before the election."

Roosevelt jumped at the touch of Root's hand, then blinked his eyes rapidly, as if suddenly realizing his surroundings. "I'm sorry, Elihu," he said. "The election is all but over, and here I am, still campaigning."

"It's an issue worth campaigning for," said the plain-looking woman.

"The problem is that nobody who agrees with me is allowed to vote for me," said Roosevelt with a wry smile.

"That's not so, Theodore," said Pinchot. "*I* agree with you."

"And I," added Root.

"Me, too, Teddy," said McCoy. "You know that."

"That's probably why none of you hold elected office," remarked the President with dry irony.

The party continued for another three hours, as still more relatives and old friends stopped by to pay their respects, and to see Roosevelt one last time while he was still the President of the United States. Politicians and Rough Riders, New York dandies and Indian chiefs, men of letters and men of action, black men and white, women of all political stripes, mingled and rubbed shoulders in the Hyde Park mansion, for the President had made many friends in his 58 years. Even F. C. Selous had taken time off from a safari to cross the Atlantic and celebrate his most famous client's birthday. Roosevelt, for his part, was soon so busy greeting guests that there were no more outbursts.

At ten o'clock, Edith had the servants bring out a case of champagne, which everyone except the President imbibed. Then came the cake, and a chorus of "For He's a Jolly Good Fellow", and then, one by one, the guests began departing.

By midnight only a handful of people remained: Root, McCoy, Selous, two grizzled old Rough Riders, and the plain-looking woman.

"I see your husband's left without you again," noted Roosevelt.

"He had business to conduct," replied the woman. "Politicians are just the opposite of flowers: they don't bloom until the sun goes down."

Roosevelt chuckled. "You always did have a fine wit."

"Thank you."

"I'll never know what perverse whim caused you to marry a Democrat," he continued, "but I suppose he's no worse than most and probably better than some. Grow him out and I imagine he'll turn out all right."

"I plan to, Cousin Theodore." She paused. "By the way, I fully agree with what you said before. The party that reaches out to the disenfranchised will dominate the next half century of American politics."

"I'm glad *someone* was listening," said Roosevelt.

"Listening and taking notes." She smiled. "Well, mental notes, anyway."

"How about your husband?" said Roosevelt. "I've never asked before—but what's *his* position on enfranchisement?"

"The same as yours."

"Really?" said Roosevelt, suddenly interested. "I didn't know that."

"He doesn't know it, either," answered the plain-looking woman, "but he will when I get through speaking to him."

Roosevelt grinned. "You're a remarkable woman, Eleanor."

She smiled back at him. "Why, thank you, Cousin Theodore."

"Play your cards right and you may be the second First Lady named Roosevelt."

"I plan to," she assured him.

OVER THERE

Roosevelt spent most of 1915 and 1916 writing articles and making speeches all across the country in favor of America entering World War I. It isn't generally known, but he actually volunteered to reconstitute the Rough Riders and take them to France, but Woodrow Wilson slapped that idea down the second he heard of it.

But what if he *had* been allowed to go? What if the greatest hero of the late 19th Century had come face-to-face with what warfare had become in the 20th Century? It was an irresistible notion. I wrote it for one of Greg Benford's *What Might Have Been?* anthologies, and he graciously let me sell it to *Asimov's* as well.

(Side note. I have had maybe fifteen of my stories and two of my novels read aloud for various audio recordings. Some were okay, some were embarrassingly bad. Only one was outstanding—this one, read by the fine actor William Windom for an audio anthology Marty Greenberg assembled. After I heard it, I wrote Windom a letter telling him that I thought it was a pretty good story when I wrote it, but I had no idea *how* good it was until I heard him read it.)

I respectfully ask permission immediately to raise two divisions for immediate service at the front under the bill which has just become law, and hold myself ready to raise four divisions, if you so direct. I respectfully refer for details to my last letters to the Secretary of War.
—Theodore Roosevelt
Telegram to President Woodrow
Wilson, May 18, 1917

> *I very much regret that I cannot comply with the request*
> *in your telegram of yesterday. The reasons I have stated in a*
> *public statement made this morning, and I need not assure you*
> *that my conclusions were based upon imperative considerations*
> *of public policy and not upon personal or private choice.*
> —Woodrow Wilson,
> Telegram to Theodore Roosevelt,
> May 19, 1917

The date was May 22, 1917.

Woodrow Wilson looked up at the burly man standing impatiently before his desk.

"This will necessarily have to be an extremely brief meeting, Mr. Roosevelt," he said wearily. "I have consented to it only out of respect for the fact that you formerly held the office that I am now privileged to hold."

"I appreciate that, Mr. President," said Theodore Roosevelt, shifting his weight anxiously from one leg to the other.

"Well, then?" said Wilson.

"You know why I'm here," said Roosevelt bluntly. "I want your permission to reassemble my Rough Riders and take them over to Europe."

"As I keep telling you, Mr. Roosevelt—that's out of the question."

"You haven't told *me* anything!" snapped Roosevelt. "And I have no interest in what you tell the press."

"Then I'm telling you now," said Wilson firmly. "I can't just let any man who wants to gather up a regiment go fight in the war. We have procedures, and chains of command, and…"

"I'm not just *any* man," said Roosevelt. "And I have every intention of honoring our procedures and chain of command." He glared at the President. "I created many of those procedures myself."

Wilson stared at his visitor for a long moment. "Why are you so anxious to go to war, Mr. Roosevelt? Does violence hold so much fascination for you?"

"I abhor violence and bloodshed," answered Roosevelt. "I believe that war should never be resorted to when it is honorably possible to avoid it. But once war has begun, then the only thing to do is win it as swiftly and decisively as possible. I believe that I can help to accomplish that end."

"Mr. Roosevelt, may I point out that you are 58 years old, and according to my reports you have been in poor health ever since returning from Brazil three years ago?"

"Nonsense!" said Roosevelt defensively. "I feel as fit as a bull moose!"

"A one-eyed bull moose," replied Wilson dryly. Roosevelt seemed about to protest, but Wilson raised a hand to silence him. "Yes, Mr. Roosevelt, I know that you lost the vision in your left eye during a boxing match while you were President." He couldn't quite keep the distaste for such juvenile and adventurous escapades out of his voice.

"I'm not here to discuss my health," answered Roosevelt gruffly, "but the reactivation of my commission as a Colonel in the United States Army."

Wilson shook his head. "You have my answer. You've told me nothing that might change my mind."

"I'm about to."

"Oh?"

"Let's be perfectly honest, Mr. President. The Republican nomination is mine for the asking, and however the war turns out, the Democrats will be sitting ducks. Half the people hate you for entering the war so late, and the other half hate you for entering it at all." Roosevelt paused. "If you will return me to active duty and allow me to organize my Rough Riders, I will give you my personal pledge that I will neither seek nor accept the Republican nomination in 1920."

"It means that much to you?" asked Wilson, arching a thin eyebrow.

"It does, sir."

"I'm impressed by your passion, and I don't doubt your sincerity, Mr. Roosevelt," said Wilson. "But my answer must still be no. I am serving my second term. I have no intention of running again in 1920, I do not need your political support, and I will not be a party to such a deal."

"Then you are a fool, Mr. President," said Roosevelt. "Because I am going anyway, and you have thrown away your only opportunity, slim as it may be, to keep the Republicans out of the White House."

"I will not reactivate your commission, Mr. Roosevelt."

Roosevelt pulled two neatly-folded letters out of his lapel pocket and placed them on the President's desk.

"What are these?" asked Wilson, staring at them as if they might bite him at any moment.

"Letters from the British and the French, offering me commissions in *their* armies." Roosevelt paused. "I am first, foremost, and always an American, Mr. President, and I had entertained no higher hope than leading my men into battle under the Stars and Stripes—but I am going to participate in this war, and you are not going to stop me." And now, for the first time, he displayed the famed Roosevelt grin. "I have some thirty reporters waiting for me on the lawn of the White House. Shall I tell them that I am fighting for the country that I love, or shall I tell them that our European allies are more concerned with winning this damnable war than our own President?"

"This is blackmail, Mr. Roosevelt!" said Wilson, outraged.

"I believe that is the word for it," said Roosevelt, still grinning. "I would like you to direct Captain Frank McCoy to leave his current unit and report to me. I'll handle the rest of the details myself." He paused again. "The press is waiting, Mr. President. What shall I tell them?"

"Tell them anything you want," muttered Wilson furiously. "Only get out of this office."

"Thank you, sir," said Roosevelt, turning on his heel and marching out with an energetic bounce to his stride.

Wilson waited a moment, then spoke aloud. "You can come in now, Joseph."

Joseph Tummulty, his personal secretary, entered the Oval Office.

"Were you listening?" asked Wilson.

"Yes, sir."

"Is there any way out of it?"

"Not without getting a black eye in the press."

"That's what I was afraid of," said Wilson.

"He's got you over a barrel, Mr. President."

"I wonder what he's really after?" mused Wilson thoughtfully. "He's been a governor, an explorer, a war hero, a police commissioner, an author, a big-game hunter, and a President." He paused, mystified. "What more can he want from life?"

"Personally, sir," said Tummulty, making no attempt to hide the contempt in his voice, "I think that damned cowboy is looking to charge up one more San Juan Hill."

Roosevelt stood before his troops, as motley an assortment of warriors as had been assembled since the last incarnation of the Rough Riders. There were military men and cowboys, professional athletes and adventurers, hunters and ranchers, barroom brawlers and Indians, tennis players and wrestlers, even a trio of Maasai *elmoran* he had met on safari in Africa.

"Some of 'em look a little long in the tooth, Colonel," remarked Frank McCoy, his second-in-command.

"Some of *us* are a little long in the tooth too, Frank," said Roosevelt with a smile.

"And some of 'em haven't started shaving yet," continued McCoy wryly.

"Well, there's nothing like a war to grow them up in a hurry."

Roosevelt turned away from McCoy and faced his men, waiting briefly until he had their attention. He paused for a moment to make sure that the journalists who were traveling with the regiment had their pencils and notebooks out and then spoke.

"Gentlemen," he said, "we are about to embark upon a great adventure. We are privileged to be present at a crucial point in the history of the world. In the terrible whirlwind of war, all the great nations of the world are facing the supreme test of their courage and dedication. All the alluring but futile theories of the pacifists have vanished at the first sound of gunfire."

Roosevelt paused to clear his throat, then continued in his surprisingly high-pitched voice. "This war is the greatest the world has ever seen. The vast size of the armies, the tremendous slaughter, the loftiness of the heroism shown and the hideous horror of the brutalities committed, the valor of the fighting men and the extraordinary ingenuity of those who have designed and built the fighting machines, the burning patriotism of the peoples who defend their homelands and the far-reaching complexity of the plans of the leaders—all are on a scale so huge that nothing in past history can be compared with them.

"The issues at stake are fundamental. The free peoples of the world have banded together against tyrannous militarism, and it is not too much to say that the outcome will largely determine, for those of us who love liberty above all else, whether or not life remains worth living."

He paused again, and stared up and down the ranks of his men.

"Against such a vast and complex array of forces, it may seem to you that we will just be another cog in the military machine of the allies, that one regiment cannot possibly make a difference." Roosevelt's chin jutted forward pugnaciously. "I say to you that this is rubbish! We represent a society dedicated to the proposition that every free man makes a difference. And I give you my solemn pledge that the Rough Riders will make a difference in the fighting to come!"

It was possible that his speech wasn't finished, that he still had more to say…but if he did, it was drowned out beneath the wild and raucous cheering of his men.

One hour later they boarded the ship to Europe.

Roosevelt summoned a corporal and handed him a hand-written letter. The man saluted and left, and Roosevelt returned to his chair in front of his tent. He was about to pick up a book when McCoy approached him.

"Your daily dispatch to General Pershing?" he asked dryly.

"Yes," answered Roosevelt. "I can't understand what is wrong with the man. Here we are, primed and ready to fight, and he's kept us well behind the front for the better part of two months!"

"I know, Colonel."

"It just doesn't make any sense! Doesn't he know what the Rough Riders did at San Juan Hill?"

"That was a long time ago, sir," said McCoy.

"I tell you, Frank, these men are the elite—the cream of the crop! They weren't drafted by lottery. Every one of them volunteered, and every one was approved personally by you or by me. Why are we being wasted here? There's a war to be won!"

"Pershing's got a lot to consider, Colonel," said McCoy. "He's got half a million American troops to disperse, he's got to act in concert with the French and the British, he's got to consider his lines of supply, he's…"

"Don't patronize me, Frank!" snapped Roosevelt. "We've assembled a brilliant fighting machine here, and he's ignoring us. There *has* to be a reason. I want to know what it is!"

McCoy shrugged helplessly. "I have no answer, sir."

"Well, I'd better get one soon from Pershing!" muttered Roosevelt. "We didn't come all this way to help in some mopping-up operation after the battle's been won." He stared at the horizon. "There's a glorious crusade being fought in the name of liberty, and I plan to be a part of it."

He continued staring off into the distance long after McCoy had left him.

A private approached Roosevelt as the former President was eating lunch with his officers.

"Dispatch from General Pershing, sir," said the private, handing him an envelope with a snappy salute.

"Thank you," said Roosevelt. He opened the envelope, read the message, and frowned.

"Bad news, Colonel?" asked McCoy.

"He says to be patient," replied Roosevelt. "Patient?" he repeated furiously. "By God, I've been patient long enough! Jake —saddle my horse!"

"What are you going to do, Colonel?" asked one of his lieutenants.

"I'm going to go meet face-to-face with Pershing," said Roosevelt, getting to his feet. "This is intolerable!"

"We don't even know where he is, sir."

"I'll find him," replied Roosevelt confidently.

"You're more likely to get lost or shot," said McCoy, the only man who dared to speak to him so bluntly.

"Runs With Deer! Matupu!" shouted Roosevelt. "Saddle your horses!"

A burly Indian and a tall Maasai immediately got to their feet and went to the stable area.

Roosevelt turned back to McCoy. "I'm taking the two best trackers in the regiment. Does that satisfy you, Mr. McCoy?"

"It does not," said McCoy. "I'm coming along, too."

Roosevelt shook his head. "You're in command of the regiment in my absence. You're staying here."

"But—"

"That's an order," said Roosevelt firmly.

"Will you at least take along a squad of sharpshooters, Colonel?" persisted McCoy.

"Frank, we're forty miles behind the front, and I'm just going to talk to Pershing, not shoot him."

"We don't even know where the front *is*," said McCoy.

"It's where we're *not*," said Roosevelt grimly. "And that's what I'm going to change."

He left the mess tent without another word.

The first four French villages they passed were deserted, and consisted of nothing but the burnt skeletons of houses and shops. The fifth had two buildings still standing—a manor house and a church—and they had been turned into allied hospitals. Soldiers with missing limbs, soldiers with faces swathed by filthy bandages, soldiers with gaping holes in their bodies lay on cots and floors, shivering in the cold damp air, while an undermanned and harassed medical team did its best to keep them alive.

Roosevelt stopped long enough to determine General Pershing's whereabouts, then walked among the wounded to offer words of encouragement while trying to ignore the unmistakable stench of gangrene and the stinging scent of disinfectant. Finally he remounted his horse and joined his two trackers.

They passed a number of corpses on their way to the front. Most had been plundered of their weapons, and one, laying upon its back, displayed a gruesome, toothless smile.

"Shameful!" muttered Roosevelt as he looked down at the grinning body.

"Why?" asked Runs With Deer.

"It's obvious that the man had gold teeth, and they have been removed."

"It is honorable to take trophies of the enemy," asserted the Indian.

"The Germans have never advanced this far south," said Roosevelt."This man's teeth were taken by his companions." He shook his head. "Shameful!"

Matupu the Maasai merely shrugged. "Perhaps this is not an honorable war."

"We are fighting for an honorable principle," stated Roosevelt. "That makes it an honorable war."

"Then it is an honorable war being waged by dishonorable men," said Matupu.

"Do the Maasai not take trophies?" asked Runs With Deer.

"We take cows and goats and women," answered Matupu. "We do not plunder the dead." He paused. "We do not take scalps."

"There was a time when *we* did not, either," said Runs With Deer. "We were taught to, by the French."

"And we are in France now," said Matupu with some satisfaction, as if everything now made sense to him.

They dismounted after two more hours and walked their horses for the rest of the day, then spent the night in a bombed-out farmhouse. The next morning they were mounted and riding again, and they came to General Pershing's field headquarters just before noon. There were thousands of soldiers bustling about, couriers bringing in hourly reports from the trenches, weapons and tanks being dispatched, convoys of trucks filled with food and water slowly working their way into supply lines.

Roosevelt was stopped a few yards into the camp by a young lieutenant.

"May I ask your business here, sir?"

"I'm here to see General Pershing," answered Roosevelt.

"Just like that?" said the soldier with a smile.

"Son," said Roosevelt, taking off his hat and leaning over the lieutenant, "take a good look at my face." He paused for a moment. "Now go tell General Pershing that Colonel Roosevelt is here to see him."

The lieutenant's eyes widened. "By God, you *are* Teddy Roosevelt!" he exclaimed. Suddenly he reached his hand out. "May I shake your hand first, Mr. President? I just want to be able to tell my parents I did it."

Roosevelt grinned and took the young man's hand in his own, then waited astride his horse while the lieutenant went off to Pershing's quarters. He gazed around the camp: there were ramshackle buildings and ramshackle soldiers, each of which had seen too much action and too little glory. The men's faces were haggard, their eyes haunted, their bodies stooped with exhaustion. The main paths through the camp had turned to mud, and the constant drizzle brought rust, rot, and disease with an equal lack of Cosmic concern.

The lieutenant approached Roosevelt, his feet sinking inches into the mud with each step.

"If you'll follow me, Mr. President, he'll see you immediately."

"Thank you," said Roosevelt.

"Watch yourself, Mr. President," said the lieutenant as Roosevelt dismounted. "I have a feeling he's not happy about meeting with you."

"He'll be a damned sight less happy when I'm through with him," said Roosevelt firmly. He turned to his companions. "See to the needs of the horses."

"Yes, sir," said Runs With Deer. "We'll be waiting for you right here."

"How is the battle going?" Roosevelt asked as he and the lieutenant began walking through the mud toward Pershing's quarters. "My Rough Riders have been practically incommunicado since we arrived."

The lieutenant shrugged. "Who knows? All we hear are rumors. The enemy is retreating, the enemy is advancing, we've killed thousands of them, they've killed thousands of us. Maybe the General will tell you; he certainly hasn't seen fit to tell *us*."

They reached the entrance to Pershing's quarters.

"I'll wait here for you, sir," said the lieutenant.

"You're sure you don't mind?" asked Roosevelt. "You can find some orderly to escort me back if it will be a problem."

"No, sir," said the young man earnestly. "It'll be an honor, Mr. President."

"Well, thank you, son," said Roosevelt. He shook the lieutenant's hand again, then walked through the doorway and found himself facing General John J. Pershing.

"Good afternoon, Jack," said Roosevelt, extending his hand.

Pershing looked at Roosevelt's outstretched hand for a moment, then took it.

"Have a seat, Mr. President," he said, indicating a chair.

"Thank you," said Roosevelt, pulling up a chair as Pershing seated himself behind a desk that was covered with maps.

"I mean no disrespect, Mr. President," said Pershing, "but exactly who gave you permission to leave your troops and come here?"

"No one," answered Roosevelt.

"Then why did you do it?" asked Pershing. "I'm told you were accompanied only by a red Indian and a black savage. That's hardly a safe way to travel in a war zone."

"I came here to find out why you have consistently refused my requests to have my Rough Riders moved to the front."

Pershing lit a cigar and offered one to Roosevelt, who refused it.

"There are proper channels for such a request," said the general at last. "You yourself helped create them."

"And I have been using them for almost two months, to no avail."

Pershing sighed. "I *have* been a little busy conducting this damned war."

"I'm sure you have," said Roosevelt. "And I have assembled a regiment of the finest fighting men to be found in America, which I am placing at your disposal."

"For which I thank you, Mr. President."

"I don't want you to thank me!" snapped Roosevelt. "I want you to unleash me!"

"When the time is right, your Rough Riders will be brought into the conflict," said Pershing.

"When the time is right?" repeated Roosevelt. "Your men are dying like flies! Every village I've passed has become a bombed-out ghost town! You needed us two months ago, Jack!"

"Mr. President, I've got half a million men to maneuver. I'll decide when and where I need your regiment."

"When?" persisted Roosevelt.

"You'll be the first to know."

"That's not good enough!"

"It will have to be."

"You listen to me, Jack Pershing!" said Roosevelt heatedly. "I *made* you a general! I think the very least you owe me is an answer. When will my men be brought into the conflict?"

Pershing stared at him from beneath shaggy black eyebrows for a long moment. "What the hell did you have to come here for, any-way?" he said at last.

"I told you: to get an answer."

"I don't mean to my headquarters," said Pershing. "I mean, what is a 58-year-old man with a blind eye and a game leg doing in the middle of a war?"

"This is the greatest conflict in history, and it's being fought over principles that every free man holds dear. How could I not take part in it?"

"You could have just stayed home and made speeches and raised funds."

"And you could have retired after Mexico and spent the rest of your life playing golf," Roosevelt shot back. "But you didn't, and I didn't, because neither of us is that kind of man. Damn it, Jack—I've assembled a regiment the likes of which hasn't been seen in almost 20 years, and if you've any sense at all, you'll make use of us. Our horses and our training give us an enormous advantage on this terrain. We can mobilize and strike at the enemy as easily as this fellow Lawrence seems to be doing in the Arabian desert."

Pershing stared at him for a long moment, then sighed deeply.

"I can't do it, Mr. President," said Pershing.

"Why not?" demanded Roosevelt.

"The truth? Because of you, sir."

"What are you talking about?"

"You've made my position damnably awkward," said Pershing bitterly. "You are an authentic American hero, possibly the first one since Abraham Lincoln. You are as close to being worshipped as a man can be." He paused. "You're a goddamned icon, Mr. Roosevelt."

"What has *that* got to do with anything?"

"I am under direct orders not to allow you to participate in any action that might result in your death." He glared at Roosevelt across the desk. "*Now* do you understand? If I move you to the front, I'll have to surround you with at least three divisions to make sure nothing happens to you—and I'm in no position to spare that many men."

"Who issued that order, Jack?"

"My Commander-in-Chief."

"Woodrow Wilson?"

"That's right. And I'd no more disobey him than I would disobey you if you still held that office." He paused, then spoke again more gently. "You're an old man, sir. Not old by your standards, but too damned old to be leading charges against the Germans. You should be home writing your memoirs and giving speeches and rallying the people to our cause, Mr. President."

"I'm not ready to retire to Hyde Park and have my face carved on Mount Rushmore yet," said Roosevelt. "There are battles to be fought and a war to be won."

"Not by you, Mr. President," answered Pershing. "When the enemy is beaten and on the run, I'll bring your regiment up. The press can go crazy photographing you chasing the few German stragglers back to Berlin. But I cannot and will not disobey a direct order from my Commander-in-Chief. Until I can guarantee your safety, you'll stay where you are."

"I see," said Roosevelt, after a moment's silence. "And what if I relinquish my command? Will you utilize my Rough Riders then?"

Pershing shook his head. "I have no use for a bunch of tennis players and college professors who think they can storm across the trenches on their polo ponies," he said firmly. "The only men you have with battle experience are as old as you are." He paused. "Your regiment might be effective if the Apaches ever leave the reservation, but they are ill-prepared for a modern, mechanized war. I hate to be so blunt, but it's the truth, sir."

"You're making a huge mistake, Jack."

"You're the one who made the mistake, sir, by coming here. It's my job to see that you don't die because of it."

"Damn it, Jack, we could make a difference!"

Pershing paused and stared, not without sympathy, at Roosevelt. "War has changed, Mr. President," he said at last. "No one regiment can make a difference any longer. It's been a long time since Achilles fought Hector outside the walls of Troy."

An orderly entered with a dispatch, and Pershing immediately read and initialed it.

"I don't mean to rush you, sir," he said, getting to his feet, "but I have an urgent meeting to attend."

Roosevelt stood up. "I'm sorry to have bothered you, General."

"I'm still Jack to you, Mr. President," said Pershing. "And it's as your friend Jack that I want to give you one final word of advice."

"Yes?"

"Please, for your own sake and the sake of your men, don't do anything rash."

"Why would I do something rash?" asked Roosevelt innocently.

"Because you wouldn't be Teddy Roosevelt if the thought of ignoring your orders hadn't already crossed your mind," said Pershing.

Roosevelt fought back a grin, shook Pershing's hand, and left without saying another word. The young lieutenant was just outside the door, and escorted him back to where Runs With Deer and Matupu were waiting with the horses.

"Bad news?" asked Runs With Deer, as he studied Roosevelt's face.

"No worse than I had expected."

"Where do we go now?" asked the Indian.

"Back to camp," said Roosevelt firmly. "There's a war to be won, and no college professor from New Jersey is going to keep me from helping to win it!"

"Well, that's the story," said Roosevelt to his assembled officers, after he had laid out the situation to them in the large tent he had reserved for strategy sessions. "Even if I resign my commission and return to America, there is no way that General Pershing will allow you to see any action."

"I knew Black Jack Pershing when he was just a captain," growled Buck O'Neill, one of the original Rough Riders. "Just who the hell does he think he is?"

"He's the supreme commander of the American forces," answered Roosevelt wryly.

"What are we going to do, sir?" asked McCoy. "Surely you don't plan to just sit back here and then let Pershing move us up when all the fighting's done with?"

"No, I don't," said Roosevelt.

"Let's hear what you got to say, Teddy," said O'Neill.

"The issues at stake in this war haven't changed since I went to see the General," answered Roosevelt. "I plan to harass and harry the enemy to the best of our ability. If need be we will live off the land while utilizing our superior mobility in a number of tactical strikes, and we will do our valiant best to bring this conflict to a successful conclusion."

He paused and looked around at his officers. "I realize that in doing this I am violating my orders, but there are greater principles at stake here. I am flattered that the President thinks I am indispensable to the American public, but our nation is based on the principle that no one man deserves any rights or privileges not offered to all men." He took a deep breath and cleared his throat. "However, since I *am* contravening a direct order, I believe that not only each one of you, but every one of the men as well, should be given the opportunity to withdraw from the Rough Riders. I will force no man to ride against his conscience and his beliefs. I would like to you go out now and put the question to the men; I will wait here for your answer."

To nobody's great surprise, the regiment voted unanimously to ride to glory with Teddy Roosevelt.

3 August, 1917

My Dearest Edith:

As strange as this may seem to you (and is seems surpassingly strange to me), I will soon be a fugitive from justice, opposed not only by the German army but quite possibly by the U.S. military as well.

My Rough Riders have embarked upon a bold adventure, contrary to both the wishes and the direct orders of the President of the United States. When I think back to the day he finally approved my request to reassemble the regiment, I cringe with chagrin at my innocence and naivete; he sent us here only so that I would not have access to the press, and he would no longer have to listen to my demands. Far from being permitted to play a leading role in this noblest of battles, my men have been held far behind the front, and Jack Pershing was under orders from Wilson himself not to allow any harm to come to us.

When I learned of this, I put a proposition to my men, and I am extremely proud of their response. To a one, they voted to break camp and ride to the front so as to strike at the heart of the German military machine. By doing so, I am disobeying the orders of my Commander-in-Chief, and because of this somewhat peculiar situation, I doubt that I shall be able to send too many more letters to you until I have helped to end this war. At that time, I shall turn myself over to Pershing, or whoever is in charge, and argue my case before whatever tribunal is deemed proper.

However, before that moment occurs, we shall finally see action, bearing the glorious banner of the Stars and Stripes. My men are a finely-tuned fighting machine, and I daresay that they will give a splendid account of themselves before the conflict is over. We have not made contact with the enemy yet, nor can I guess where we shall finally meet, but we are primed and eager for our first taste of battle. Our spirit is high, and many of the old-timers spend their hours singing the old battle songs from Cuba. We are all looking forward to a bully battle, and we plan to teach the Hun a lesson he won't soon forget.

Give my love to the children, and when you write to Kermit and Quentin, tell them that their father has every intention of reaching Berlin before they do!

All my love,
Theodore

Roosevelt, who had been busily writing an article on ornithology, looked up from his desk as McCoy entered his tent.

"Well?"

"We think we've found what we've been looking for, Mr. President," said McCoy.

"Excellent!" said Roosevelt, carefully closing his notebook. "Tell me about it."

McCoy spread a map out on the desk.

"Well, the front lines, as you know, are *here*, about fifteen miles to the north of us. The Germans are entrenched *here*, and we haven't been able to move them for almost three weeks." McCoy paused. "The word I get from my old outfit is that the Americans are planning a major push on the German left, right about *here*."

"When?" demanded Roosevelt.

"At sunrise tomorrow morning."

"Bully!" said Roosevelt. He studied the map for a moment, then looked up. "Where is Jack Pershing?"

"Almost ten miles west and eight miles north of us," answered McCoy. "He's dug in, and from what I hear, he came under pretty heavy mortar fire today. He'll have his hands full without worrying about where an extra regiment of American troops came from."

"Better and better," said Roosevelt. "We not only get to fight, but we may even pull Jack's chestnuts out of the fire." He turned his attention back to the map. "All right," he said, "the Americans will advance along this line. What would you say will be their major obstacle?"

"You mean besides the mud and the Germans and the mustard gas?" asked McCoy wryly.

"You know what I mean, Hank."

"Well," said McCoy, "there's a small rise here—I'd hardly call it a hill, certainly not like the one we took in Cuba—but it's manned by four machine guns, and it gives the Germans an excellent view of the territory the Americans have got to cross."

"Then that's our objective," said Roosevelt decisively. "If we can capture that hill and knock out the machine guns, we'll have made a positive contribution to the battle that even that Woodrow Wilson will be forced to acknowledge." The famed Roosevelt grin spread across his face. "We'll show him that the dodo may be dead, but the Rough Riders are very much alive." He paused. "Gather the men, Hank. I want to speak to them before we leave."

McCoy did as he was told, and Roosevelt emerged from his tent some ten minutes later to address the assembled Rough Riders.

"Gentlemen," he said, "tomorrow morning we will meet the enemy on the battlefield."

A cheer arose from the ranks.

"It has been suggested that modern warfare deals only in masses and logistics, that there is no room left for heroism, that the only glory remaining to men of action is upon the sporting fields. I tell you that this is a lie. *We matter!* Honor and courage are not outmoded virtues, but are the very ideals that make us great as individuals and as a nation. Tomorrow, we will prove it in terms that our detractors and our enemies will both understand." He paused, and then saluted them. "Saddle up—and may God be with us!"

They reached the outskirts of the battlefield, moving silently with hooves and harnesses muffled, just before sunrise. Even McCoy, who had seen action in Mexico, was unprepared for the sight that awaited them.

The mud was littered with corpses as far as the eye could see in the dim light of the false dawn. The odor of death and decay permeated the moist, cold morning air. Thousands of bodies lay there in the pouring rain, many of them grotesquely swollen. Here and there they had virtually exploded, either when punctured by bullets or when the walls of the abdominal cavities collapsed. Attempts had been made during the previous month to drag them back off the battlefield, but there was simply no place left to put them. There was almost total silence, as the men in both trenches began preparing for another day of bloodletting.

Roosevelt reined his horse to a halt and surveyed the carnage. Still more corpses were hung up on barbed wire, and more than a handful of bodies attached to the wire still moved feebly. The rain pelted down, turning the plain between the enemy trenches into a brown, gooey slop.

"My God, Hank!" murmured Roosevelt.

"It's pretty awful," agreed McCoy.

"This is not what civilized men do to each other," said Roosevelt, stunned by the sight before his eyes. "This isn't war, Hank—it's butchery!"

"It's what war has become."

"How long have these two lines been facing each other?"

"More than a month, sir."

Roosevelt stared, transfixed, at the sea of mud.

"A month to cross a quarter mile of *this*?"

"That's correct, sir."

"How many lives have been lost trying to cross this strip of land?"

McCoy shrugged. "I don't know. Maybe eighty thousand, maybe a little more."

Roosevelt shook his head. "*Why*, in God's name? Who cares about it? What purpose does it serve?"

McCoy had no answer, and the two men sat in silence for another moment, surveying the battlefield.

"This is madness!" said Roosevelt at last. "Why doesn't Pershing simply march around it?"

"That's a question for a general to answer, Mr. President," said McCoy. "Me, I'm just a captain."

"We can't continue to lose American boys for *this*!" said Roosevelt furiously. "Where is that machine gun encampment, Hank?"

McCoy pointed to a small rise about three hundred yards distant.

"And the main German lines?"

"Their first row of trenches are in line with the hill."

"Have we tried to take the hill before?"

"I can't imagine that we haven't, sir," said McCoy. "As long as they control it, they'll mow our men down like sitting ducks in a shooting gallery." He paused. "The problem is the mud. The average infantryman can't reach the hill in less than two minutes, probably closer to three—and until you've seen them in action, you can't believe the damage these guns can do in that amount of time."

"So as long as the hill remains in German hands, this is a war of attrition."

McCoy sighed. "It's been a war of attrition for three years, sir."

Roosevelt sat and stared at the hill for another few minutes, then turned back to McCoy.

"What are our chances, Hank?"

McCoy shrugged. "If it was dry, I'd say we had a chance to take them out..."

"But it's not."

"No, it's not," echoed McCoy.

"Can we do it?"

"I don't know, sir. Certainly not without heavy casualties."

"How heavy?"

"*Very* heavy."

"I need a number," said Roosevelt.

McCoy looked him in the eye. "Ninety percent—if we're lucky."

Roosevelt stared at the hill again. "They predicted fifty percent casualties at San Juan Hill," he said. "We had to charge up a much steeper slope in the face of enemy machine gun fire. Nobody thought we had a chance—but I did it, Hank, and I did it alone. I charged up that hill and knocked out the machine gun nest myself, and then the rest of my men followed me."

"The circumstances were different then, Mr. President," said McCoy. "The terrain offered cover and solid footing, and you were facing Cuban peasants who had been conscripted into service, not battle-hardened professional German soldiers."

"I know, I know," said Roosevelt. "But if we knock those machine guns out, how many American lives can we save today?"

"I don't know," admitted McCoy. "Maybe ten thousand, maybe none. It's possible that the Germans are dug in so securely that they can beat back any American charge even without the use of those machine guns."

"But at least it would prolong some American lives," persisted Roosevelt.

"By a couple of minutes."

"It would give them a *chance* to reach the German bunkers."

"I don't know."

"More of a chance than if they had to face machine gun fire from the hill."

"What do you want me to say, Mr. President?" asked McCoy. "That if we throw away our lives charging the hill that we'll have done something glorious and affected the outcome of the battle? I just don't know!"

"We came here to help win a war, Hank. Before I send my men into battle, I have to know that it will make a difference."

"I can't give you any guarantees, sir. We came to fight a war, all right. But look around you, Mr. President—*this* isn't the war we came to fight. They've changed the rules on us."

"There are hundreds of thousands of American boys in the trenches who didn't come to fight this kind of war," answered Roosevelt. "In less than an hour, most of them are going to charge across this sea of mud into a barrage of machine gun fire. If we can't shorten the war, then perhaps we can at least lengthen their lives."

"At the cost of our own."

"We are idealists and adventurers, Hank—perhaps the last this world will ever see. We knew what we were coming here to do." He paused. "Those boys are here because of speeches and decisions that politicians have made, myself included. Left to their own devices, they'd go home to be with their families. Left to ours, we'd find another cause to fight for."

"This isn't a cause, Mr. President," said McCoy. "It's a slaughter."

"Then maybe this is where men who want to prevent further slaughter belong," said Roosevelt. He looked up at the sky. "They'll be mobilizing in another half hour, Hank."

"I know, Mr. President."

"If we leave now, if we don't try to take that hill, then Wilson and Pershing were right and I was wrong. The time for heroes is past, and I *am* an anachronism who should be sitting at home in a rocking chair, writing memoirs and exhorting younger men to go to war." He paused, staring at the hill once more. "If we don't do what's required of us this day, we are agreeing with them that we don't matter, that men of courage and ideals can't make a difference. If that's true, there's no sense waiting for a more equitable battle, Hank—we might as well ride south and catch the first boat home."

"That's your decision, Mr. President?" asked McCoy.

"Was there really ever any other option?" replied Roosevelt wryly.

"No, sir," said McCoy. "Not for men like us."

"Thank you for your support, Hank," said Roosevelt, reaching out and laying a heavy hand on McCoy's shoulder. "Prepare the men."

"Yes, sir," said McCoy, saluting and riding back to the main body of the Rough Riders.

"Madness!" muttered Roosevelt, looking out at the bloated corpses. "Utter madness!"

McCoy returned a moment later.

"The men are awaiting your signal, sir," he said.

"Tell them to follow me," said Roosevelt.

"Sir..." said McCoy.

"Yes?"

"We would prefer you not lead the charge. The first ranks will face the heaviest bombardment, not only from the hill but from the cannons behind the bunkers."

"I can't ask my men to do what I myself won't do," said Roosevelt.

"You are too valuable to lose, sir. We plan to attack in three waves. You belong at the back of the third wave, Mr. President."

Roosevelt shook his head. "There's nothing up ahead except bullets, Hank, and I've faced bullets before—in the Dakota Bad Lands, in Cuba, in Milwaukee. But if I hang back, if I send my men to do a job I was afraid to do, then I'd have to face myself—and as any Democrat will tell you, I'm a lot tougher than any bullet ever made."

"You won't reconsider?" asked McCoy.

"Would you have left your unit and joined the Rough Riders if you thought I might?" asked Roosevelt with a smile.

"No, sir," admitted McCoy. "No, sir, I probably wouldn't have."

Roosevelt shook his hand. "You're a good man, Hank."

"Thank you, Mr. President."

"Are the men ready?"

"Yes, sir."

"Then," said Roosevelt, turning his horse toward the small rise, "let's do what must be done."

He pulled his rifle out, unlatched the safety catch, and dug his heels into his horse's sides.

Suddenly he was surrounded by the first wave of his own men, all screaming their various war cries in the face of the enemy.

For just a moment there was no response. Then the machine guns began their sweeping fire across the muddy plain. Buck O'Neill was the first to fall, his body riddled with bullets. An instant later Runs With Deer screamed in agony as his arm was blown away. Horses had their legs shot from under them, men were blown out of their saddles, limbs flew crazily through the wet morning air, and still the charge continued.

Roosevelt had crossed half the distance when Matupu fell directly in front of him, his head smashed to a pulp. He heard McCoy groan as half a dozen bullets thudded home in his chest, but looked neither right nor left as his horse leaped over the fallen Maasai's bloody body.

Bullets and cannonballs flew to the right and left of him, in front and behind, and yet miraculously he was unscathed as he reached the final hundred yards. He dared a quick glance around, and saw that he was the sole survivor from the first wave, then heard the screams of the second wave as the machine guns turned on them.

Now he was seventy yards away, now fifty. He yelled a challenge to the Germans, and as he looked into the blinking eye of a machine gun, for one brief, final, glorious instant it was San Juan Hill all over again.

18 September, 1917

Dispatch from General John J. Pershing to Commander-in-Chief, President Woodrow Wilson.

Sir:

I regret to inform you that Theodore Roosevelt died last Tuesday of wounds received in battle. He had disobeyed his orders and led his men in a futile charge against an entrenched German position. His entire regiment, the so-called "Rough Riders", was lost. His death was almost certainly instantaneous, although it was two days before his body could be retrieved from the battlefield.

I shall keep the news of Mr. Roosevelt's death from the press until receiving instructions from you. It is true that he was an anachronism, that he belonged more to the 19th Century than the 20th, and yet it is entirely possible that he was the last authentic hero our country shall ever produce. The charge he led was ill-conceived and foolhardy in the extreme, nor did it diminish the length of the conflict by a single day, yet I cannot help but believe that if I had 50,000 men with his courage and spirit, I could bring this war to a swift and satisfactory conclusion by the end of the year.

That Theodore Roosevelt died the death of a fool is beyond question, but I am certain in my heart that with his dying breath he felt he was dying the death of a hero. I await your instructions, and will release whatever version of his death you choose upon hearing from you.

—Gen. John J. Pershing

22 September, 1917

Dispatch from President Woodrow Wilson to General John J. Pershing, Commander of American Forces in Europe.

John:

That man continues to harass me from the grave.

Still, we have had more than enough fools in our history. Therefore, he died a hero.

Just between you and me, the time for heroes is past. I hope with all my heart that he was our last.

—Woodrow Wilson

And he was.

1919:

THE LIGHT THAT BLINDS, THE CLAWS THAT CATCH

The first and greatest love of Roosevelt's life was his wife, Alice. He all but worshipped her, and when she died (on the same day, and in the same house, as his mother) he left New York, moved to the Dakota Bad Lands, and never allowed her name to be mentioned in his presence again.

It's no secret that I consider him our greatest and most accomplished American. And from time to time I wondered what his life would have been like had Alice lived. And finally I wrote the story.

Like most of the Roosevelt stories, it ran in *Asimov's*. This is its first appearance since then. It has certainly garnered less notice than any of my other Teddy stories, but it's always been my favorite of them, and seems a fitting chronological end to his alternate historical career.

"And when my heart's dearest died, the light went from my life for ever."
—Theodore Roosevelt
In Memory of my Darling Wife (1884)

"Beware the Jabberwock, my son!
The jaws that bite, the claws that catch!"
—Lewis Carroll
Through the Looking-Glass (1872)

The date is February 14, 1884.

Theodore Roosevelt holds Alice in his arms, cradling her head against his massive chest. The house is cursed, no doubt about it, and he resolves to sell it as soon as Death has claimed yet another victim.

His mother lies in her bed down the hall. She has been dead for almost eight hours. Three rooms away his two-day-old daughter wails mournfully. The doctors have done all they can for Alice, and now they sit in the parlor and wait while the 26-year-old State Assemblyman spends his last few moments with his wife, tears running down his cheeks and falling onto her honey-colored hair.

The undertaker arrives for his mother, and looks into the room. He decides that perhaps he should stay, and he joins the doctors downstairs.

How can this be happening, wonders Roosevelt. Have I come this far, accomplished this much, triumphed over so many obstacles, only to lose you both on the same day?

He shakes his head furiously. *No!*, he screams silently. *I will not allow it! I have looked Death in the eye before and stared him down. Draw your strength from me, for I have strength to spare!*

And, miraculously, she *does* draw strength from him. Her breathing becomes more regular, and some thirty minutes later he sees her eyelids flutter. He yells for the doctors, who come up the stairs, expecting to find him holding a corpse in his arms. What they find is a semi-conscious young woman who, for no earthly reason, is fighting to live. It is touch and go for three days and three nights, but finally, on February 17, she is pronounced on the road to recovery, and for the first time in almost four days, Roosevelt sleeps.

And as he sleeps, strange images come to him in his dreams. He sees a hill in a strange, sunbaked land, and himself riding up it, pistols blazing. He sees a vast savannah, filled with more beasts than he ever knew existed. He sees a mansion, painted white. He sees many things and many events, a pageant he is unable to interpret, and then the pageant ends and he seems to see a life filled with the face and the scent and the touch of the only woman he has ever loved, and he is content.

New York is too small for him, and he longs for the wide open spaces of his beloved Dakota Bad Lands. He buys a ranch near Medora, names it Elkhorn, and moves Alice and his daughter out in the summer.

The air is too dry for Alice, the dust and pollen too much for her, and he offers to take her back to the city, but she waves his arguments away with a delicate white hand. If this is where he wants to be, she will adjust; she wants only to be a good wife to him, never a burden.

Ranching and hunting, ornithology and taxidermy, being a husband to Alice and a father to young Alice, writing a history of the West for Scribner's and a series of monographs for the scientific journals are not enough to keep him busy, and he takes on the added burden of Deputy Marshall, a sign of permanence, for he has agreed to a two-year term.

But then comes the Winter of the Blue Snow, the worst blizzard ever to hit the Bad Lands, and Alice contracts pneumonia. He tries to nurse her himself, but the condition worsens, her breathing becomes labored, the child's wet nurse threatens to leave if they remain, and finally Roosevelt puts Elkhorn up for sale and moves back to New York.

Alice recovers, slowly to be sure, but by February she is once again able to resume a social life, and Roosevelt feels a great burden lifted from his shoulders. Never again will he make the mistake of forcing the vigorous outdoor life upon a frail flower that cannot be taken from its hothouse.

He sleeps, more restlessly than usual, and the images return. He is alone, on horseback, in the Blue Snow. The drifts are piled higher than his head, and ahead of him he can see the three desperadoes he is chasing. He has no weapons, not even a knife, but he feels confident. The guns they used to kill so many others will not work in this weather; the triggers and hammers will be frozen solid, and even if they should manage to get off a shot, the wind and the lack of visibility will protect him.

He pulls a piece of beef jerky from his pocket and chews it thoughtfully. They may have the guns, but he has the food, and within a day or two the advantage will be his. He is in no hurry. He knows where he will confront them, he knows how he will take them if they offer any resistance, he even knows the route by which he will return with them to Medora.

He studies the tracks in the snow. One of their horses is already lame, another exhausted. He dismounts, opens one of the sacks of oats he is carrying, and holds it for his own horse to eat.

There is a cave two miles ahead, large enough for both him and the horse, and if no one has found it, there is a supply of firewood he laid in during his last grizzly-hunting trip.

In his dream, Roosevelt sees himself mount up again and watch the three fleeing figures. He cannot hear the words, but his lips seem to be saying: *Tomorrow you're mine...*

He runs for mayor of New York in 1886, and loses—and immediately begins planning to run for Governor, but Alice cannot bear the rigors of campaigning, or the humiliation of defeat. *Please*, she begs him, *please don't give the rabble another chance to reject you.* And because he loves her, he accedes to her wishes, and loses himself in his writing. He begins work on a history of the opening of the American West, then stops after the first volume when he realizes that he will have to actually return to the frontier to gather more material if the series is to go on, and he cannot bear to be away from her. Instead, he writes the definitive treatise on taxidermy, for which he is paid a modest stipend. The book is well received by the scientific community, and Roosevelt is justifiably proud.

This dream is more disturbing than most, because his Alice is not in it. Instead an old childhood friend, Edith Carow, firm of body and bold of spirit, seems to have taken her place. They are surrounded by six children, his own daughter and five more whom he does not recognize, and live in a huge house somewhere beyond the city. Their life is idyllic. He rough-houses with both the boys and the girls, writes of the West, takes a number of governmental positions.

But there is no Alice, and eventually he wakes up, sweating profusely, trembling with fear. He reaches out and touches her, sighs deeply, and lies back uncomfortably on the bed. It was a frightening dream, this dream of a life without Alice, and he is afraid to go back to sleep, afraid the dream might resume.

Eventually he can no longer keep his eyes open, and he falls into a restless, dreamless sleep.

It is amazing, he thinks, staring at her: *she is almost 40, and I am still blinded by her delicate beauty, I still thrill to the sound of her laughter.*

True, he admits, she could take more of an interest in the affairs of the nation, or even in the affairs of the city in which she lives, a city that has desperately needed a good police commissioner for years (he has never told her that he was once offered the office); but it is not just her health, he knows, that is delicate—it is Alice herself, and in truth he would not have her any other way. She could read more, he acknowledges, but he enjoys reading aloud to her, and she has never objected; he sits in his easy chair every night and reads from the classics, and she sits opposite him, sewing or knitting or sometimes just watching him and smiling at him, her face aglow with the love she bears for him.

So what if she will not allow talk of this newest war in the house? Why should such a perfect creature care for war, anyway? She exists to be protected and cherished, and he will continue to dedicate his life to doing both.

He has seen this image in a dream once before, but tonight it is clearer, more defined. His men are pinned down by machine gun fire from atop a hill, and finally he climbs onto his horse and races up the hill, pistols drawn and firing. He expects to be shot out of the saddle at any instant, but miraculously he remains untouched while his own bullets hit their targets again and again, and finally he is atop the hill, and his men are charging up it, screaming their battle cry, while the enemy races away in defeat and confusion.

It is the most thrilling, the most triumphant moment of his life, and he wants desperately for the dream to last a little longer so that he may revel in it for just a few more minutes, but then he awakens, and he is back in the city. There is a garden show to be visited tomorrow, and in the evening he would like to attend a speech on the plight of New York's immigrants. As a good citizen, he will do both.

On the way home from the theater, two drunks get into a fight and he wades in to break it up. He receives a bloody nose for his trouble, and Alice castigates him all the way home for getting involved in a dispute that was none of his business to begin with.

The next morning she has forgiven him, and he remarks to her that, according to what he has read in the paper, the trusts are getting out of hand. Someone should stop them, but McKinley doesn't seem to have the gumption for it.

She asks him what a trust is, and after he patiently explains it to her, he sits down, as he seems to be doing more and more often, to write a letter to the *Times*. Alice approaches him just as he is finishing it and urges him not to send it. The last time the *Times* ran one of his letters they printed his address, and while he was out she had to cope with three different radical reformers who found their way to her door to ask him to run for office again.

He is about to protest, but he looks into her delicate face and pleading eyes and realizes that even at this late date he can refuse her nothing.

It is a presumptuous dream this time. He strides through the White House with the energy of a caged lion. This morning he attacked J. P. Morgan and the trusts, this afternoon he will make peace between Russia and Japan, tonight he will send the fleet around the world, and tomorrow...tomorrow he will do what God Himself forgot to do and give American ships a passage through the Isthmus of Panama.

It seems to him that he has grown to be twenty feet tall, that every challenge, far from beating him down, makes him larger, and he looks forward to the next one as eagerly as a lion looks forward to its prey. It is a bully dream, just bully, and he hopes it will go on forever, but of course it doesn't.

Alice's health has begun deteriorating once again. It is the dust, the pollution, the noise, just the incredible *pace* of living in the city, a pace he has never noticed but which seems to be breaking down her body, and finally he decides they must move out to the country. He passes a house on Sagamore Hill, a house that fills him with certain vague longings, but it is far too large and far too expensive, and eventually he finds a small cottage that is suitable for their needs. It backs up to a forest, and while Alice lays in bed and tries to regain her strength, he secretly buys a rifle—she won't allow firearms in the house—and spends a happy morning hunting rabbits.

In this dream he is standing at the edge of a clearing, rifle poised and aimed, as two bull elephants charge down upon him. He drops the first one at 40 yards, and though his gunbearer breaks and runs, he waits patiently and drops the second at ten yards. It falls so close to him that he can reach out and touch its trunk with the toe of his boot.

It has been a good day for elephant. Tomorrow he will go out after rhino.

Alice hears the gunshots and scolds him severely. He feels terribly guilty about deceiving her and vows that he will never touch a firearm again. He is in a state of utter despair until she relents—as she always relents—and forgives him.

Why, he wonders as he walks through the woods, following a small winding stream to its source, does he always disappoint her when he wants nothing more than to make her happy?

He sleeps sitting down with his back propped against a tree, and dreams not of a stream but a wild, raging river. He is on an expedition, and his leg has abscessed, and he is burning with fever, and he is a thousand miles from the nearest city. Tapirs come down to drink, and through the haze of his fever, he thinks he can see a jaguar approaching him. He yells at the jaguar, sends it skulking back into the thick undergrowth. He will die someday, he knows, but it won't be here in this forsaken wilderness. Finally he takes a step, then another. The pain is excruciating, but he has borne pain before, and slowly, step by step, he begins walking along the wild river.

When he awakens it is almost dark, and he realizes that the exploration of the winding stream will have to wait for another day, that he must hurry back to his Alice before she begins to worry.

Within a year she dies. It is not a disease or an illness, just the fading away of a fragile spirit in an even more fragile body. Roosevelt is disconsolate. He stops reading, stops walking, stops eating. Before long he, too, is on his deathbed, and he looks back on his life, the books he's written, the birds he's discovered, the taxidermy he's performed. There was a promise of something different in his youth, a hint of the outdoor life, a brief burst of political glory, but it was a road he would have had to walk alone, and he knows now, as he knew that day back when he almost lost her for the first time, that without his Alice it would have been meaningless.

No, thinks Roosevelt, *I made the right choices, I walked the right road. It hasn't been a bad or an unproductive life, some of my books will live, some of my monographs will still be read—and I was privileged to spent every moment that I could with my Alice. I am content; I would have had it no other way.*

And History weeps.

Appendix

THE UNSINKABLE TEDDY ROOSEVELT

Bill Fawcett doesn't just write and edit science fiction. Recently he put together a book titled *Oval Office Oddities* (which thankfully were not confined to the Oval Office, or even to the years of the subject's Presidency), and since my tastes are well-known to him, he asked me for the following chapter on Roosevelt.

So here we are, with one last look at the real Theodore (he hated the nickname "Teddy".) Kind of hard to believe some of these anecdotes don't belong in the stories you just read, isn't it?

His daughter, Alice, said it best: "He wanted to be the bride at every wedding and the corpse at every funeral."

Of course, he had a little something to say about his daughter, too. When various staff members complained that she was running wild throughout the White House, his response was: "Gentlemen, I can either run the country, or I can control Alice. I cannot do both."

He was Theodore Roosevelt, of course: statesman, politician, adventurer, naturalist, ornithologist, taxidermist, cowboy, police commissioner, explorer, writer, diplomat, boxer, and President of the United States. John Fitzgerald Kennedy was widely quoted after inviting a dozen writers, artists, musicians and scientists to lunch at the White House when he announced that "This is the greatest assemblage of talent to eat here since Thomas Jefferson dined alone." It's a witty statement, but JFK must have thought Roosevelt ate all his meals out.

Roosevelt didn't begin life all that auspiciously. "Teedee" was a sickly child, his body weakened by asthma. It was his father who decided that he was not going to raise an invalid. Roosevelt was encouraged to swim, to take long hikes, to do everything he could to build up his body. He was picked on by bullies, who took advantage of his weakened condition, so he asked his father to get him boxing lessons. They worked pretty well. By the time he entered Harvard, he had the body and reactions of a trained athlete, and before long he was a member of the boxing team. It was while fighting for the light-weight championship when an incident occurred that gave everyone an insight into Roosevelt's character. He was carrying the fight to his opponent, C. S. Hanks, the defending champion, when he slipped and fell to his knee. Hanks had launched a blow that he couldn't pull back, and he opened Roosevelt's nose, which began gushing blood. The crowd got ugly and started booing the champion, but Roosevelt held up his hand for silence, announced that it was an honest mistake, and shook hands with Hanks before the fight resumed.

It was his strength of character that led to his developing an equally strong body. His doctor, W. Thompson, once told a friend: "Look out for Theodore. He's not strong, but he's all grit. He'll kill himself before he'll ever say he's tired." In 59 years of a vigorous, strenuous life, he never once admitted to being tired.

Roosevelt was always fascinated by Nature, and in fact had seriously considered becoming a biologist or a naturalist before discovering politics. The young men sharing his lodgings at Harvard were probably less than thrilled with his interest. He kept a number of animals in his room. Not cute, cuddly one, but rather snakes, lobsters, and a tortoise that was always escaping and scaring the life out of his landlady. Before long most of the young men in his building refused to go anywhere near his room.

Roosevelt "discovered" politics shortly after graduating Harvard (*phi beta kappa* and *summa cum laude*, of course). So he attacked the field with the same vigor he attacked everything else. The result? At 24 he became the youngest Assemblyman in the New York State House, and the next year he became the youngest-ever Minority Leader. He might have remained in New York politics for years, but something happened that changed his life. He had met and fallen in love with Alice Hathaway Lee while in college, and married her very soon thereafter. His widowed mother lived with them. And then, on February 14, 1884, Alice and his mother both died (Alice in childbirth, his mother of other causes) twelve hours apart in the same house. The blow was devastating to Roosevelt. He never mentioned Alice again and refused to allow her to be mentioned in his presence. He put his former life behind him and decided to lose himself in what was left of the Wild West.

He bought a ranch in the Dakota Bad Lands...and then, because he was Theodore Roosevelt and couldn't do anything in a small way, he bought a second ranch as well. He spent a lot more time hunting than ranching, and more time writing and reading than hunting. (During his lifetime he wrote more than 150,000 letters, as well as close to 30 books.) He'd outfitted himself with the best "Western" outfit money could buy back in New York, and of course he appeared to the locals to be a wealthy New York dandy. By now he was wearing glasses, and he took a lot of teasing over them; the sobriquet "Four Eyes" seemed to stick. Until the night he found himself far from his Elkhorn Ranch and decided to rent a room at Nolan's Hotel in Mingusville, on the west bank of the Beaver River. After dinner he went down to the bar—it was the only gathering point in the entire town—and right after Roosevelt arrived, a huge drunk entered, causing a ruckus, shooting off his six-gun, and making himself generally obnoxious. When he saw Roosevelt, he announced that "Four Eyes" would buy drinks for everyone in the bar—or else. Roosevelt, who wasn't looking for a fight, tried to mollify him, but the drunk was having none of it. He insisted that the effete dandy put up his dukes and defend himself. "Well, if I've got to, I've got to," muttered Roosevelt, getting up from his chair. The bully took one swing. The boxer from Harvard ducked and bent the drunk in half with a one-two combination to the belly, then caught him flush on the jaw. He kept pummeling the drunk until the man was out cold, and then, with a little help from the appreciative onlookers, he carried the unconscious man to an outhouse behind the hotel and deposited him there for the night. He was never "Four Eyes" again.

The dude from New York didn't limit himself to human bullies. No horse could scare him either. During the roundup of 1884, he and his companions encountered a horse known only as "The Devil". He'd earned his name throwing one cowboy after another, and was generally considered to be the meanest horse in the Bad Lands. Finally Roosevelt decided to match his will and skills against the stallion, and all the other cowboys gathered around the corral to watch the New Yorker get his comeuppance—and indeed, The Devil soon bucked him off. Roosevelt got on again. And got bucked off again. According to one observer, "With almost every other jump, we would see about twelve acres of bottom land between Roosevelt and the saddle." The Devil sent him flying a third and then a fourth time. But Roosevelt wasn't about to quit. The Devil couldn't throw him a fifth time, and before long Roosevelt had him behaving "as meek as a rabbit", according to the same observer. The next year there was an even wilder horse. The local cowboys knew him simply as "The Killer", but Roosevelt decided he was going to tame him, and a tame horse needed a better name than that, so he dubbed him "Ben Baxter". The cowboys, even those who had seen him break The Devil, urged him to keep away from The Killer, to have the horse destroyed. Roosevelt paid them no attention. He tossed a blanket over Ben Baxter's head to keep him calm while putting on the saddle, an operation that was usually life-threatening in itself. Then he tightened the cinch, climbed onto the horse, and removed the blanket. Two seconds later, Roosevelt was sprawling in the dirt of the corral. A minute later, he was back in the saddle, and five seconds later, he was flying through the air again, to land with a bond-jarring *thud!* They kept it up most of the afternoon; Roosevelt climbing back on every time he was thrown, and finally the fight was all gone from Ben Baxter. Roosevelt had broken his shoulder during one of his spills, but it hadn't kept him from mastering the horse. He kept Ben Baxter, and from that day forward "The Killer" became the gentlest horse on his ranch. Is it any wonder that he never backed down from a political battle?

Having done everything else one could do in the Bad Lands, Roosevelt became a Deputy Sheriff. And in March of 1886, he found out that it meant a little more than rounding up the town drunks on a Saturday night. It seems that a wild man named Mike Finnegan, who had a reputation for breaking laws and heads that stretched from one end of the Bad Lands to the other, had gotten drunk and shot up the town of Medora, escaping—not that anyone dared to stop him—on a small flatboat with two confederates. Anyone who's ever been in Dakota in March knows that it's still quite a few weeks away from the first signs of spring. Roosevelt, accompanied by Bill Sewell and Wilmot Dow, was ordered to bring Finnegan in, and took off after him on a raft a couple of days later. They negotiated the ice-filled river, and finally came to the spot where the gang had made camp. Roosevelt, the experienced hunter, managed to approach silently and unseen until the moment he stood up, rifle in hands, and announced that they were his prisoners. Not a shot had to be fired. But capturing Finnegan and his friends was the easy part. They had to be transported overland more than 100 miles to the town of Dickenson, where they would stand trial. Within a couple of days the party of three lawmen and three outlaws was out of food. Finally Roosevelt set out on foot for a ranch—*any* ranch—and came back a day later with a small wagon filled with enough food to keep them alive on the long trek. The wagon had a single horse, and given the weather and conditions of the crude trails, the horse couldn't be expected pull all six men, so Sewell and Dow rode in the wagon while Roosevelt and the three captives walked behind it on an almost non-existent trail, knee-deep in snow, in below-freezing weather. And the closer they got to Dickenson, the more likely it was that Finnegan would attempt to escape, so Roosevelt didn't sleep the last two days and nights of the forced march. But he delivered the outlaws, safe and reasonably sound. He would be a lawman again in another nine years, but his turf would be as different from the Bad Lands as night is from day. He became the Police Commissioner of New York City.

New York was already a pretty crime-ridden city, even before the turn of the 20th Century. Roosevelt, who had already been a successful politician, lawman, lecturer and author, was hired to change that—and change it he did. He hired the best people he could find. That included the first woman on the New York police force—and the next few dozen as well. (Before long every station had police matrons around the clock, thus assuring that any female prisoner would be booked by a member of her own sex.) Then came another innovation: when Roosevelt decided that most of the cops couldn't hit the broad side of a barn with their sidearms, target practice was not merely encouraged but made mandatory for the first time in the force's history. When the rise of the automobile meant that police on foot could no longer catch some escaping lawbreakers, Roosevelt created a unit of bicycle police (who, in the 1890s, had no problem keeping up with the cars of that era which were traversing streets that had not been created with automobiles in mind.) He hired Democrats as well as Republicans, men who disliked him as well as men who worshipped him. All he cared about was that they were able to get the job done. He was intolerant only of intolerance. When the famed anti-Semitic preacher from Berlin, Rector Ahlwardt, came to America, New York's Jewish population didn't want to allow him in the city. Roosevelt couldn't bar him, but he came up with the perfect solution: Ahlwardt's police bodyguards were composed entirely of very large, very unhappy Jewish cops whose presence convinced the bigot to forego his anti-Semitic harangues while he was in the city. Roosevelt announced that all promotions would be strictly on merit and not political pull, then spent the next two years proving he meant what he said. He also invited the press into his office whenever he was there, and if a visiting politician tried to whisper a question so that the reporters couldn't hear it, Roosevelt would repeat and answer it in a loud, clear voice.

APPENDIX: THE UNSINKABLE TEDDY ROOSEVELT

As Police Commissioner, Roosevelt felt the best way to make sure his police force was performing its duty was to go out in the field and see for himself. He didn't bother to do so during the day; the press and the public were more than happy to report on the doings of his policemen. No, what he did was go out into the most dangerous neighborhoods, unannounced, between midnight and sunrise, usually with a reporter or two in tow, just in case things got out of hand. (Not that he thought they would help him physically, but he expected them to accurately report what happened if a misbehaving or loafing cop turned on him.) The press dubbed these his "midnight rambles", and after awhile the publicity alone caused almost all the police to stay at their posts and do their duty, because they never knew when the Commissioner might show up in their territory, and either fire them on the spot or let the reporters who accompanied him expose them to public ridicule and condemnation.

Roosevelt began writing early and never stopped. You'd expect a man who was Governor of New York and President of the United States to write about politics, and of course he did. But Roosevelt didn't like intellectual restrictions any more than he liked physical restrictions, and he wrote books—not just articles, mind you, but *books*—about anything that interested him. While still in college he wrote *The Naval War of 1812*, which was considered at the time to be the definitive treatise on naval warfare. Here's a partial list of the non-political books that followed, just to give you an indication of the breadth of Roosevelt's interests:

Hunting Trips of a Ranchman
The Wilderness Hunter
A Book-Lover's Holidays in the Open
The Winning of the West, Volumes 1-4
The Rough Riders
Literary Treats
Papers on Natural History

African Game Trails
Hero Tales From American History
Through the Brazilian Wilderness
The Strenuous Life
Ranch Life and the Hunting Trail

I've got to think he'd be a pretty interesting guy to talk to. On any subject. In fact, it'd be hard to find one he hadn't written up.

A character as interesting and multi-faceted as Roosevelt's had to be portrayed in film sooner or later, but surprisingly, the first truly memorable characterization was by John Alexander, who delivered a classic and hilarious portrayal of a harmless madman who *thinks* he's Teddy Roosevelt and constantly screams "Charge!" as he runs up the stairs, his version of San Juan Hill, in *Arsenic and Old Lace*. Eventually there were more serious portrayals: Brian Keith, Tom Berenger, even Robin Williams…and word has it that, possibly by the time you read this, you'll be able to add Leonardo Di Caprio to the list.

Roosevelt believed in the active life, not just for himself but for his four sons—Kermit, Archie, Quentin, and Theodore Junior, and two daughters, Alice and Edith. He built Sagamore Hill, his rambling house on equally rambling acreage, and he often took the children—and any visiting dignitaries—on what he called "scrambles", cross-country hikes that were more obstacle course than anything else. His motto: "Above or below, but never around." If you couldn't walk through it, you climbed over it or crawled under it, but you never ever circled it. This included not only hills, boulders, and thorn bushes, but rivers, and frequently he, the children, and the occasional visitor who didn't know what he was getting into, would come home soaking wet from swimming a river or stream with their clothes on, or covered with mud, or with their clothes torn to shreds from thorns. Those wet, muddy, and torn clothes were their badges of honor. It meant that they hadn't walked around any obstacle.

"If I am to be any use in politics," Roosevelt wrote to a friend, "it is because I am supposed to be a man who does not preach what he fears to practice. For the year I have preached war with Spain..." So it was inevitable that he should leave his job as Undersecretary of the Navy and enlist in the military. He instantly became Lieutenant Colonel Roosevelt and began putting together a very special elite unit, one that perhaps only he could have assembled. The Rough Riders consisted, among others, of cowboys, Indians, tennis stars, college athletes, the marshal of Dodge City, the master of the Chevy Chase hounds, and the man who was reputed to be the best quarterback ever to play for Harvard. They were quite a crew, Colonel Roosevelt's Rough Riders. They captured the imagination of the public as had no other military unit in United States History. They also captured San Juan Hill in the face of some serious machine gun fire, and Roosevelt, who led the charge, returned home an even bigger hero than when he'd left.

While on a bear hunt in Mississippi, Colonel Roosevelt, as he liked to be called after San Juan Hill and Cuba, was told that a bear had been spotted a few miles away. When Roosevelt and his entourage—which always included the press—arrived, he found a small, undernourished, terrified bear tied to a tree. He refused to shoot it, and turned away in disgust, ordering a member of the party to put the poor creature out of its misery. His unwillingness to kill a helpless animal was captured by *Washington Post* cartoonist Clifford Berryman. It made him more popular than ever, and before long toy companies were turning out replicas of cute little bears that the great Theodore Roosevelt would certainly never kill, rather than ferocious game animals. Just in case you ever wondered about the origin of the Teddy Bear.

Some 30 years ago, writer/director John Milius gave the public one of the truly great adventure films, *The Wind and the Lion*, in which the Raisuli (Sean Connery), known as "the Last of the Barbary Pirates", kidnapped an American woman, Eden Perdicaris (Candice Bergan) and her two children, and held them for ransom at his stronghold in Morocco. At which point President Theodore Roosevelt (Brian Keith, in probably the best representation of Roosevelt ever put on film) declared that America wanted "Perdicaris alive or Raisuli dead!" and sent the fleet to Morocco. Wonderful film, beautifully photographed, well-written, well-acted, with a gorgeous musical score. Would you like to know what *really* happened? First of all, it wasn't *Eden* Perdicaris; it was *Ion* Perdicaris, a 64-year-old man. And he wasn't kidnapped with two small children, but with a grown stepson. And far from wanting to be rescued, he and the Raisuli became great friends. Roosevelt felt the President of the United States had to protect Americans abroad, so he sent a telegram to the Sultan of Morocco, the country in which the kidnapping took place, to the effect that America wanted Perdicaris alive or Raisuli dead. He also dispatched seven warships to Morocco. So why wasn't there a war with Morocco? Two reasons. First, during the summer of 1904, shortly after the kidnapping and Roosevelt's telegram, the government learned something that was kept secret until after all the principles in the little drama—Roosevelt, Perdicaris, and the Raisuli—had been dead for years…and that was that Ion Perdicaris was *not* an American citizen. He had been born one, but he later renounced his citizenship and moved to Greece, years before the kidnapping. The other reason? Perdicaris's dear friend, the Raisuli, set him free. Secretary of State John Hay knew full well that Perdicaris had been freed before the Republican convention convened, but he whipped the assembled delegates up with the "America wants Perdicaris alive or Raisuli dead!" slogan anyway, and Roosevelt was elected in a landslide.

Roosevelt was as vigorous and active as President as he'd been in every previous position. Consider: even though the country was relatively empty, he could see land being gobbled up in great quantities by settlers and others, and he created the national park system. He arranged for the overthrow of the hostile Panamanian government and created the Panama Canal, which a century later is *still* vital to international shipping. He took on J. P. Morgan and his cohorts, and became the greatest "trust buster" in our history, then created the Department of Commerce and the Department of Labor to make sure weaker Presidents in the future didn't give up the ground he'd taken. We were a regional power when he took office. Then he sent the Navy's "Great White Fleet" around the world on a "goodwill tour". By the time it returned home, we were, for the first time, a world power. Because he never backed down from a fight, a lot of people thought of him as a warmonger—but he became the only American President ever to win the Nobel Peace Price while still in office, when he mediated a dispute between Japan and Russia before it became a full-fledged shooting war. He created and signed the Pure Drug and Food Act. He became the first President to leave the United States while in office, when he visited Panama to inspect the Canal.

Roosevelt remained physically active throughout his life. He may or may not have been the only President to be blind in one eye, but he was the only who to ever go blind in one eye from injuries received in a boxing match *while serving as President*. He also took years of *jujitsu* lessons while in office, and became quite proficient at it. And, in keeping with daughter Alice's appraisal of him, he was the first President to fly in an airplane, and the first to be filmed.

Roosevelt's last day in office was February 22, 1909. He'd already been a cowboy, a rancher, a soldier, a marshal, a police commissioner, a governor, and a President. So did he finally slow down? Just long enough to pack. Accompanied by his son, Kermit, and the always-present journalists, on March 23 he boarded a ship that would take him to East Africa for the first organized safari on record. It was sponsored by the American and Smithsonian museums, which to this day display some of the trophies he shot and brought back. His two guides were the immortal F. C. Selous, widely considered to be the greatest hunter in African history, and Philip Percival, who was already a legend among Kenya's hunting fraternity. What did Roosevelt manage to bag for the museums? 9 lions, 9 elephants, 5 hyenas, 8 black rhinos, 5 white rhinos, 7 hippos, 8 wart hogs, 6 Cape buffalo, 3 pythons, and literally hundreds of antelope, gazelle, and other herbivores. Is it any wonder that he needed 500 uniformed porters? And since he paid as much attention to the mind as to the body, one of those porters carried 60 pounds of Roosevelt's favorite books on his back, and Roosevelt made sure he got in his reading every day, no matter what. While hunting in Uganda, he ran into the noted rapscallion John Boyes and others who were poaching elephants in the Lado Enclave. According to Boyes's memoir, *The Company of Adventurers*, the poachers offered to put a force of 50 hunters and poachers at Roosevelt's disposal if he would like to take a shot at bringing American democracy, capitalism and know-how to the Belgian Congo (not that they had any right to it, but from their point of view, neither did King Leopold of Belgium). Roosevelt admitted to being tempted, but he had decided that his chosen successor, William Howard Taft, was doing a lousy job as President and he'd made up his mind to run again. But first, he wrote what remains one of the true classics of hunting literature, *African Game Trails*, which has remained in print for just short of a century as these words are written. (And half a dozen of the journalists sold *their* versions of the safari to the book publishers, whose readers simply couldn't get enough of Roosevelt.)

William Howard Taft, the sitting President (and Roosevelt's hand-picked successor), of course wanted to run for re-election. Roosevelt was the clear choice among the Republican rank and file, but the President controls the party's machinery, and due to a number of procedural moves Taft got the nomination. Roosevelt, outraged at the backstage manipulations, decided to form a third party. Officially it was the Progressive Party, but after he mentioned that he felt "as fit as bull moose", the public dubbed it the Bull Moose Party. Not everyone was thrilled to see him run for a third term. (Actually, it would have been only his second election to the Presidency; he became President in 1901 just months after McKinley's election and assassination, so though he'd only been elected once, he had served in the White House for seven years.) One such unhappy citizen was John F. Schrank. On October 14, 1912, Roosevelt came out of Milwaukee's

Hotel Gillespie to give a speech at a nearby auditorium. He climbed into an open car and waved to the crowd—and found himself face-to-face with Schrank, who raised his pistol and shot Roosevelt in the chest. The crowd would have torn Schrank to pieces, but Roosevelt shouted: "Stand back! Don't touch that man!" He had Schrank brought before him, stared at the man until the potential killer could no longer meet his gaze, then refused all immediate medical help. He wasn't coughing up blood, which convinced him that the wound wasn't fatal, and he insisted on giving his speech before going to the hospital. He was a brave man...but he was also a politician and a showman, and he knew what the effect on the crowd would be when they saw the indestructible Roosevelt standing before them in a blood-soaked shirt, ignoring his wound to give them his vision of what he could do for America. "I shall ask you to be as quiet as possible," he began. "I don't know whether you fully understand that I have just been shot." He gave them the famous Roosevelt grin. "But it takes more than that to kill a Bull Moose!" It brought the house down. He lost the election to Woodrow Wilson—even Roosevelt couldn't win as a third-party candidate—but William Howard Taft, the President of the United States, came in a distant third, capturing only eight electoral votes.

That was enough for one vigorous lifetime, right? Not hardly. Did you ever hear of the River of Doubt? You can be excused if your answer is negative. It no longer exists on any map. On February 27, 1914, at the request of the Brazilian government, Roosevelt and his party set off to map the River of Doubt. It turned out to be not quite the triumph that the African safari had been. Early on they began running short of supplies. Then Roosevelt developed a severe infection in his leg. It got so bad that at one point he urged the party to leave him behind. Of course they didn't, and gradually his leg and his health improved to the point where he was finally able to continue the expedition. Eventually they mapped all 900 miles of the river, and Roosevelt, upon returning home, wrote another bestseller, *Through the Brazilian Wilderness*. And shortly thereafter, the *Rio da Duvida* (River of Doubt) officially became the river you can now find on the maps, the *Rio Teodoro* (River Theodore). He was a man in his mid-fifties, back when the average man's life expectancy was only 55.

He was just recovering from being shot in the chest (and was still walking around with the bullet inside his body). Unlike East Africa, where he would be hunting the same territory that Selous had hunted before and Percival knew like the back of his hand, no one had ever mapped the River of Doubt. It was uncharted jungle, with no support network for hundreds of miles. So why did he agree to map it? His answer is so typically Rooseveltian that it will serve as the end to this chapter: "It was my last chance to be a boy again."